THE

SANTA CLAUS AGREEMENT

BY

DEREK McFADDEN

This paperback edition compiled by

Papillon du Père Publishing

ISBN: 978-1-915221-05-6

PAPILLON DU PÈRE
PUBLISHING

Cover design

Papillon du Père Publishing

www.papillon-du-pere.com

@PapillonPere

Copyediting

Jay Allchin
@ The Editing-Store.com

www.editing-store.com

ALSO BY
DEREK McFADDEN

Novels

What Death Taught Terrence

The Santa Claus Agreement

Short Stories

What Eternity Taught Eve

The Last Christmas Gift

Written by the Victors (forthcoming)

Nonfiction

Prose from a Grandson to a Senior Fellow

DEDICATION

For my brothers, specifically my brothers who helped both inspire and form the character of Brendan. Ben and Brandon, with love and thanks that knows no bounds. For our talks and laughter and joy when we can hang, and how it all resounds.

For my sisters, Katie and Delaney. For your humor, your laughter, your own unbridled joy—qualities you both share—when life is good. Your understanding, compassion, and deep kindness when it is not.

For my Santas, Richard Kenbok and Bradley Harper, with deep appreciation for all your encouragement, love, and belief.

And for everyone in The Fearless Writers Writing Club. Specifically to Chante, Reese, and Molly. My Tuesdays wouldn't be the same and this book wouldn't *exist* without you guys.

And finally, for my editor, "Mr. Lewis." Jay, first and foremost, may this little story bring you both hope and joy. Life can kick our butts sometimes, and at those times it can feel like it's kicking our butts *all the time*, but real friends know that being there sometimes just means staying where you are and saying, "I'm here if you need me." Secondly, you told me when I began this tale that I shouldn't limit the scope of this story, so I didn't.

Thus, what follows is kind of your fault.

CONTENTS

THE SANTA CLAUS AGREEMENT

This is the story of an agreement. It's about a magical apprenticeship and a life wrenched askew.

It's about Santa and Mrs. Claus and the elves and Rudolph and Frosty the Snowman and the North Pole and how they're all real. And it's about a kid with cerebral palsy who became a man with cerebral palsy.

That kid was me. That man *is* me.

And, right now—in the heart of another holiday season—they're both *broken*.

Perhaps irreparably so.

The Santa Claus Agreement

PROLOGUE

A Real Man Provides

"A *real* man provides for his family, David," Aubrey said, *again*, last night. Our last night. "When have you ever done that?"

A sharpened barb. Aubrey was parroting her father, a man I hadn't liked because he hadn't liked me. Though, unlike me, he hadn't even tried. She was using the man's community-college teacher lecture-tone.

I bet that tone makes them both feel superior, I'd thought.

This time, when Aubrey left my house—unlike all the other times she'd left in a huff—this time, I hadn't tried to stop her. I was too emotionally tired to try. To remind her of our long history. To apologize for nothing while taking the blame for everything. To word-salad our way through another night together. To go to bed depressed and depleted. When my front door shut behind her with a final, too-loud click of its latch, and when I was sure Aubrey was gone and wasn't coming back for anything, least of all me, I took a deep breath, exhaled a sigh, and thought of sleep.

No, that's not happening. Instead, I called my brother, Brendan, and told him what had just happened.

"Aubrey and I broke up tonight."

He'd heard this before.

"For good?" he asked.

"Yeah. I think for good."

"Oh, brother, I'm so sorry. We'll be right over."

"No, you guys don't need to do that. Really. I don't mean to ruin *your* night, too. I'll be alright." I said all of this, but Brendan hung up, probably before he'd heard half of it. When I dialed him again, the call went straight to voicemail.

They were on my porch in ten minutes, the two of them, bearing food. A lasagna for me.

"You should really eat, Davey," my sister-in-law, Jess, said. And so I did. Unaware yet, as I might well have been in some form of shock, that—in losing Aubrey—I'd lost far more than a relationship that never would have worked.

***

My hair used to be light brown, matching my light-brown eyes. What my Grandma Joan had called my "puppy-dog eyes."

I have no one to blame for this agreement debacle but myself. I didn't follow the rules so clearly set out so many years ago; the passage of so much time boggles my mind. And I knew not following the rules would endanger my once-in-centuries opportunity. All I can say is it's not entirely my fault.

Not entirely.

It isn't just my broken heart I'm depressed about, either. This local mall just south of Seattle—housed in a concrete behemoth of a building with little signage to indicate its purpose, this mall where I've performed as Santa for two straight years now—is done with me.

Actually, we're done with each other.

My boss, Calvin, is a small, brown-haired man with hair fleeing the top of his head at a clip that would impress bootleggers. And he's ashen-faced, well, except for when

Cal's angry, which is about half the time. Then the man's face goes beet-red and will stay that way for a long time.

Calvin told me two weeks ago, when I gave my notice, that this actually made things easier, as management had decided—but hadn't yet informed me—that I would not return for a third season.

"That's perfectly fine, Mr. Boyd. We need a Santa who's believable, anyway. One who looks ... I hate to say it, I *really* do ... but one who looks ... normal." At the word, Calvin's posture relaxed. A great weight gone. Lifted.

He'd hated to say it, but he'd said it. With some measure of unabashed pleasure that I didn't miss. So how much had he actually hated to say it?

"That's not fair, Cal," I argued, not even sure why I was arguing. I was seated before my boss's imposing jet-black oak desk, in his huge third-floor office, with its floor-to-ceiling windows behind him, which was the only thing about the man that was remotely imposing, aside from his ability to—as my Grandma Joan and her husband, my Papa Dale, would say—"yell and scream and carry on." The mall's third floor was the point on high from which management looked down on all they lorded over.

"Since when has fairness meant anything?" Calvin asked. "Besides, you're leaving, anyway. You're the one who wants to leave."

Fair points, I thought. Ironically. My leaving was the reason I'd asked for this meeting.

"I'm a businessman, Boyd," Calvin said. "How do you think I got to where I've gotten to in my life?"

He was accepting the resignation of a mall-Santa at the beginning of what would be my final fortnight in the mall's too-small North Pole. Not to mention its too-small, moth-eaten Santa suit. So, where exactly had he gotten to in his life?

Not as far as he'd thought.

"You know, I knew the real Santa, and the real Santa would say—"

"Boyd! For Christ's sake, man, save your fantasies for the kids out there or for someone else who cares! That is not me!"

Clearly.

If I said this, I'd be fired on the spot, and our North Pole would be closed for the day, our elves sent home. Kids disappointed. So I kept it to myself.

I couldn't help but grimace at Cal, though. Luckily, he didn't see it, too absorbed in telling me what a peon I was. "I know you tell that story of yours five or six times a year. And I know the kids love it. But you don't have to convince me you know the real Santa. Not me, Boyd. I live in the real world. Got it?"

A world without magic, he meant. Must be a pretty boring place to live.

"I got it," I said.

"Good. Now, you owe us two more weeks. Get down there and make those kids happy. And tell their parents to shop like this mall depends on it."

What Calvin Grigsby didn't say, because he didn't need to say it, was the mall did depend on it. It was only the holiday season that put this outdated artifact in the black each year.

Leaving wasn't hard for me.

I had another job lined up. A better job. The best job I could ever dream of was about to be mine. Or it would have been mine, if only I could have followed the rules. Now, two weeks later, it's too late to change my mind about quitting. And it's far too late to ever change Calvin Grigsby's mind. I couldn't ask for this mall job back. He'd simply (and gladly) tell me he was sorry (which he wasn't); following my stepping aside, management had had no choice but to move in the different direction Calvin had wanted to move in for some time. It didn't matter one iota that his wife, Rose, and I were casual friends.

They'd have another Santa in the chair next year. A Santa without my unique mild form of cerebral palsy. My palsy is mild, yes, though I'd be remiss if I didn't note how dispiriting it can be at times.

When I *let* it dispirit me.

CHAPTER 1

One More Day in a Moth-Eaten Santa Suit at a Sad Suburban Mall

As my story begins—or, more accurately, as the telling of the beginning of the end of my story gets underway—I owe Calvin Grigsby and the third-floor higher-ups just one more day in the big chair. It's December 23, and I ubered to work this morning—as I always do these days—when all around me was still early winter darkness. Ten years ago and ... heck ... maybe even five years ago ... back then, I wouldn't have been comfortable doing this. My explanation is simple; the fear it can bring to my mind. As a disabled man, I am often fearful of attack, and inviting a stranger to both drive me places and to see that I'm all by myself, my body compromised as ever, a prime target for the opportunistic mugger or the off-his-rocker loner fascinated with firearms ... that can be a very scary deal. I've ubered off and on over the past decade, and in this job I'm always doing it.

It was also easier than usual ducking into someone else's Toyota Prius this early morning, knowing I only had one more day left in a very famous suit. However, that doesn't mean my stomach wasn't doing flips of unease, though those were more about the job I loved ending than any fear for my physical safety.

Because it *was* doing flips.

It still is as I get out of that Prius. My stomach is flipping like my Papa Dale used to flip stacks of blueberry pancakes on his hot griddle. I liked to watch when he'd make breakfast. I was just a little kid then. I really liked to watch when he'd bake cookies.

***

"Is this really your last day?" Carrie the Elf asks me, disbelieving, when I arrive, rushing through a side entrance no one would know was an entrance unless you worked here, and we give each other our usual head-elf/big-guy daily greeting just inside that door.

Beyond the kids, Carrie is who I'll miss most about this place. Carrie's blonde, with hair that stops at her shoulders, blue-eyed, not much beyond five feet tall. The kids really buy her as the head of Santa's elves, and we've developed a pleasant work rapport with one another to the point where I think she might actually miss me, too, come tomorrow—when everyone but me comes back to clean out their lockers and to say farewell to one more Christmas season. I'll clean out my own locker tonight when the mall closes and the children and their parents or guardians disappear from our North Pole for another year.

Yep, that's the plan. After what happened last night, I don't want to be in a cheery, happy place—or at least a place pretending cheer and happiness the way our mall's North Pole display does—for one more second than I have to. If you're ever in the midst of a breakup with the woman you've loved with all you have for five whole years, some advice: try not to structure your life so that you have to wake up the morning after she pulverizes your heart, the heart she doesn't care about anymore—and maybe she never did—and become Santa Claus again for so many believers.

Another Christmas is in two days. I can hardly believe it. Both that the holiday's so close at hand—and that, with it, a big career change should be in the offing for me—and that my girlfriend, Aubrey, who I'd once thought key to this career change, and I are now so far apart.

Breakups always happen at the worst times possible. Or maybe it's that we look back on our breakups and think of them as the worst of times.

Either way ...

"Santa? Earth to Santa!"

"What did you say?" I ask, distracted. *Carrie is talking to you*, I remind myself.

"Is this your last day?" my head-elf repeats.

"How did you kn—?"

"Cal told me."

Of course he had. And of course, the question she left unspoken was, "Why didn't you tell me, Davey?"

"I'm afraid so, Carrie. Hanging up the big red suit after today." And probably forever. Who would buy a Santa Claus without his missus?

"Why would you go?"

"I'm retiring." Simple. But not the full answer she's seeking. The full answer is I'm retiring and I'm depressed. A breakup will do that to a guy. The kids looking to have an audience with Santa are lucky I got out of bed this morning. But let's not add that. *Who gets depressed in the North Pole, anyway?* I morosely muse. (Well, in this mall's incarnation of the North Pole, I can imagine the answer is many people, including every Santa before me.).

There is, of course, another job offer on the table, the best job offer I could ever get and the very reason I was leaving this one, in fact. But I can't take the new job now, not anymore.

I won't be allowed to take it.

When they come to see me about the new job tonight, as I know they will—this meeting's been scheduled, on the books, as they say, for years—I'll just have to tell them the truth.

I can't do it, and I'm sorry to have wasted their time.

My plans have changed.

My plans have been changed for me.

***

There had been signs of trouble in the relationship for a good while. Aubrey sure was staying at her sister's an awful lot lately; she was doing what I'd consider a couple things, like seeing movies, going to dinner, or spending time with her family; yet I—her devoted boyfriend of five years—was not invited. As Christmas approached, I knew what that meant.

I wouldn't think it, let alone say it, but I *knew.*

"It's just a family thing, David," Aubrey would say, trying to breeze out the door and avoid confrontation, jacket and rain boots on (Seattle essentials both).

I wouldn't let her leave, not yet; I blocked the door, though not in a menacing way; I deserved to know why I wasn't coming with her. "Why aren't I coming with you?"

"You wouldn't want to go," she continued. "You don't get along with my parents, anyway."

She meant her father, the man who thought my passion for writing nothing more than a directionless hobby. Who said that, if I didn't get a job that paid better, a job that paid *anything*, something he considered practical, then I was, "an example of the height of laziness."

What did he know? Besides how to be a machinist at Boeing (or somewhere like that) and then a teacher who teaches future machinists at Boeing (or somewhere like that), and how to remodel bathrooms in his retirement?

The man never took into account my palsy, the life I was forced to lead by the disability I'd never wanted. How writing was my outlet and, in that way, its own reward for having to suffer all the pain my disability caused. How this outlet helped cushion the aloneness I couldn't deny.

"And besides, you've never published anything, David," Aubrey said.

"Not yet I haven't. Writing is a long game."

"It's *too long* a game for my father. He's not gonna wait for you to write that big novel you're always going on about."

"No, he won't, Aubrey. I wouldn't expect him to. The question is ... will you wait?"

Aubrey was right about one thing. I didn't get along with her parents, either of them really, and the less time I had to spend pretending to care about what they thought about me, or anything else, the better.

But I *did* care what they thought. That was the most messed-up part about it. I cared what two people who didn't like me thought because Aubrey cared what her parents thought above all others.

This was far from the only time I'd been passed over by the woman I loved in favor of anyone or anything who wasn't me. When she'd go to her sister's for the day or the weekend, there was always a reason why I didn't, why I couldn't, and she had it ready for me.

"It's just a day (a weekend, a fishing trip, a camping trip) with my sister and my nephews, David. You'd be bored. You wouldn't want to come." Her sister, Susan, who'd told Aubrey I was annoying because I tried to engage her in conversation once while she prepared dinner, and Aubrey thought this supposed anecdote important enough to use it in the derailing of one of our usual nighttime phone calls.

"Susan thinks you're annoying."

"Why wouldn't she tell me herself? Is she afraid I can't take it or something?"

"She doesn't want to speak with you. And I know you don't want to talk to her."

She had that right. "Well, no, not now." *Especially not now.*

As to Aubrey's work Christmas party: "David, it's just dinner with the girls from work." It wasn't. "And, yes, they know who you are, but this is a no-significant-others-dinner." It wasn't. "You get it, right?" I didn't. "You'll be busy with the Santa-thing, anyway. You understand?"

I did. Or I wanted to. In my head. But in my heart ...

Had Aubrey ever called me Davey, as the rest of my friends did? As I'd asked her to do years ago? Going through our countless memories together in a quick flipbook retrospective, our relationship flashing by on a big movie screen my mind erected, I couldn't find one instance when I was Davey to Aubrey instead of David. Where she'd chosen time with me over time alone or amongst her family. Maybe this meant nothing. But maybe it meant something. Perhaps it meant everything.

I didn't want to admit it, but for a while now, I hadn't been all that significant to Aubrey, whom I considered the most significant person in my life.

Last night, I'd finally confronted her. Sitting in her car for the last time—she'd always driven whenever we went anywhere because I've never been able to drive (thanks, cerebral palsy; double-thanks to the state of Washington), which she'd said, since day one, she was more than okay with—I asked, "Aubrey, how important am I to you?"

"What do you mean, David? I don't understand the question."

"If you needed help ... like, right away ... and you had to call someone, where would I be on your list of helpers?"

Aubrey considered this. I waited, hopeful. Maybe our relationship could be saved, after all.

"Well, let's see ... there're my parents. They're one and two. Then my sister. Susan is three. My brother-in-law would be four. Then my nephews—"

"Your nephews?" I blurted. "But they're, like, five and three."

"You asked who would be on my list, David. My nephews would be on my list at number five and number six. So I guess that means you would be number seven."

I couldn't help but be dejected, and I'm sure it showed on my face. I've never been good at hiding my emotions. Ask my mother.

"Why? Where would I be on *your* list?" Aubrey finally asked after a too-long, uncomfortable pause, both of us shifting in our seats.

"Number one. You would be number one." *I think we're done.*

Not much later that night, Aubrey said the last two things she'd ever say to me. "You know we're done, right?"

I did. I nodded.

"It's the only reason I'm here right now, David."

All my life, all I'd ever wanted was to be included, and here I was dating someone who absolutely refused to include me.

Through tears and shared sadness for the unrealized potential of *us*, we called it quits yesterday. Aubrey came over to my house, what used to be *our* house, to get the last of her stuff. We'd talked in her car, but there had been no real conversation after she'd said I wasn't a real man. Because what could be said after that? As I got out of her car, she got out, too, and went to the bathroom. And then, at my door, she said, "I'm gonna go stay with my sister."

For good, she didn't need to add.

I nodded again. And, with that, after half a decade, we were, now officially, done.

***

Lost in thoughts of what was lost, I've completely forgotten Carrie the Elf is talking to me, trying to engage me in our usual morning banter, as she always does. I am glad she is doing this. Whether she knows it or not, talking with someone who actually wants to talk to me soothes something deep within me. Something I cannot name or place.

I feel old, I think, not quite conscious of the fact that, as I think it, I just declared as much aloud.

"You're not that old." Thirty-five-year-old Carrie breaks off of whatever she has been saying as I snap back into the present. Whenever people word *that sentence* that way—*you're not that old*—they're acknowledging you're getting old and hoping you haven't noticed how old you've already gotten.

I have noticed. With my naturally sluggish body, I can't help but notice.

"Not that old, huh? Tell that to my doctor, why dontcha? Tell him to keep his hands where I can see them, too," I chuckle. "In case you're wondering, cerebral palsy is less fun at forty-eight than it's ever been."

"I would think," Carrie said.

"And it's almost Christmas, anyway. We're all but done here," I remind her. "One more day."

"I know that. And, trust me, I know how it is, Davey ..." Carrie tries to rationalize with me. She used my name on purpose right there.

She's never once called me David, has she? Friends call me Davey, as I told her on the day we met. (I told Aubrey, too. She just ... didn't listen.).

"I guess I'll call you Davey, then," Carrie had said way back when I revealed my preference on our first day together. "Merry Christmas, Davey," she'd said and winked at me.

If the mall were open right now, she'd call me Santa, out of professional courtesy. But the doors are still locked tight for another hour.

"I know how it is," Carrie repeats. I'm not sure what this means until she continues. "These days," she says, "you almost have to work two jobs to make ends meet. I understand that, believe me. And this job is seasonal. You know that better than anyone. When it's over, I'm back to hauling freight for Kroger and making sandwiches at Subway on third shift. People want roast beef at weird times." I didn't know those were Carrie's regular jobs. "But the kids just adore you, Davey. How could you leave knowing that?"

"You act like I'm letting them down. Like I'm abandoning them."

"Maybe you are."

"This is my last day," I reaffirm. "There will be other Santas. Besides, they can't wait to hire someone else, someone ... normal." I pause, stung by the word anew. Stung even though I'm the one doing the stinging this time. And I'm stung by, "Besides ... Aubrey and I ... It didn't ... Never mind." I think better of delving too deep into my

17

cratering personal life. This is not the place. Did she catch my momentary slip-up? I don't think so. "I just need a new start, Carrie, that's all. We rode out the season, didn't we? We got through another one, you and me. This will just … this'll be it. I'll miss you, Carrie. I will. You've been a great head-elf."

There is no hyperbole in this compliment.

She puts her hand lightly on my shoulder, understanding at last in her eyes. "And you've been an amazing Santa. The best we've ever had."

"Well, the bar wasn't all that high when I came along now, was it?" As a matter of fact, you barely needed to limbo underneath that thing. The guy before me liked his bartender and whatever was on tap much more than he enjoyed telling the kids he'd look into their myriad of gift requests.

"One more day?" I say to my head-elf. *Are you ready for this?* the question means.

"One more day," Carrie seconds. "Go get into your suit. The kids will be here soon. And Merry Christmas, Davey. Merry Christmas, Santa."

"Merry Christmas, Carrie. Ho, ho, ho."

Carrie grins at my added flourish. I put my whole body into it.

I take her advice and head straight for my private dressing room. (In any season when Santa isn't becoming Santa behind its locked door, this dressing room serves as a broom closet.)

At least they gave me a mirror. *Thanks, third floor.* It figures that the mirror would be too small; I'd expect nothing else, but at least I have one. It's hung precariously above the broom-closet door and looking like it might fall to its glass-shattering doom at any moment. I stare into it, at the last time my reflection will ever reflect Santa as I think hard about the broken life I've led to get here, the mistakes I've made, the not-enough I've been. A tear I tried hard not to let fall trickles and tickles at my cheek, inertia its only guide. I wipe the tear away with a white-gloved Santa hand before it can wet my beard.

I wish I looked better.

I'm always wishing I looked better. Which probably isn't a healthy thought. But I'll always have my cerebral palsy, so I'll never look as good as I ...

Ah, hell. One more day. Hold it together for one more day, Davey Boyd.

***

About an hour and a half or so into my last day in the big chair—I've already seen about ten little ones and learned their Christmas wishes and said I'd look into them; that's how efficient we are—story time begins. And I can't help it. I'm wading into a pool of sentimentality whose temperature I appreciate, as I now realize—in a way I haven't before—how this will *actually* be my last day.

Maybe it was the sentimentality that got me to tell this particular story.

Or maybe I would have told it, anyway. Because I enjoy telling it, and I've told it over and over. Again and again. And besides, the story is finally about to end tonight.

Will it end happily?

That I can't say.

What I can say is it's story time, and a large circle of tiny tots with their eyes all aglow has now formed before me, sat in my Santa-seat. It is once again time for Santa to hold court.

***

My story—the version I tell the little ones—always begins in the same way: "Don't get the wrong idea, boys and girls," I'll say. "It's fair to call this story a Christmas story. It's a good one, I daresay (even though I just made the questionable choice of using the word daresay), though I am a little biased. It's my story, after all.

"While mine is a Christmas story, it's not about Jesus. Plenty of Christmas stories tell *that* story. Plenty of Bible stories, too. This story, boys and girls," I tell them, "is about me, my family, and the two Christmases that changed my life forever."

***

First, there was my seventh Christmas, when my heart broke into a million bajillion pieces. And then came my eighth, when that heart—this heart (I point at my chest) was restored and made even stronger than before.

Did I mention, folks, how I met the real Santa Claus around that time? No? I left that part out, you say? Ah, silly me! Should have led with that. Well, I met the real Santa Claus. Do you want to hear how it happened?

I see a couple hands raise.

You do? Good. Because that's the story I'm telling today. You can sit and listen while your adults shop. I see that we have a fair number of parents or grandparents here with us, too. Of course, you're welcome to stay and enjoy my story with your kiddos. This story shouldn't take too long to tell ... I say that, but what they don't know is how I've never gotten to the end of this story before, because the end of this story hasn't happened yet. You'll be able to go across the way to get a Cinnabon very soon. I wouldn't mind one myself.

For now, when it comes to what I have to say, I simply ask the older set—kid or adult—to be open to the possibility of magic being a real thing in the world.

If you can remain open, I tell them, it will make the story easier for your youngsters to take in. When I'm through, some of you might not buy into my story, and I wouldn't exactly blame you if you didn't. If I weren't the one telling it (and if I hadn't told it every Christmas season for almost forty years now, to anyone who'll listen), I'd think it more than a little far-fetched, too. Maybe you're an unsentimental sort who'll leave here scoffing about how this isn't the real North Pole ... Just a cheap and somewhat shabby Santa setup at a suburban Seattle mall a couple days before Christmas. Then you might add—for emphasis— how my story was complete hogwash, and you still don't believe any of it could possibly be true. Not even after I, your humble storyteller, have promised you that mine is a true story without even a bit of fantasy to it ...

Just the facts, ma'am. It all happened.

For real.

And yet, while there is no fantasy about it, my story is quite fantastical, let me tell you, boys and girls. With some magic to it, even though there is no Christmas miracle. You know, Santa himself once told me, when we were in his sleigh awaiting liftoff on my eighth Christmas Eve, "Miracles happen, Davey. But they're rare. And Christmas miracles are *extremely* rare. The word miracle is used far too often in the world, anyway."

Yes, you heard that right, boys and girls. That quote came from Santa Claus himself.

Speaking of which, I've never seen anyone eat so many cookies. I imagine his dentist worked overtime. And if he ever had a nutritionist, they likely gave up after one house call! Oh boy, no one has ever eaten more gingerbread than that supposed one-night-a-year third-shifter, either. And that makes sense, too, since gingerbread is everywhere in the workshop.

But I'm getting ahead of myself.

So, this all happened—really happened—just about forty years ago. When both I, and the world, were a little more innocent.

Some people think the story began on that chilly evening out on my family's front lawn when my brother, Brendan, and I met the big guy in the red suit. Met him in the flesh. Shook his hand. But that's not when this story started at all. The whole thing began two weeks before my seventh Christmas, a full year before Santa showed up on our lawn. That's when my best friend, Luke, gave me a great idea.

CHAPTER 2

What Are You Gonna Ask Santa For This Year?

This part of the story always comes with a minor caveat, something that says *before we continue, here's one thing you'll most definitely need to know.*

Raise your hand, boys and girls, I'll say to my audience, and I say it now. Raise your hand if you think I'm the real Santa. Good. A few of you. I always love seeing believers out there. Now, raise your hand if you think I'm one of Santa's helpers. Good. A few more of you. You guys are believers, too, but you're believers who'd like to see proof. I respect that. Today, I hope to get you that proof.

But, before any of that, I need to tell you about something called cerebral palsy. Do you know what that is? Most of you are shaking your heads. No? That's okay. I'll tell you. Cerebral palsy is something I have. Some people think of it as a birth defect, but it usually happens when a doctor makes a big mistake and a baby gets hurt.

As a baby, I got hurt.

Now I stand so the kids can see how my legs aren't like their legs, how my right foot, more than any other part of my body, turns too far the wrong way, evidence of my brokenness. How my right arm stays too close to my body. Aubrey called this my "T-Rex" arm. Some of the kids murmur at this. Carrie smiles a they're-learning smile and tosses me a look of encouragement. Then I sit again.

When I was a kid, I used to wish I hadn't gotten hurt because most kids who were my age didn't know what to think of me. Some were downright mean. I'm not sure my parents knew what to think, either. Well, when I was about seven, I'd had about all I could take of not being normal or not being enough of what other people expected me to be. You need to know this, boys and girls, in order to understand what it meant to me when Luke told me what he thought I should ask Santa for that seventh Christmas ...

That was forty-one years ago, when seven-year-old Luke, my best friend, and seven-year-old Davey—that's me, for those not paying close attention (I often add so the kids can better follow along)—sat at the kitchen counter, drinking hot cocoa my mom had made for us that mid-December morning after a sleepover. The two of us were both so glad to have been released from school until after New Year's. Luke was, is, and will always be taller than me. As an adult, I'm not much taller than five and a half feet. As a kid, I was taller than my younger brother, although Brendan is taller than me now, of course. I had brown hair then. It definitely isn't *as* brown anymore, though I'm loath to admit as much. Well, maybe except for when the Christmas season comes around again; then its whiteness serves me well. My hair is also thinner these days, though it was never exactly known for its thickness. Luke's hair was blond and curly when we were kids. These days, he keeps it short, and it never has the chance to grow out and regain its former curl.

Back then, as my seventh Christmas approached, we sat and drank our cocoa and considered constructing a gingerbread house. We never did build the house, the considering never got that far, but Mom bought the candy that would have gone on the roof, if we hadn't eaten our entire supply of skittles and junior mints before they—and a dollop or two of frosting—could act as roof shingles. Mom also bought the kit we were supposed to use, and we sure liked to *consider* building it.

We were doing this, upholding the second-annual Gingerbread House Consideration Council, of which we were the only members, when Luke asked me the question all seven-year-old believers ask: "What are you gonna ask Santa for this year, Davey?"

True, there were only two weeks 'til Christmas. And both of us knew what Luke wanted, what he'd be asking for from Santa—we'd known for months: a brand-new red ten-speed bike and—if he was really good and Santa was feeling generous—a new baseball glove. His favorite glove had a hole in the webbing. But I, Davey Boyd, was still without a solid gift idea for the big man.

"I don't know," I said, and I lowered my head to my still-too-hot-to-drink cocoa.

I was embarrassed because it was the truth. I didn't know what to ask Santa for. I stirred two ice cubes into my drink with a spoon, hoping to cool the cocoa quick.

"I got an idea what you could ask for," Luke said, giddy.

"You do?" I glanced over at the kid who'd been my best friend since we were five, two whole years—which, at seven, was an eternity—and he was smiling in that mischievous way that told me he'd just come up with something brilliant. Or, as we would have said at seven, something *really cool*.

"I can't believe you've never thought of it before, Davey," he said.

"What is it?" I scooted toward Luke in my seat, meaning I nearly fell off the side of one of the two swivel chairs that lived in our kitchen. "Tell me, c'mon!"

"You should ask Santa to take away your cerebral palsy!"

I sat back. Struck. Hurt. I couldn't believe Luke would suggest such a thing. "What?" was all I could manage to say.

My cerebral palsy made me who I was. Kind. Caring. Understanding of people who weren't normal in different ways than I wasn't normal. Why would my best friend want me to get rid of such a big part of *me*? Then I was struck by something else—how badly I wanted to be rid of it, too. I'd just never let myself think about it before.

"Wouldn't you love to play sports like I can, Davey?" Luke asked.

My best friend was what the other kids and the adults we knew called "normal," which they'd whisper when they saw us walking around school together and they didn't want me to hear.

Luke risked a dangerously large sip of his own cocoa at that moment. His tongue burned. I could see it on his face, even though he tried to hide his discomfort.

"I would, yeah. It'd be so much fun to play baseball or basketball with you." I smiled. A smile soon replaced by its cousin, the frown. "But I can't. I can't play sports. *You know* I can't. That's just part of *this*." I used my hands to indicate my entire body in much the same way as a gameshow model would show off a new car, the gesture saying, *Do you see this?* and so much more. "I can't ask for that as my Christmas present."

"Why can't you?" Luke challenged.

The thing about Luke is he wasn't just my best friend *then*; he was my best friend then, and he's still one of my best friends now. And he's long been one of the few people who could level his gaze at me in that unique way he does to make a point. Actually, both he and my grandfather could do this. The man I called Papa Dale. They both have (had, in Papa's case) special talents for it, admittance into an exclusive club.

Luke knew why I couldn't ask Santa to make me a great athlete. As he sometimes would ask the big guy to do for himself. Why I wouldn't ask for such a thing.

My cerebral palsy.

I couldn't run. I couldn't jump more than a few inches off the ground. I was lucky even to be able to walk, in my own halting, weaving, I-can't-believe-that-actually-works, uncertain stride that turned my face red with the effort. Or I'd turn red with anger or embarrassment whenever people saw me walking and then turn abruptly away from me and pretend they hadn't seen.

I'm broken, I knew then. Yet I also knew how some people with palsy couldn't walk at all. Some couldn't *talk* at all.

My parents made sure to impress this fact upon little Davey Boyd.

***

"You're really quite lucky, Davey," my mother had shared with me the previous summer at a baseball game. Luke was there, too, but when my mom spoke to me like she was speaking to me then, he knew to stay quiet. I'd just told Mom how unlucky I was. I couldn't play sports like the baseball men we were watching. Like Luke could play sports. "There are some people who'd give anything to be you, Davey, to have your abilities."

What abilities? I'd thought, squinting into the summer-bright sunshine.

On top of everything else—my palsy, my legs that hurt if I used them too much—my little brother, Brendan, had just entered his terrible twos. The fact that Mom came to the baseball game with Luke and me was a huge departure from the usual. My dad had bought the tickets. Luke and I had been so excited to go with him for a "guys' day out." Then, at the last minute, Dad found out he had to work on a Saturday, so Mom asked Grandma Joan to come over to our house and watch little Brendan, which Grandma was more than happy to do, and off to the game we went. My best friend, my mom, and me. I was so glad I was still going to the game that I didn't quite know how to be grateful for the outing.

The terrible twos were "a tough age," my father had said, nodding at me as the two of us had a man-to-man talk in my room about a week before the baseball game. His point was made, but he spelled it out for me, anyway. "Don't make trouble for your mother and me. Your brother does plenty of that. Help us when you can and when you can't, Davey, the best thing you can do is to just stay out of the way."

"Grandma Joan says that to me sometimes."

"Well, she's right."

My family would have even less time for me now that they had to chase after my brother, the demon-child, whose black hair matched old photographs of Grandma Joan. My parents made me look at these whenever Mom dragged out the family photo albums once each year.

Brendan, who didn't have palsy. Who ran like he was coming out of starter's blocks whenever he ran anywhere. Which he did all the time now.

***

At that moment, sitting with my best friend at the kitchen counter, remembering last summer's man-to-man talk with Dad and the baseball game with Mom and Luke, I looked out our kitchen window at a steadily falling snow Dad had said would be gone by noon, so I should enjoy it while it lasted. The only ability seven-year-old me was grateful for just then was how I hadn't burned my tongue on my cocoa like Luke did. I still had the ability to taste food. That didn't mean Luke wanted to be me or anything. He was smarter than that.

He was also smart enough to be an only child.

Luke didn't make me answer his *why-can't-you* question. Which is good. I had so much in my head at that moment that I'd pretty much forgotten about it. Instead, he asked another.

"What do you usually ask Santa for, Davey?"

"Toys. You know that. Remember last year I got those army men?" Of course he remembered. We'd played with them every time he'd come over to my house since. Except today. Today was gingerbread and hot cocoa (emphasis on hot, de-emphasis on gingerbread).

Luke nodded. "Santa's good about bringing toys, isn't he?"

Santa was. He hadn't failed me yet. Seven-year-old me knew Santa to be friendly, approachable, and good-humored, what with his ho-ho-hos and his bowl-full-of-jelly belly. Maybe most important of all, Santa was dependable. If I asked for something, he'd deliver.

It's this dependability that truly set my story in motion.

"What would you really want for Christmas this year?" Luke asked. "If you could ask for whatever you wanted?"

I thought about this. At the same time, I finally took a sip of my cocoa. *The perfect temperature!* I celebrated silently. *You did the right thing letting it cool, Davey!*

"Do you think Santa would take Brendan back?" I asked my best friend, half-joking, half-hopeful. I wouldn't make this joke if I thought Mom could hear me. It'd hurt her too much, my not accepting Brendan yet. Sure, I grudgingly tolerated the kid, but Mom didn't want grudgingly tolerated. That wasn't good enough.

Luke shook his head. "My mom says Santa does deliveries, but he's not so good at returns. 'The sleigh only comes around once a year, Lukie. And Santa only does off-loads. The elves aren't expecting him to bring anything back with him.'"

I took another sip of cocoa and considered this for a long moment. Luke's mom was pretty reliable. She took us to baseball games, out for breakfast on the weekends when I stayed over at Luke's house—which was most weekends—and she always had plenty of sodas in the fridge for us to drink. Mostly for me to drink. I was the only one of Luke's friends who could finish a full can of soda and wouldn't leave open cans around the house to flatten. Though she warned us that too much soda could rot our teeth out and make us as fat as Santa Claus himself, we figured she was joking about that last bit because no one could be as fat as Santa Claus himself, but we checked our teeth after each can of soda we drank to make sure they were still in our heads.

Luke's mom was named Corinne, and if she said returns weren't a Santa-thing, we believed her. Still, I was stumped ... What to ask for, if not the removal of an annoying little brother I'd never asked for in the first place, a little brother who'd taken all my parents' attention for two whole years now?

I frowned. "Then ... what I want more than anything in the whole, whole world," I told Luke, "is what you want. For Santa to take my palsy away." I explained my logic, which was probably the same logic Luke had used when coming up with the idea. "Santa can do this. I *know* he can!

My palsy happened because a doctor messed up. All Santa has to do is take his sleigh back through time and keep the doctor away from me until I've been born. That way, I won't be lifted into the world by an old doctor using forceps. I won't get hurt. Santa travels to every house on Christmas Eve night, right?"

This was true, common knowledge, and Luke gave a quick nod. "Well, everyone who believes," he said.

"Right! Like us! So he shouldn't have any trouble going back in time and keeping that doctor away from me," I reasoned.

"He shouldn't," my best friend agreed.

Luke left my house that afternoon, once the snow had melted away (as Dad had said it would). Luke's mom picked him up and drove him away in their family Suburban, both of us hopeful. There was a chance—a fairly good chance— that I'd wake up normal in two weeks.

Normal.

Just the thought made me tear up and brought a sizable lump to my throat. Normal. All I've ever wanted, ever since I could barely walk, but I never actually dreamed I could be normal.

Until then.

No more palsy. No more pain. No more Charlie Cage stealing my lunch money every day at school just because he could. Luke had tried to convince the school bully, Charlie—a year older and a head taller than us—not to do this anymore because it was mean and bad and Santa was watching him.

"Santa is watching you, Charlie Cage," Luke had told him on the playground.

Amazingly, this worked. For about a week.

Then big, bad Charlie Cage went back to his big, bad ways, and he came to school one day with a story none of us wanted to hear, which Charlie's older brother had told him. Charlie said that Santa—yes, *that* Santa—wasn't real!

"You think one guy can go to that many houses in only one night?" Charlie challenged. "He can't."

"Then how do all those presents get under our trees, Charlie?" Luke demanded.

"Someone we know does the presents, obviously," Charlie said with confidence. Or with pretend confidence, anyway. Something you'll learn when you're older, boys and girls: bullies often show pretend confidence because they can't find the real thing anywhere.

"Are you sure?" I asked Charlie Cage. "You got proof Santa isn't real?"

At seven, proof is everything. Some of you kids are nodding at me. You know. Without proof, seven-year-old me knew no one should listen to this Santa-isn't-real business.

"I don't have any proof," Charlie said. "But—"

"No buts!" Luke insisted. "We believe in Santa! We know he's real because Davey and I talk to him every year, and we send our lists to him. I don't need you telling me and my best friend that someone we believe in isn't real!"

We didn't choose to sit at the same lunch table as Charlie Cage; Luke and I weren't stupid. Charlie Cage had chosen to steal my lunch money ... again because I was "crippled"—that's not a good word to use, boys and girls; I don't want to hear it from any of you, okay?—and somehow, in Charlie's mind, my condition entitled him to my money. We were confused. Luke and I chose not to tell a teacher what Charlie had done, what he always did, for fear that both of us would get beat to a smooth, mashed-potato texture.

I've never liked mashed potatoes, maybe because, somehow, they make me think of Charlie Cage.

Either way, we didn't much want to eat our next month of meals through two matching straws. Charlie also chose that moment to sit at our lunch table and try and ruin our childhoods, mine and Luke's alike. Because ... why not?

Luke refused to let him, though. After what Luke had said, Charlie Cage didn't speak for a second. He looked at me, then back at Luke.

"You two are losers!" he blurted. "You know that, right?" He got up and turned and walked away with my lunch money in the back pocket of his jeans. He didn't even spend it on anything to eat. We figured he didn't need to; Charlie Cage ate plenty as it was.

We didn't like Charlie Cage much. Obviously. Thought he'd for sure get coal in his stocking from the big guy for the next ten Christmases, and we thought this was fine.

More than fine. We thought it was fair, even. What a bully like Charlie Cage deserved.

CHAPTER 3

Santa and His Head-Elf

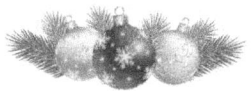

The Mall

My thoughts often wander. As they're wandering now.

I'm careful not to share all of these thoughts with the children. For the little ones, I stick to the simplified, mall-approved version of my tale. Mall-approved means I told the story to Cal once, and he unenthusiastically gave it his blessing. "If this is the story you want to tell, Boyd, that's fine. There's nothing objectionable in what you've told me, so I won't stop you. But if I hear you've deviated from this script of yours one iota, you won't last long after that. Are we clear, Boyd?"

I was being watched by the third-floor higher-ups. Granted, not *intensely* watched, but watched nonetheless. So I'm careful. Partly because Cal or his spies could be watching at any time, partly because kids have more active imaginations than adults (and they don't need explanations for *absolutely everything*), and partly because kids' attention spans can be almost nil.

Don't bore them, under any circumstance, ever. This is the edict handed down not by the third floor but by the kids themselves.

They definitely don't need to know why Carrie is so good at what she does. They don't need me to tell them. They can *see* it in the way she carries herself, in our easy interaction, and in the exuberance she must have been born exuding.

That's why this part of the story isn't for them. No, it's for you, the non-believer. The skeptic.

The doubter among all of us.

Carrie's a forever cheery, often chatty, rosy-cheeked woman. She's been on the job alongside me for two Christmases. I like her. She's easy to like.

Not like *that*, though. Don't get the wrong idea. Before last night, I'd been with Aubrey for forever. Besides, Carrie would never think of me that way.

I have cerebral palsy, don't forget. I sure can't.

Carrie is single, though. I do know that about her.

"By choice," she's told me. "None of the guys out there these days seem to *get* me."

The guys may not have gotten her, but the people she worked with sure did. She's been voted head-elf by her colleagues each year we've worked together, at least in part because she doesn't need to paint her cheeks rosy with make-up like the other elves do. For Carrie, the rosy cheeks are one hundred percent natural. She might even still believe in Santa. That's how chipper she is every morning when she greets me as I make my way to my mall dressing room.

"Hi, Santa! Did you have a good night?" she'll say. It's always something like that. She knows my name is Dave and that my friends—Carrie included—call me Davey. But she'll always call me Santa if there's even the slightest chance little ears might overhear us.

I wish I could be more like Carrie. But I can't even fake it, at least never that early in the day.

"Mm-hm," I grunted two weeks back. Right after I'd left Cal Grigsby's third-floor office. Right after I'd given my notice and my boss had taken it with too much glee.

When would I tell Carrie? I didn't know. Maybe I wouldn't need to. I could just slip out on our last day, December 23, and she'd never see me again and her life wouldn't be impacted at all by my leaving it. I still had two weeks before I needed to worry about that, though.

"What did you do last night, Santa?"

"Not much." I'd done *nothing*, to be precise. Nothing but talk myself up in my bedroom. "You can quit. You will quit. There are better days ahead for you, Davey Boyd. You know that."

But did I? When I'd called Aubrey, looking for moral support, my call went unanswered.

She must be busy, I thought. That wasn't unusual these days. *Don't bother her.*

"I went to the Nutcracker with my father. Have you seen it, Santa?" Carrie asked.

"I haven't," I said.

"It's wonderful!" she gushed.

"I assumed. People have been performing it and going to see it forever."

"My mother and I used to go every year! She loved it, and she taught me to love it. 'Carrie,' she told me every holiday season, 'my grandmother, your great-grandmother, was a ballerina. She told me she was a sugar plum fairy years ago.'"

"Was she?" I asked my head-elf.

"We don't have any pictures to prove it," Carrie said, "but we don't *doubt* it, either."

"And you shouldn't. Ho, ho, ho." If you don't practice the Santa laugh, your Santa laugh won't be any good. So sometimes I'll practice it with Carrie. Just throw it in at the end of whatever it is I'm saying. She'll often give me a mouth-closed smile in response.

I wished Carrie the Elf a Merry Christmas, and I headed into my dressing room. Ten minutes later, I was ready to take my seat amid the mall's North Pole display. Red-suited. Black-booted. The beard has always been real, so I have no need for the fake beard plus adhesive that some mall-Santas use. My girth is real, too, unfortunately, and my doctor has warned me it needs to go.

***

It's a week ago, December 16, at around 9:25 in the morning. The line to see me is already too long, and the first child of the day approaches my lap. Were he and his parents here when the mall opened?

"And who might you be?" I ask him.

"I'm Nick," he says as he climbs onto my lap. Then he whispers into my ear, "It's short for Nicholas."

Nick's parents stand with their hands on each other's shoulders just down the stairs from Santa's seat. Mom's an attractive brown-eyed brunette in her late twenties. She isn't tall, but I wouldn't call her petite, either. She's got her phone out, taking a video of little Nick. Nicholas. Dad is about six feet tall, dishwater blond, in his mid-thirties. He's smiling wide. It's a smile I recognize. It denotes contentment.

They're lucky. That's not a smile I often see this time of year. More often than not, any smile I see from an adult when it's this cold and the Seattle weather is a mix between rain, snow, and wind—any smile is, at best, tight and, at worst, forced for the good of a child making memories.

"And what would you like for Christmas this year, young Nicholas?"

"I want a dog," says the boy. "Did you get my letter?"

"I did," I say. "But I'm afraid there are a lot of boys your age named Nicholas out there. My name is Nicholas, too." At least some people would say it is, so I can get away with telling the boy this. "Did you know that?"

"I didn't." He smiles as wide as his father. The same smile.

"It's a good name. Could you remind me what kind of dog you want?"

"A black lab. They're my favorite kind of dog."

"Ah, I see. Did you know that's Santa's favorite kind of dog, too? I'll look into it for you. For now, let's take a picture, shall we? Look to your left … no, your left … yes, like that. And smile."

The camera flashes, and Nicholas and his parents say thank you to me and to Carrie the Elf, who took the photo—as she's taken so many other photos—and they are gone.

***

There's a rule here at the mall. It's really *my* rule. It came along when I came along. It isn't posted anywhere, so none of the kids know anything about it, but all of the elves know it, and so should you, dear reader.

I hope my telling you of this "rule" gives you a better idea of who I am.

Davey's Rule: No kids are allowed into the North Pole before Santa has taken his seat and gotten settled in.

Once I'm situated just so, I don't get up for hours. I can't. I can't let the kids see my wobbly walk or the way my right foot is on my body nearly backwards; these things that bother me might do worse if seen by any kids who see me inside the Santa persona. My reality might bust the Santa of it all for them, and I, for one, won't let my brokenness—my palsy—be the what that ruins the illusion. Since I'm stationed in one place for so long—and since I don't dare move when any child might chance upon seeing how their long-believed and cherished fantasy is really an imperfect, agreed-upon, sometimes-choreographed real lie—I don't drink anything for a good portion of the day, either. No one wants Santa to pee the suit, or his chair, least of all Santa himself.

I start work at 9 a.m. most days. Story time starts at around 11, with a scheduled break at noon. That's when the North Pole closes for a hurried forty-five minutes, and I both eat my lunch (which I've packed today, since there isn't and has never been a full-fledged Mrs. Claus in my life), and I take care of any business I need to take care of.

Yes, boys and girls, I'll often tell my little listeners, even Santa goes to the bathroom. (I always say something like this when I'm telling this particular story. I pick a spot when they're looking bored or checked out, and I'll insert the joke.)

At my declaration, there is never not a not-small giggle-fit amongst the story time crowd. I expect it. I wait for the fit to subside before going on.

Another thing I don't ever tell the kids, because they don't want to hear it, is how Carrie the Elf always has a hot coffee waiting for me to go with my lunch. My one cup for the day. On our second day ever working together, I'd let slip how I preferred my coffee with cream and two sugars, and she's never forgotten this. We've taken our lunches together for so long it's become the expectation—our two-year-old, in-season routine. We didn't really plan it that way. It just sort of happened.

Our lunch conversations often start not unlike our morning greetings; with the usual small talk my head-elf is so good at. Carrie asking me something like, "How was your night last night, Santa?" Which is precisely how today's lunch conversation on December 23—our last lunch conversation ever—began.

Followed by me telling her how I spent my evening bingeing a time-travel TV series I loved as a kid. I've seen each episode at least ten times. What I don't tell her is how I've gotten used to watching the episodes alone and how my heart is broken today. Because who wants to hear that from Santa?

Not even his head-elf.

"I did some scrapbooking with my niece last night, and then we made spaghetti for dinner," Carrie shares.

"You have a niece?"

She nods, a wide smile breaking across her face. "I love her so much. She called spaghetti 'nooda' last night. 'Auntie Carrie, can we make nooda?' Have I never told you about Emily?"

I shake my head. We've talked about a lot of things in two years, but we've never delved far into personal lives beyond my saying I had a girlfriend and Carrie saying Aubrey was a lucky girl. Which is just, you know, something you say, even if you don't think it. To be polite.

Whose decision was this minimal-personal-life-discussion? Mine? I'm not sure. It was likely mutual, a decision arrived at without words.

"Do you have kids?" I ask, uncertain if I should be asking.

"No. One of these days, maybe. I haven't found the right guy yet."

"Well, do you have a type in mind? What kind of guy are you looking for? If you don't mind me asking? Or you could tell me to shut up. That's option two. And you'd be fully within your rights to say it."

I'm not asking in hopes of making myself a candidate for the position. Carrie would never choose me, anyway. Any women who *do* choose me eventually return this broken-down jalopy of a man to the sketchy online-dating dealership from which they obtained him. They all return him worse for wear, it seems, dented and leaking tears instead of oil and falling apart in his palsied middle age. But if Carrie the Elf is looking, there should be plenty of candidates willing to put in applications.

My lunch is underwhelming today; I packed the leftovers Brendan and Jess brought over. I called them last night to say things were finally and fully over with Aubrey, and they asked how I was, and I said I was fine (which was a lie, and they knew it but didn't call me on it). And they got in their car without being asked to get in their car—even though I'd told them not to—a little red, we-haven't-had-kids-yet hatchback, and drove right over, showing up on my porch with a casserole dish full of lasagna, my sister-in-law saying I should eat.

Brendan agreed, saying, as only he could: "This is a hard time, brother. I get it. But you can't forget to eat. As your brother, I insist that you eat."

I did then, and I am now. Yet, as good as the meal was last night, I'm not a fan of it reheated. I know that most people are and that I'm a definite outlier here, but my opinion is what it is. Maybe the lasagna doesn't taste right because it's the main course of the first lunch I packed after Aubrey left for good.

Carrie thinks my question over, repeats it aloud to herself. "What type of guy am I looking for? Well, I ... I don't know if I've ever told anyone this, but ever since I was a kid ... No, I can't say it; you're gonna think I'm nuts, Davey. Either that or you'll laugh at me."

"No, I won't. I won't think you're nuts and I won't laugh. Tell me." Now I'm intrigued. Carrie the Elf has a secret she's never told anyone, and she's about to let me in on it.

"Well, okay. But please don't laugh. You have to promise."

"I promise not to laugh, Carrie. Santa's honor."

"Excuse me?"

"It's like scout's honor, but I was never a scout. I've been Santa for a while, though, so ... Santa's honor."

Carrie grins. "Okay. Well, ever since I was a kid, I've always wanted to marry ... Santa Claus."

"You have not!"

"I have too! As a little girl, I thought it sounded romantic. Marry Santa, live in the North Pole surrounded by snow and Christmas colors, and celebrate Christmas—the best holiday there is year-round."

I learn something new every day I do this job. But I never thought I'd learn that about Carrie the Elf.

The last twenty minutes of lunch I spend scraping my congealed jaw off the mall's food court floor. Then I give myself a reality check. I don't do this often enough.

She said Santa, buddy, I remind myself. *She never said she wanted to marry you, a forty-something disabled man who's been playing Santa for two years and who always makes sure none of the kids who believe in Santa ever actually see him walk anywhere. You're a sad man at the tail end of the breakup of a toxic relationship on the last day of a job your bosses don't even want you in any longer. You're not the real Santa, Davey Boyd, and you know it.*

Could I ever be the real Santa?

I thought I could once. But now? No chance.

***

"Are you one of my elves?" I'd asked her, way back when Carrie and I had our first-ever confab. Our first-ever interaction. That chilly morning feels like so long ago now. How is it that it was just over twenty-four months ago in real time? A day that served as both my first and the first day of Carrie's second month in our respective positions. The previous Santa, mall lore told, had been fired because he liked bars and drink more than he liked ho-ho-hoing and making kids happy.

"I'm actually your head-elf!" Carrie said cheerily. She was obviously proud of this distinction and, as if to underscore this pride, was already garbed in full elf regalia; I had yet to don Santa's famous ensemble, as it was still two hours before the doors opened.

I wasn't nearly as cheer-filled; it was too early. But then I don't know that I've ever been as cheer-filled as Carrie. "I see," I said, my voice flatter than it should have been. Flatter than I'd intended it.

"How did you come to be our Santa?" Carrie asked.

I've since learned she meant nothing by the question. She wasn't looking for reasons to get rid of me already, like some people would when they saw the palsy on me. They treated it like an ugly sweater I'd chosen to wear. *If the body's no good, the person must be no good, too.* A knee-jerk reaction. For Carrie, it was simple small talk between newly minted colleagues. But that's certainly not how I took it then.

Did she notice your walk, Davey? How could she not notice?

Both Luke and Brendan and—to a lesser extent—my parents have always made allowances for me and my palsy. They'd grown used to it over many years; it was routine to them. If we went out to eat, for example, someone who wasn't me would cut up my meal for me. Unless I was smart and ordered a burger. No one need slice into a burger for me to eat it. Though one of them might offer to halve it, and I'd usually take them up on this option.

Davey can't drive, so someone will need to make sure he has a ride when we decide to go out. Though I often felt like a burden, one of the two of them—either my brother or my best friend—always made sure the ride was taken care of.

Therefore, whenever *anybody* appeared to question my place in the world, I bristled. I couldn't help it.

"Would you rather the job went to someone else?" I asked Carrie. She'd hurt me without knowing it.

"No, no. It's just that I noticed ..." She looked down at my legs, then back up at me.

"And you were wondering why the mall was so desperate?" I forced a smile my heart wasn't in.

"No, that's not it at all. I *know* why the mall is so desperate. What I mean to say is ... I'm so sorry, we've gotten off on the wrong foot here, and I'm sorry about that. I think it's my fault." She stuck out a green-gloved hand. "I'm Carrie. And you are?"

"Dave. But my family and most of my friends call me Davey. Childhood nicknames die hard."

She laughed. "May *I* call you Davey?"

I eyed her warily. Trust is not something I give over easily. "I suppose," I said.

"If it makes you feel any better, Davey, my childhood nickname was Bookworm."

"Who gave you that name? A bully?"

Now she smiled wide. "Far from it. My mother. She wasn't making fun of me or anything, though. She considered herself a bookworm, too."

"Ah. Well, you asked how I ended up as Santa. Word is your previous seat-filler was a bit of a lush."

"That he was," Carrie verified. "I was wondering when they'd finally can him." She only told me this a year later, but before my predecessor's exit, she'd complained to the third floor for months.

"Yes, well ... my landlady ... her husband is the head honcho here at the mall."

"You know Calvin?" She was not impressed.

"I know Calvin's wife, Rose. She called me this past weekend and said her husband and the folks here at the mall were in a big bind. They'd just let their Santa go and could I possibly step in? I play Santa every year in my apartment building's Christmas pageant."

"Your apartment building has a Christmas pageant?" *That's weird*, Carrie didn't have to say. We both knew it was.

"What can I say? It's mostly older folks with young grandkids who wanted a reason for their families to come around for the holidays besides the holidays themselves. And none of the old guys in the building have any experience playing Santa. So they asked me if I'd do it because, I don't know, maybe I looked the part? I was hesitant at first; I have cerebral palsy, as you can see." I bounced my on-half-backwards right foot up and down so that she'd notice how it was turned the wrong way on its leg. (Essentially, no sandals or flip-flops for me; not that either of those would have ever been my preferred footwear.) "But the group insisted, and I didn't have the heart to turn them down."

"And you couldn't turn Rose down, either, could you?"

I shook my head. "I gave her the same out I'd given the apartment people." It's also the same out I give *all* people when I first meet them, and by mentioning it I was offering it to Carrie the Elf. "I told Rose I had palsy, and was she sure she wanted me to do it and I'd understand if she didn't." This wasn't true, and Carrie and I both knew it wasn't true. So did Rose. "She said I was talking nonsense and that she'd had the good fortune to see my Santa when visiting a friend of hers who lived in my building, that you'd all be lucky to have me, and that all concessions to my physical impairments that needed to be made would be."

"Cal agreed to that?"

"Not sure he had much of a choice, if he didn't want to be sleeping on the couch for months."

She chuckled. "Well, it sounds to me like you have a good heart, Davey." She was already using the friends-only form of my name, as though she'd used it a thousand times. "And Rose was right. You tell me what you need. I'll do everything I can to make this work for you, Santa, as long as you stay away from excessive amounts of alcohol on North Pole days."

"I think I can do that," I said. "I don't drink."

Then Carrie surprised me. "Would It be too forward of me to ask you to lunch, Santa?"

"Too forward? No, it wouldn't. But I'm afraid I pack my lunch every day, and Rose said we only get about forty-five minutes for lunch. 'Calvin's tight with his lunch breaks,' she warned me. 'They start at the stroke of noon, and if they're not over by forty-five after, he starts docking pay.'"

"That's true, unfortunately, he does do that. He's kind of an ass. But he's older and he's been here forever, so none of us have stood up to him yet. Maybe we never will. I don't know." She spent a moment with her thoughts. "Okay, well ... if you pack your lunch, we could eat at the same table in the food court. Are you good with that?"

What was this, high school again? "What is this, high school again?" I said with a half-smirk. *If so, get me out of here.*

"The way I see it, Davey, once you've gotten out of high school—but somehow *only* once you've gotten out of high school—you realize how all of life is basically different versions of high school relived, over and over again."

She wasn't wrong, and despite the fact that we'd first met in the early morning, when I'm notoriously at my most cantankerous, Carrie the Elf and I became fast friends, to the point where I soon learned her lunchtime go-to was a grilled cheese sandwich she'd stand in line for each day from a booth in our court called "Just Cheese, Please!" followed by a Cinnabon for dessert. Sometimes, she'd even share the bun with me, cut it in half, though I never asked her to do this, and I never thought much of the gesture beyond, *She's just trying to fatten me up for the role I'm playing, so that I can keep up appearances.*

Of course, Carrie never failed to get me a coffee when she got her bun, either; always with cream and two sugars. My one cup for the day. I'd never asked for this, either, but I appreciated it, and I'd give Carrie a nod of thanks when she'd set down the steaming cup before me and my brown-bag lunch each day.

CHAPTER 4

The List

And now, back to the mall-approved story. The one I tell so often I could tell it in my sleep.

Let's see. Where was I? Oh, sure, my best friend, Luke, had just given seven-year-old me the idea to ask Santa to get rid of my palsy. Now it was up to me to write my list to Santa, to make the all-important request with both passion and humility. Or, as seven-year-old me thought of it, I needed to "ask Santa right."

***

How many of you have ever written a letter to Santa, boys and girls? (Myriad hands wave high.) That's good. How can Santa know what you want if you don't write him a list, right? (Many nods.) Well, the next part of my story is about the list *I* wrote to Santa before my seventh Christmas.

Hang on, seven-year-old me thought, alone in my bedroom after Luke left with his mom that afternoon. The cocoa was gone, our spent cups soaking in the kitchen sink, the gingerbread house still (and forever) unbuilt. The snow was gone, too. Now I sat at my childhood desk, typing my Christmas list for Santa himself on my ancient computer. Well, *you* would think it was ancient, boys and girls; back then, the home computer was fairly new, a technological marvel. Downstairs, my parents tried to keep up with little two-year-old Brendan, and from what I could hear—pots and pans clanging in the dining room and then in the kitchen and then in the dining room again—Brendan was running a marathon. Was that glass breaking?

I can't write by hand, and I never have been able to, so my computer was the only way for me to write down things like a list to the big guy.

Do I want to ask Santa to make Charlie Cage be nicer to me, too? Besides the big thing I want? Or maybe I could ask if he'd skip Charlie's house completely? Coal is one thing; the horror of being fully skipped by Santa and having to tell your classmates about it when we all go back to school and someone innocently asks what he got from Santa would be even better.

Or maybe I should ask Santa to make my little brother grow up faster.

Brendan was only two and a half, and my mom and dad were all about him back then. I missed how Mom used to spend every second she could with me. Now I was up in my room working on my list and she hadn't even noticed I was gone. Dad probably figured I was staying out of the way like he and Grandma sometimes asked me to do.

No, I decided. I wouldn't ask for any of those things. If Santa can get rid of my palsy, he'll get rid of the reason Charlie Cage bullies me. And so much more. If he can get rid of my palsy, I'd actually have the chance to be Brendan's big brother instead of what I was afraid I'd turn into one day and then be his whole life: a burden. And he'd have to spend that whole life making sure I hadn't fallen, that I was comfortable, that I had enough food for dinner, that it was cut up well enough and I could eat it without any more help. Brendan would spend so much of his time on Earth making sure his big brother didn't get left behind.

That's not fair. To him or to me, I told myself.

***

My letter to Santa, December 1981.

Dear sir (Mom says all the thank-you cards or letters I write should start out "formal but polite." I told her I'd try it. I hope you like it, Santa sir!)

Davey Boyd here! In case you talk to a lot of Davey Boyds, I'm the one from Seattle, Washington, United States, who has cerebral palsy.

I'm seven now, and I know I always ask for too much every Christmas. Mom tells me I do. Somehow, you always come through, though, sir, and I have to thank you for that.

This year, my list isn't a big one. No video game systems. No expensive TVs I won't get. Dad says the one I have in my room is "perfectly fine." It isn't a long list, either. I'm not expecting twenty-five presents under our tree (I know you have other kids to build toys for, kids who've probably been better than me this year, but in my defense, it's hard adjusting to being the second-most important kid in a house after being the most important kid in the house), and I won't be counting my presents to see if I have more this year than last.

My parents are busy with their new-ish baby, Brendan, who's learned to walk since I wrote you last. Mom says he's a terror, but she loves him anyway. Dad says he hopes Brendan stops drawing on the walls. Brendan says he's drawing Mommy and Daddy. He doesn't understand why Daddy gets so mad. It makes him cry.

Everything makes him cry, really. Such a baby. He'll grow up soon, won't he?

Brendan can babble now, which my mom and dad think is so cute it's annoying, but he still doesn't talk much. He's kind of boring, too, because he doesn't do anything but eat and sleep and poop and pee and cry and Crayola all over the walls.

Honest.

For a letter without a long list, this one is going long. I know. That's because what I'm going to ask you for, Santa, is something I've never asked you for before. But my best friend, Luke (you know Luke. He asks for new shoes every year because he's good at sports and he runs a lot and his shoes wear out), Luke says that if anyone can help me, you can.

I believe him. Just like I believe in you. Even though the older kids at my school, like Charlie Cage, say you're not real and that everyone who says you are is lying.

I want to prove them wrong. It would also be so nice to wake up in a body that didn't have my cerebral palsy anymore. That didn't always hurt. That didn't always wobble when I walk.

So here's my list. It's short and, I hope, simple. I'm not asking you and your elves to build me a helicopter, after all.

<u>1. (& only): Get rid of my palsy please.</u>

For good please.

I want to wake up Christmas morning and run—really run—down the stairs to the tree and get there just as fast as the kids who don't have what I have. I want to call Luke and celebrate two things: how you're real, which we've known all along, and, more importantly, how I'm not handicapped anymore. I'm sick of being a burden to my parents. I shouldn't know that word. That's what Grandma says. It's a big word. But Dad and Mom use it all the time when they're fighting in their room and they think I can't hear them. Mom will speak in a muffled, whispery voice so she's hard to hear, but at the end of whatever she says there's usually Dad's name, Robert, plus that word I'm not supposed to know.

Burden.

Then Dad will say something like, "He's not a burden, Sylvia! How can you say that?" I can hear Dad loud and clear because when he says what he says he's yelling it. It's also the first and only time I've heard Dad use Mom's actual name in my whole life.

She says she's sorry and she didn't mean it, but Dad says he's not sure he believes her. I'm not sure, either.

Santa, I know that if you get rid of my palsy, my parents will stop fighting. I'm the reason they fight, and I don't want to be the reason anymore. It hurts too much. It hurts more than being handicapped, which hurts a lot. I want them to stop fighting not just for me but for Brendan, too.

My right leg doesn't work right. It never has. You know that. You see me when I'm sleeping, you know when I'm awake, so it's hard to miss the way my right foot is almost always the reason I'll trip over nothing.

"What was that, a gum wrapper?" my dad will say, his eyes smiling even though his expression is serious as he gives me his hand and picks me up off the ground.

Again.

Dad and I like to go walking every Saturday. To strengthen my legs, Dad says. I think we also go so Dad can get out of the house and give Mom a tiny break. She's got Brendan to worry about now, and she needs a break from having two kids sometimes. If Mom's with us on our walks (she comes along once in a month of Sundays, says Dad), she'll give him a dirty look for saying that thing about the gum wrapper, but I can see how upset it makes her when I fall. When I lose my balance. Whenever my palsy shows up to bother us.

Dad might say, "You can't ask Santa for that. To get rid of your palsy? That's asking for way too much, bud. Be realistic, Davey." I can hear Dad in my head right now.

But let's be honest. Just between you and me, Santa (and I know you can keep a secret; you keep so many), I've always had more faith in you than Dad has.

Two Christmases ago, when I'd just turned five and Mom left and Dad said she was gone for good this time, you were there for me. You remember, don't you? I wrote you a week after Mom left and said all I wanted for Christmas was for my mommy to come back (Mommy is such a five-year-old word to use, isn't it?). I didn't even tell Dad I'd sent the letter, and I didn't send it from here at home because he's the one who sends out our mail. I had my Grandma Joan send it from her post office. She said she was happy to do it and that every little boy should get to write a letter to Santa and have it sent all the way to your workshop at the North Pole.

I hope she won't mind sending my list this year, too. Mom and Dad are just too busy. I don't want to bother them.

Anyway, two Christmases ago, as I came running downstairs (or as close to running as I could get with my palsy) early on Christmas morning, the doorbell rang. I knew who it was before Dad even opened the door.

Mom had returned.

As she came through the door, her arms open for a hug from me—her baby boy—I said a silent thank you, Santa. I hope you heard it. Grandma says you hear everything and that you have great ears. I'm not sure I believe her, considering how old you are (a hundred? Two hundred?), but I hope she's right.

Anyway, Mom always says, if I want something, I should be able to tell people why I want it, not just that I want it. She says it's no different with you, Santa.

"If you can't tell Santa why you want a toy, or whatever it is you ask him for, Davey, then you won't get it."

I would think not being bullied by Charlie Cage and being able to really be Brendan's big brother would be enough for you to understand me wanting my palsy gone, but in case they're not … I don't want to hurt anymore; I don't want people to think I'm mentally handicapped anymore. I want Brendan to look up to his big brother. I want him to look up to me. I don't want him to be embarrassed by me or for just looking at me to scare him, like it can sometimes in the mornings when my legs are weak and walking is hard for me. He thinks I walk like a monster, and he's not exactly wrong.

And, yes, I want to play sports like Luke can. I want to be on his baseball team. I'll play second base. He can play shortstop. We'll turn double-plays together.

For all these reasons, and more, please, Santa, take my palsy. Take it far, far away.

If you can do this—and I know you can; I have faith in you—this will be the merriest Christmas I've ever had.

With so much hope and Christmas joy, a devoted believer. (Grandma Joan helped me with that sign-off over the phone),

Davey Boyd

Seattle, Washington,

United States

CHAPTER 5

The Night Before Christmas

The Mall

It is my long-practiced habit to take a break after I mention the list, however long it takes me to get there. Though I've never exactly sped through it, today the story's taken me a while. In these breaks, I'll tell the story of Rudolph and a certain foggy Christmas Eve. Or the story of Frosty and how he and a group of lucky kid-followers once had some fun before he melted away. Good standbys, both of them.

Carrie knows the routine. She knows the beats I'll hit with this story. Usually, she can time them pretty well, too, but not today.

I'm going slower today, savoring the tale.

"How many of you have actually met my friend, Carrie the Elf?" I ask the circled children.

A couple tiny hands raise high and wave there in the air like small, self-powered wind chimes. A few little voices call out, "I have! I have!" "Me, me, me!" "I know her! I know her!"

I smile at their excitement. They personally know a celebrity. One of Santa's elves. His head-elf, no less. At the age when anyone qualifies as a celebrity: a teacher who's just patiently taught them their times-tables; the bus driver who's picked them up from their stop for three years straight; their school's custodian.

"I ask because it's Carrie you boys and girls have to thank for story time. For this circle we're in right now."

"Oooooo," comes the collective coo.

Story time is something of a workaround Carrie devised. She came to this understanding by simply observing me and then she asked if I was in pain.

"I know you have palsy, but are you in pain, Davey?"

I saw no reason to lie to her—she realized sitting for as long as was required of Santa-me left non-magical-me stiff and hurting by day's end. Really by day's middle, to be honest.

"Our Santa needs to be able to stretch his legs so he doesn't end every day stiff as a board," Carrie had argued up on the third floor. She told me about this conversation the first day we ever had story time with Santa. About a year ago. She didn't tell me she was thinking about challenging Cal on my behalf because she had to know I would have told her not to do it. She was standing, she said, while Calvin Grigsby sat—short, fat, grumpy, and old— behind his massive desk. "What if we put the kids in a circle and Davey—I mean Santa—told them a story? He could even sit with them and stretch out as needed."

"If we do that," Calvin replied, unmoved by Carrie's plea, "the kids will know there's something *wrong* with him. We can't have that. I know Mr. Boyd himself takes pains to make sure that doesn't happen. And whoever heard of a mall employing a Santa and not using him for proper Santa-ing, anyway? Let the kids sit on his lap, ask for their toys, everyone smiles for pictures, and then we all go home. Simple."

"And if you don't take me up on this story time idea and give Mr. Boyd a tiny break each day—besides lunch, I mean," Carrie had threatened, knowing she was the one with leverage, "you'll lose both a Santa—the best one this place has ever had, and you know it—and his head-elf. And if you don't think I'll walk, you just try me, Cal. Simple."

Cal hadn't tried her. He'd relented. He hadn't liked it, but he'd relented. I don't doubt his wife, Rose, was somehow involved. If nothing else, she likely came to Cal's mind at that moment. And thus story time was born.

And on that story time-birthing day, completely unplanned and unprompted, at least on my end (I wouldn't have known how to prompt such a thing), Carrie the Elf and I had our first—and, so far, our only—kiss; a chaste little peck I hadn't expected that she gave me at lunch over our shared Cinnabon after I'd learned of the new story time.

"You said *what?*" I chuckled. "He said *what?* How did you do that, Carrie? *Why* did you do that?"

She'd said she'd done it for me, and then came the peck. It hadn't gone any further than that, though. For two reasons. I had a girlfriend whom I loved deeply, who would have been crushed if she knew my head-elf was kissing me or if she knew I thought about kissing her back, and I wouldn't let it go any further. Besides, the mall frowned upon workplace relationships. The higher-ups, like Cal, thought them highly inappropriate, and any such "romances" would have been, in Cal's own words, "grounds for dismissal."

Anyway, back to story time ...

Carrie steps forward to address the circle. "Who's got questions for Santa? Ask away!" This is to help keep story time a little more interactive.

I'm curious. Will this group of kids inquire as to how Santa can get all his work done in one freezing, solitary night? Sometimes, they'll ask this; sometimes, older kids will ask how Santa and Mrs. Claus met. Do they have any children of their own? Parents will pipe up, too. Not often, but when they do, they want to hear where Santa shops. Where they can get the best deals. I don't blame them for asking, but I'm not much help on that topic.

"The elves do all the work," I say, and it's the truth, if a little deceptive. Sometimes, the elves shop, either late at night when no one's looking or whenever the fewest people will see them. It's likely they even shop online these days. But, for our purposes, the elves do all the work. "Santa himself is an elf. Just a really big elf."

This afternoon, a little boy asks about the first time Santa ever laughed. "Did it sound like ho, ho, ho when you laughed the first time, Santa? What about when you were a kid like me? Like us? What did your laugh sound like then?"

Sometimes, the kids are extra-inquisitive like this and they can't quite decide which question they want to ask, which they want answered. Sometimes, they're more reticent and Carrie will redirect the conversation and suggest a quick added story. As she does today.

"How about *The Night Before Christmas*? What if Santa read that story for all of you? Would you like that?"

"Yes!" they answer together, not in unison though very loud.

The Night Before Christmas it is. I've read this story a thousand times. Probably more. I look at Carrie and give a nod of appreciation. She notices the nod and gives me one of her wide, toothy smiles. Her trademark. I like to imagine they remain on her face even when she's not wearing elf-green, but I've never seen my head-elf in any other garb.

When I've finished reading Clement Clarke Moore's beloved poem, then we'll get back to the story I need to finish before I'm finished with work tonight.

***

"… A Merry Christmas to all. And to all a good night."

The kids clap—and a couple squeal excitedly—as I set the picture-book aside. Carrie the Elf claps the loudest.

Now, where did we leave off? I ask the kids this, and they tell me, so loudly and talking all at once …

Ah, yes. I'd just written my list for Santa and gotten it to Grandma Joan in secret so she could mail it for me—no small feat. After that, off Brendan and I went to visit the big guy at a not-so-sad suburban mall.

CHAPTER 6

Visiting the Big Guy

Forty-One Years Ago

Mom was frantic. Panicked.

If we didn't leave the house right now, she was convinced Brendan would miss his chance to meet Santa. And she would miss *her* chance to get a perfectly posed picture of Brendan meeting Santa. That's when my dad made the mistake many men before him have made.

As we all put on our coats and Mom was in the process of losing it, poor Dad took her by the shoulders, not roughly, and spoke six words. I counted. Those words almost killed him because Mom almost killed him after she heard them.

"Sylvia, will you please calm down?"

Mon's face went deep red with rage. "Excuse me?" She turned on Dad, who instantly spotted his error and began his verbal backpedal.

"I'm sorry, honey. I only meant that—"

"What *did* you mean? Tell me! I'd love to know!"

As they fought, we ran out the door. Well, they were running, with Brendan latched onto Mom's hand. They dragged him to the car on his feet. I was just trying to keep up, lagging behind as I so often did. Good thing for me we were taking the car to the mall. If we'd been walking the whole way, there would have been no Santa-visit for me.

"Calm down? You want me to calm down?" Mom repeated, angry.

"I know that's what I said. What I meant was we should take our time. You know Davey walks slower than we—"

"This isn't about Davey, Robert!" Those days, nothing ever was. She hugged Brendan close. "Are you excited to meet Santa, honey?" she said to him.

Before then, he'd been too young or too into crying in public for the whole Santa experience. The week before, Mom had told me, as the two of us ate a quiet lunch while Brendan napped, "I'm afraid your brother'll throw a tantrum on Santa's lap."

I understood her fear. This was a big year for Brendan. It was even bigger for Mom, who insisted on pictures every time our family did anything together.

"Brendan meeting Santa for the first time ... we have to get a picture."

"Honey, the elves take the photos. And Brendan isn't the only kid meeting Santa today," Dad attempted to reassure her with reason.

No, he isn't, I thought. *I'll be there, too. If anyone cares. Will Mom even know I'm there?* Whether Mom did or not, Santa would know me. *I hope he got my letter. I can't wait to wake up without my cerebral palsy on Christmas morning!*

***

"Who have we got here?" Santa asked, not the mall-Santa smelling of pipe tobacco I'd gotten used to, when Mom last took me to visit Santa (and insisted on pictures of me with him.)

"This is Brendan," Mom said. We'd been waiting in line for so long. Too long. When I asked her how long we waited, when we finally got to Santa, Mom whispered that it was half an hour or so, but it felt like a whole day. She placed Brendan on Santa's lap.

"What would you like for Christmas, little guy?" Santa asked him.

"Dog," Brendan said, excitedly wiggling around. "Dog for Christmas!" He grinned just the way he did when he'd stolen a cookie and Mom didn't see.

Santa nodded. "I'll look into it, Brendan."

Yeah, right, I thought. There would be no dog. I'd asked to get a dog for years. Now I knew enough to know that Santa and Mom and Dad talked a lot and that Mom had told Santa a dog was not happening, so I'd stopped asking.

Let the new kid ask for a dog. Let him be disappointed like I was when it doesn't come. Life's tough, kid. And then you grow up and the parents don't think you're cute anymore. I've been there. You'll be there someday, too.

"Look at my elf now. Yes, that-a-way. That's right. Or look at your mom. That's okay, too. It's time for our picture. Smile for Santa, Brendan."

Brendan did. A camera flashed.

"And who's big brother here?" Santa turned his eyes on me. They were twinkling like the stars.

"This is our Davey," Mom said, dismissive. She placed both of her hands on my shoulders and moved me toward him.

"Davey Boyd, sir. David. But my friends call me Davey. I sent you a letter about two weeks ago. Did you get it?" I wobbled forward in my unique, unsteady way.

Santa saw the wobble. I knew he'd seen it. No one could miss it, and no one could hide when they'd first taken it in. How their face would harden suddenly, then soften with a cross between empathy and sadness. The person would look down at their shoes and keep their eyes down there as long as was socially acceptable. Usually longer. I hated what I thought when people saw me wobble like I did.

Did I even deserve to be on this planet if I couldn't walk normally?

Well, on Christmas morning, I wouldn't have those thoughts anymore. I'd finally *be* normal. And not just in my dreams. When no one else was looking.

"Davey Boyd?" Santa repeated.

"Yes, sir. Davey Boyd from Seattle, Washington, United States."

My dad always said I should add the country. For accuracy, and in case there were any other Davey Boyds out there "randomly roaming the planet." Guess there had to be.

"You know, I think I did receive your letter, young man."

Success! Grandma Joan had come through for me again. Same as last year.

"So you remember what I asked for then?" I was relieved.

"Can you refresh my memory, young man? What was it you wanted for Christmas?"

What? How could he forget? There was only one thing on that dang list. If he's read the letter, he knows what it is.

Suspicious, I asked, "Are you the real Santa?"

I'd been standing in front of him for too long now. Other kids were getting impatient, and kids my age and younger weren't afraid to say so. Even back then. They didn't hide their displeasure well, either. They got loud about it.

"You know what I want," I challenged.

"I need you to remind me," said Santa. Under a deep breath, he added a sincere, "I'm sorry."

Behind me, a kid said to his mom waiting with him in line, "Why are they taking so long up there?" Then, louder: "Other people are waiting! Hurry up!"

My dad didn't talk much; he never has. He lets Mom do the whole verbal confrontation thing when needed (still true to this day). But if and when he did open his mouth— rare as a Charlie-Cage-is-being-nice-to-me-just-because day—you couldn't miss it, and today, while Dad didn't speak his disapproval, he did give this kid his dirtiest look. The kid quieted, and his mom pulled him out of line and talked in a firm whisper to her son, probably about making a scene in public and how he shouldn't do it; how, when he did something like that, it embarrassed *her*. Mom had had the same talk with me before.

Several times.

I climbed onto Santa's lap, and in a harsh whisper into the ear closest to me, I said, "I want you to take away my cerebral palsy for Christmas. You *know* that."

Santa swallowed hard. Even though he wasn't eating anything. He swallowed like he'd forgotten how to swallow and he was trying to remember.

Does he have a sore throat or something?

His face turned almost white. He looked like he might fall back off his seat.

He better not. He's got Brendan—who has yet to run back to Mom—and me on his lap. *If he falls back, we all fall back.*

"I'll ... I'll look into it. How's that?"

"I know you can do it!" I said. "My best friend Luke and I have spent a lot of time thinking about the first thing I'm gonna do when I don't have my palsy anymore. Do you wanna know what it is?" I didn't wait for the yes he didn't give me. "I'm gonna run at full speed. Which I've never done. But you know that. I told you that in last year's letter.

It's why I wanted those Nikes you brought me. Then I'm gonna go help Dad chop wood 'cause I figure if I don't have palsy anymore, I should help around the house. I've never been able to help around the house before. Not really. And Mom will be so happy I don't have my palsy anymore she'll forget how she's totally forgotten about me ever since Brendan was born. Oh, and if I'm real lucky, I might even be able to dunk a basketball! Maybe even play sports on the same teams as Luke! I can't wait for Christmas morning!"

"Right." A shaken Santa turned to Mom. "You want a picture with the two of them, yes?"

"We do," Mom confirmed, glancing back at Dad, who I can remember standing ready to verbally spar, should anyone else yell at his family.

Then Santa looked at my brother and me. "Okay. Look at my elf now. Yes, that-a-way. That's right. Smile for Santa, you two."

CHAPTER 7

My Heart Is Broken

The Mall

At the beginning of this Christmas season, I found myself dealing with—and, at the same time, *denying* I was dealing with—the kind of heartbreak I hadn't experienced in forty years. The kind of heartbreak about which people compose songs that aren't just melancholy; the songs I'm talking about lean more toward devastatingly beautiful, emphasis on devastating. This is the strain of heartbreak for which, it can be well argued, the art of poetry was invented. The songs I'm talking about *opine*. (Do you know what opine means, boys and girls? No?)

Carrie the Elf is looking askance at me—she doesn't know, either; all she knows is how I've deviated from the story she knows. I'll choose a different word: fair. People complain about how life just isn't fair, kids. I see some of your parents nodding at me out there. They know what I'm talking about.

You find me someone who'll claim—with a straight face—that life is fair, and I'll introduce you to someone who doesn't know the full breadth of the human experience, and probably never will.

Some of the parents call out, "He's right," "Uh-huh," and "Listen to him, kids!" at this. Others look utterly confused. The kids don't move. Are they transfixed or just bored out of their heads, wondering what the heck Santa is going on about.

One little girl raises her hand.

I point to her. "Yes?"

"Santa, I'm confused." She says it like confuse-*ed*.

The confused parents nod. As if to say, "*Us, too.*"

"Oh. Why are you confused?"

"What is heartbreak?"

Well, hell. Now I've got to tell them, don't I? But how?

"Heartbreak ... heartbreak is ... Remind me of your name, sweetheart?" This is me stalling.

"Cecilia."

"Ah, Celia, yes. Wonderful name. Cecilia, heartbreak is when you want something so much your heart breaks when or if you don't get it. Heartbreak is finally having something you want so, so much, getting the inkling that it might be slipping away, and then losing it."

"But you're Santa. Santa doesn't get his heart broken. Does he? Do you? Isn't Santa, like, always happy? He's got Mrs. Claus and the elves and the reindeer. He *must* be happy."

You would think so, wouldn't you, Cecilia? The children are gathered in the usual wide circle of story time. Cecilia leans in towards me—probably an instinctive action she doesn't even know she's taking. Celia knows empathy. Out of the corner of my eye, I think I see Carrie the Elf leaning in, too.

"Oh, Santa's had his heart broken plenty of times."

"You have?" There is a cross between sorrow and wonder in Cecelia's little blue eyes.

"I have. But you kids don't want to hear about that."

Heartbreak will come to them soon enough. Why hasten it?

Even as I say what I say, even as I think what I think, I wish I could pull the sentence back into my mouth. I wish I could rid my head of the thought I didn't want to entertain. I don't know how I haven't seen it until right now, but the story I'm telling the kids today … this story is about heartbreak, above all else. I'm so used to it that I let myself believe it to be about something else—a life changed and faith restored. But before my story can be about those things, it's first about heartbreak.

"I do," Celia says. "I want to hear."

"I do, too," seconds Carrie the Elf.

If both Celia and Carrie want to hear about heartbreak, I can tell them all about heartbreak. I'm an expert. Then again, by the time you get to be my age, who among humankind isn't?

That question is rhetorical.

My heart is broken today, boys and girls, I say, to the kids and Carrie (I haven't told Carrie about this yet; heck, I barely even told her I was seeing anyone because I figured my love life was irrelevant to her). It's broken because the girl Santa thought he loved—for the past five years, might I add—just told him she doesn't love him back. She probably never has, not in the way he loved her.

Ever.

Carrie the Elf senses oncoming melancholy, steps forward, and is preparing to call a halt to this entire story time when I change subjects, just in time.

But the heartbreak I'm going to tell you about in this story is a different kind of heartbreak altogether, boys and girls.

This is heartbreak only a child could know.

CHAPTER 8

Christmas Morning Heartbreak

Forty-One Years Ago

As my seventh Christmas morning slowly dawned, I'd barely slept.

I was giddy with anticipation, so I'd tossed and turned. Sleep was the very last thing I got to that night. And yet I woke out of a dream, a dream so authentic—that means real; it's just another way to say it—a dream so authentic I'd have sworn it was reality.

My legs didn't hurt the way they always did. My right leg didn't turn so far the wrong way that some kids asked if the doctors put it on backwards. I got out of bed and stood on normal legs for the first time. I ran to the stairs. Wind blew in my wake. Below me, my parents sipped coffee in the kitchen. Brendan was with them, already awake. At the top of those two flights of carpeted stairs, I stretched. I "limbered up," as my dad would say. (This was a baseball term, one of Dad's favorites that he'd use when we went to a game. "That pitcher's limbering up in the bullpen, Davey. Do you see him down there?")

Boy, won't they be surprised! Mom might cry; she probably will. Then, when she's done crying, if she ever stops, I'll call Luke. I'll tell him how our plan actually worked.

I stood on the bottom stair, my shocked family was turning to look at the new me, and I was saying, "I can be a big brother now!" *Like I always should have been.*

I ran to my family. And they were all rushing from the breakfast table to hug me ... the normal boy they'd always wanted ...

... When my eyes popped open and the darkness of the middle of Christmas Eve night replaced the bright, cheery tones of the false Christmas morning my mind had made up, constructed out of too many Christmas Eve candy canes and misplaced hope for my first day ever without palsy.

Had I known it was false?

I hadn't.

I'd believed in the dream, in the illusion, but only because my mind—in its eagerness to meet the actual morning and the new, normal me—had gotten way ahead of itself.

I looked at my bedside clock: 11:35 p.m. It wasn't even officially Christmas yet. And I was sure Santa hadn't come yet and that if I trundled out of bed and down the stairs to our Christmas tree, our presents would not be waiting.

Not yet.

Patience, I told myself. *Grandma Joan always tells you to take your time when you're walking down the hall in her house so that you won't trip and fall.* "It's okay to go slow," she'll tell me. "When you feel your legs teetering, take a moment or two to steady yourself. You've got to have patience, Davey, or nothing you really want will ever come. And, if you're impatient, when the thing you really want does show up, you might not even recognize it for what it is."

Yes, I'd stay in bed, at least until first light. I'd go back to sleep, if I could, until my *actual* Christmas miracle had come. When I woke again, I'd hop out of bed the same way Luke did every morning; free and easy. "Big brother is ready to open presents," I'd tell everyone, "because he's already gotten the best present ever." And Santa hadn't even used any wrapping paper to conceal it.

***

Brendan cried.

In his two-year-old, I'm-the-most-important-person-in-the-house way that only he can get away with.

I didn't wake up to the bells of Santa's sleigh as he drove away, high into the sky, headed north. Headed back home. I didn't hear him call out his Merry Christmas to all. I didn't catch one of his reindeer—probably Rudolph, their leader, seven-year-old me guessed—absconding from our house with a bushel of carrots. (We'd only left two or three carrots out because Dad said that was enough. Santa's reindeer were magic; if they wanted a bushel of carrots, they'd make it happen.)

By the way, absconding just means a person—or a reindeer, in this case—leaves with something without anyone seeing them take it. My dad was a quiet man, but as a weekend-writer of short stories when he wasn't thinking about work, abscond was one of his favorite words, and I learned it early thanks to him.

But I didn't wake up to any of that, which would have confirmed my faith and belief in something unseen. No siree. What I woke up to was my two-year-old brother crying his head off. I wondered if he'd pooped himself in the night. At least I didn't do that.

Small victories.

"Brendan, calm down, sweetheart," I heard my mother say as she passed my door, moving towards the door to Brendan's room at a fast, mama's-coming clip. "I'm coming."

Then I heard my mother scream. The sound got my dad out of bed, too.

"What's the matter?" he called down the hall from the doorway of their room. I'm pretty sure he was putting on his pants; Dad always took a second to put on his pants on Christmas morning before he came downstairs all bleary-eyed.

My mom could barely get the words out. "My baby is gone!"

"He's not gone." My dad came up behind her. Concerned, I'd gotten out of bed and now followed after him. I could still hear Brendan crying, so Dad was right; he wasn't gone. *Darn it.* "He's downstairs by the tree."

At this declaration, my mother went from panicking to rejoicing. "Oh, my baby!" she yelled and sprinted for the stairs.

Sure enough, Brendan sat on his legs by the tree. And he was scream-crying.

"What's the matter, sweetheart?" Mom asked, sweeping him up into her arms.

"No doggie!" Brendan lamented. "Christmas! Presents! No doggie!"

My little brother, the detective, was in fact correct. Crowded around the tree was a collection of presents that defied explanation. The amount, the sheer volume, of presents was massive. But so many of the gifts were tiny, meant for Brendan and not me. And not one of the gifts was the dog that Brendan really wanted.

Time to learn about life the hard way, little guy, I thought but didn't say. If I'd said this to my two-year-old brother within earshot of our mom, I'd be more likely to get my mouth washed out with soap in ten minutes or less than to be opening presents.

We'd all been so focused on the Brendan's-missing scare that I'd barely noticed when I'd gotten out of my bed and joined the search. But here it was Christmas morning, and here I was, Davey Boyd, about to show his parents how normal he was.

Finally.

Before I showed my parents my new, non-palsied self, I did a quick assessment of my body. My legs still heavy. *Too* heavy. Not normal. My right foot still partially turned the wrong way. Also not normal.

Before I could scream (which I definitely wanted to do because Santa had let me down, and nothing could hurt worse to a seven-year-old), my mom shared a surprise.

"Brendan honey, your dad and I know how much you wanted a dog," she said.

"No doggie!" Brendan reiterated. He gave the deepest frown any two-year-old has ever given anyone.

"Well, that's true. Sort of," said my dad. "You see, we didn't want to put him in a box under the tree there because he's just a puppy. He would have barked all night. So he slept in Mom and Dad's room, where we could keep him quiet. Brendan, here is your puppy." While Dad was speaking, Mom had left the room and gone back upstairs to get the puppy. She came back down with the dog, the two of them smiling.

I love when dogs smile; it makes my heart happy. But on this Christmas, when I'd been let down so dearly, I didn't think anyone else had the right to be happy.

"Oh, I see how it is," I said, my tone icy. "I ask for a dog for years and nothing. The kid asks for a dog, and he's the favorite, so guess what happens?"

Dad shoots me a look. "Davey, Brendan's not the favorite. Get over yourself. It's Christmas. Do you think we only got this dog for the little one? Don't you think we considered you, too?"

Dad had a point.

"I guess," I scoffed.

"What's really bothering you, Davey? Something's up, I can tell."

I'd been petting the dog, which was running in circles around a giggling Brendan. I couldn't help myself. Now I went to sit with Dad on our living room couch.

"I only asked Santa for one thing this year, Dad. One thing."

"Uh-huh." He and Mom shared a *did-you-know-about-this* look, and after a moment, that look changed to, *Not me. Did you?*

"And it didn't come!"

"Oh. Well ... you know, Santa's pretty busy, bud. What did you ask him for? Maybe Mom and I can help him."

"You can't help, Dad."

"Well, not with that attitude."

"You can't." Now I was near tears. You get it, don't you, boys and girls?

"How do you know?" Dad asked me. He'd been looking at Mom while talking to me. Now he turned a sympathetic gaze my way.

"Because I asked for something only Santa could give me."

"And what was that?" Mom moved to the couch, Brendan in her arms and the new dog, whom we had yet to name, at her feet.

"I sent Santa a long letter with my list this year. And I told him why I wanted him to get rid of my cerebral palsy for Christmas."

"You asked for *what*?" Dad was first to find his voice again. "You asked Santa to get rid of ...?"

"I did."

"I didn't see your list."

"Neither did I," Mom added.

"Grandma Joan sent it out from her post office." My secret revealed. I'd scold myself for it later, assuming I still believed in Santa by the time this day was done.

"Why, Davey? Why did you ask to get rid of your C.P.? Your palsy makes you who you are."

"That's why!" I said, exasperated.

"What do you mean?" said Dad.

"My palsy shouldn't *make me* who I am. I should decide that. I should decide if I want to go play sports with Luke or if I want to run fast like Luke or if I want to have a normal body like Luke has. I decide who I am, not my palsy!"

I wouldn't know the meaning of the expression that crossed my dad's face then until much later. The expression Dad wore said he'd let his boy down.

The next thing I did was to run—too slowly—to my room and call Luke. My best friend answered on the first ring. He'd expected this call.

"Did Santa come? Did he do it? Did he get rid of your—"

"No. I still have it."

"What? Why? That can't be right. Maybe Santa's just late. Maybe he lost his big list and—"

"I think I'll *always* have it, Luke." An ache settled in my soul; an ache more painful than anything palsy had ever done to me; an ache that made it hard to talk. Hard to breathe, even. "Will you still be my friend if I can't get rid of my palsy?"

"Sure I will," Luke answered without hesitation. And, hurt as I was, I knew my best friend was telling the truth.

Yet, on my seventh Christmas morning, I got to know heartbreak.

Too well.

CHAPTER 9

A Whole Year

The Mall

"How long did you stay sad for?" the little girl named Cecelia asks me (In my mind, I've already shortened her name to Celia, something my dad would do; I hope she won't mind).

Too long, I think. "A while," I tell her. "About a year."

"A *whole* year?" Otherwise known as forever to a kid.

I nod.

Another little boy dressed in blue jeans and a Christmas-red T-shirt that is otherwise blank, his brown hair a little long—as though he'd missed the last two appointments his mother made for a haircut but he doesn't seem to mind—raises his hand. I point at him.

"What's your name, son?"

"Ricky, sir."

"What's your question for Santa, Ricky?"

"Well, I want to ask you something, but I'm afraid I might get in trouble," Ricky says.

"Ask me your question, Ricky. You won't get in trouble. Where's your mom? Is she one of the parents with us today?"

"She's shopping. She'll be back in half an hour, so she told me to stay here and listen to story time. And I did, and now I have a question."

I give Ricky my best Santa-wink, along with the big guy's most earnest expression. *Go on* is written across my Santa face.

Ricky clears his throat, still a bit uncomfortable. "If you have several palsy and you can't—"

"Cerebral palsy," I correct him.

"Right. That. If you have ... ce-re-br-al palsy," he sounds out the phrase, "and you can't run, and you can't play sports, and you can barely walk, how are you allowed to be one of Santa's helpers?"

How am I *allowed?*

My mind flashes back to Charlie Cage. Besides the times when I tell my story every Christmas, I never, ever think of him anymore. *Thank you, years and years of therapy.*

I'd expected a tough question from Ricky. But this one hits me hard in the gut. "I ... um, well, I ..."

"The thing is," Ricky plows on, not caring that he's interrupting my attempt at a response, "I know you're not *the* Santa. He can't be everywhere all at once. And, this time of year, he's busy in the North Pole, checking that all the elves are doing their jobs and stuff. Making sure the reindeer are ready for the flight. So he hires people like you to help him."

"Uh-huh ..." I want to say more, but that's all that comes. Two useless syllables.

"But how are you *allowed* to be Santa's helper? You're not normal like me. Like ..." the boy glances around him, "like us."

I've checked the Santa's Helper Guide. I'm not allowed to punch Ricky—nor can I sock either of his parents—in the mouth. Which is unfortunate.

Celia jumps to my defense. "That's not fair! And who said you were normal anyways, Ricky?"

"Well, I don't have palsy, do I? I can run, I can jump, I can play sports. I've never begged Santa for a normal body."

"No," Celia replies. "But you've been begging him for a bike for three years, haven't you? All you've gotten so far is three years' worth of coal." She can't help but chuckle.

Celia hops to her feet and approaches me. She points at my lap. "Can I sit?" she asks softly.

"Sure," I mouth more than say.

She does, and then she whispers in my ear, "Don't worry about Ricky. He's a bully. I don't like him. I don't think *anybody* does. I know you're not allowed to say if you like him or not, as a Santa. But if you don't like him, too, I'd understand."

I look at Carrie the Elf, who's giving me our wrap-it-up sign. This is far from a normal story time. And Carrie has always been cognizant of not overworking me. If she senses I need a break, she jumps right in, thank you very much.

Then Celia says, "What happened next?"

"Huh?"

"In your story, Santa. What happened next in your story?"

"I think we're done with story time for today, Celia." I won't be getting through my tale after all. It's unfortunate, but ...

"No, you can't do that! You gotta tell us what happened next!" she demands. "If Ricky doesn't want to hear it, who cares? I've been in school with him forever, and he's never been nice."

I give Carrie our just-one-more-minute sign. My friend and head-elf nods her grudging acknowledgment, even though she knows it'll be far longer than a minute. And then I decide.

I'm gonna finish this story, not just for Celia, who's asked me to finish it (and who didn't correct me when I took a syllable off her name), but for everyone here, I say. A few kids and some parents and grandparents lightly clap. Ricky, if you don't want to hear it, you're free to leave. Go get yourself a Cinnabon. Whatever you do, you won't ruin this story for others. Got it?

Oh, boy. If Cal ever hears I said that, he'll ... But what do I care? This is my last day.

Ricky nods and, chastened, he doesn't move. Some bullies bully purely to bide time, because they can, because no one challenges their bullying authority. Often, when you call them out, it kills their momentum.

Plus, while he didn't want to admit it, I know what it looks like when a kid's interested in a story. And our local present-day bully is plenty interested. He might not believe I'm telling the truth, but he wants to hear how my story ends just as much as Celia does.

CHAPTER 10

Next Christmas Season

Forty Years and Two Weeks Ago

Close to a year passed without much happening.

In the first three months of that year, I barely said a word to either of my parents. They'd lied to me about Santa and his magic. About what I could ask him for and actually get—although, looking back, none of the adults in my life ever recommended I ask Santa to get rid of my palsy; that was for sure a kid-thought. But I wasn't gonna blame Luke. He was my best friend, and he'd been as excited to see what I'd look like in a normal body as I was.

When I did talk to my parents, I said things like, "I hate you," a phrase I'd never said before. As was, "I wish I had other parents," and "I wish I had parents who weren't so excited for their normal kid they forgot about me." Each time I said something like that, I could see it hurt my mom. But that was the point, wasn't it? Let her feel how much she'd let me down. How apart from our family I was in those days. After all, if it wasn't The Brendan Show, Mom just wasn't interested, and Dad—who never said much— had only one goal in life: keep Mom happy. If that meant ignoring Davey, Dad was all for it, no matter how deeply it wounded me.

So I was nursing quite the grudge—silent treatment and all—against my parents when my mom knocked on my bedroom door on a soon-to-be-snowy Saturday two weeks before my eighth Christmas. It was already Christmas-cold outside and snow was predicted, so our house was so hot with electric heat that, as worked up as I was, I wore shorts in my room to ward off the threat of baking alive. Or cooking like our Christmas turkey. By this point, although I was talking to my parents again, sometimes on a daily basis, they were lucky if they got three-word responses out of me.

At Mom's knock, I responded with a "What?"

"Davey, can I come in?" Mom asked from behind the door.

"Uh-huh," I said, my voice flat. I was sure little Brendan, Mom's favorite, would be trailing behind her, as he always was. And behind him would come our puppy, Lucky.

Dad had told Brendan and me, "You guys are pretty lucky to get a dog as cute and as good as this one." We were. And he was a black lab, just as we'd both wanted. "Why don't we name him Lucky?" We did. Well, Dad did, and I agreed, and Brendan would have done pretty much whatever Dad said to do; that's what happens when you're only three.

Mom opened my bedroom door, which squeaked a little as it widened, but neither Brendan nor Lucky were with her. Dad must have taken them somewhere, maybe to the dog park, where they could both run around awhile. This was Mom—and only Mom—come to talk to me about something.

Uh-oh. Am I in trouble? I'm probably in trouble, I thought.

Mom sat next to me on my bed. I'd been lying on my pillow, paging through a picture-book that somehow involved baseball and a squirrel and the squirrel going up the leg of one of the shortstops. I'd tried to read the words, but some of them were still too big, even for me, so I'd contented myself with looking at the funny pictures.

Now I sat up, and I put the book down on the side of me closest to the wall and farthest from Mom. She angled herself so that we could face each other.

"Davey, I know you're upset," Mom said.

"I'm not upset," I lied. I wasn't allowed to be upset, I'd made myself believe. Because I'm not Brendan. Only Brendan is allowed to cry in this house. Only Brendan is allowed to complain and get his way whenever he does in this house. Only Brendan is allowed to be ... normal in this house.

"You are upset, and it's okay that you are."

It's okay? I think. *Is it really okay?*

"I'd expect nothing less from my big boy." Mom paused, looked down, and when she looked at me again she was crying. "Grandma Joan called and told your dad and me what you asked for from Santa for Christmas last year." I'd told them already. Which meant Grandma Joan had to have done more than just tell them again how I'd asked Santa to get rid of my palsy. "Grandma Joan read us your list. Actually, she sent it, like she told you she would, but she also made a copy for herself and framed it. Because she thought it was beautiful, she said. With the holidays coming up here again soon, Grandma was back in her attic recently, gathering all her Christmas things, and she rediscovered that list of yours she'd framed all packed away. That's when she called and read it to us."

"She shouldn't have called you," I huffed, betrayed. *I've been betrayed.* I was surprised I even knew that word. That's the last time I watch a movie about pirates right before bed. Why wasn't I watching a feel-good Christmas movie or something? Because Mom and Dad were too focused on Brendan to even care what I watched, that's why.

"Why not?" Mom took both my hands in hers and looked into my eyes as she spoke. "Why wouldn't you want me and Dad to read your list?"

"My list was for *Santa*, not for my parents. You guys weren't supposed to read it! Ever! It was private!"

"I'm sorry, Davey, but you know your dad and I are two of Santa's helpers, so we *had* to know what was on—"

"You're not two of his helpers," I said, my tone matter of fact.

"We're not?"

"No."

"Why do you say that?"

"Because Santa isn't real, and you know it. You and Dad both know it. And Grandma Joan and everyone else who's lied to me about Santa knows—"

My mom cut me off, showing real anger for the first time in our exchange. "You *will not* say that in front of your brother, do you understand me? You won't take the magic of Santa and Christmas from him!"

"Why shouldn't I tell him the truth?" I challenged, feeling—for the first time in my life—superior to my parents, to my lying parents, and liking it.

My mom's eyes were alight with rage. "Tell me someone you love."

"What?"

"Tell me someone you love, Davey! Right now!"

"I don't under—"

"Your Grandma Joan. You love her, don't you?"

"Yeah."

"A lot?"

"Yeah, a lot. Why are you—"

"Okay. Now what if I flat-out told you she wasn't real?"

"But she *is* real," I countered. "My grandma is real!"

"Sure. But say I told you she wasn't and then I told you I could prove it. How would you feel if you found out, after all these years of knowing her and loving her, that your grandma wasn't real?"

I thought about this. Really thought about it. The idea of it—of the grandma I'd loved my whole life, with my whole heart, not being real—left me numb.

"Davey, you have to understand that, for your brother ... for Brendan, that's basically who Santa is right now. You can't ruin that for him."

I'd never looked at the whole Santa-thing quite like that before. Mom was right. I couldn't take it from my younger brother. As his older brother, it was my responsibility to help uphold his belief in Santa, not tear it down.

"We're gonna go see Santa with Brendan tomorrow, and I know your brother would really like it if you were there."

"Mom, he's *three*. He'd really like to eat his own boogers, and he likes running around the house naked and giggling like a crazy person when you or Dad notice." The kid wasn't fully cooked yet. There were some soft spots in his fruitcake. I'd said that since the day he was born, though no one would listen to me. "Mom, he doesn't care if I visit Santa with him or not."

"Not true, Davey. Brendan looks up to you. So much. He should. You're his big brother. I know you don't really believe anymore, but will you come with us anyway? For Brendan? And for me? I care if you come, Davey. I want you to come."

I told Mom I would. And I meant it. Even though I hadn't bothered to write out a list for Santa going into my eighth Christmas—because what the heck was the point?

We hugged.

"Merry Christmas, Davey," Mom said as we parted.

"It's not Christmas yet," I told her. We had a long time to wait still. Two whole weeks.

"I know that. I just hope you have a better Christmas this year than you did last year. And I'm truly sorry."

"What for, Mom?"

"I'm sorry you didn't get what you asked for last year. If I could take your palsy away myself, or if I could go to the store or the pharmacy and buy a pill that would take it away forever and I could give you that pill as a present, you have to know I'd do it in a heartbeat, sweetheart." Big tears welled in her eyes then, threatening to fall. She didn't want them to fall.

"I know you would, Mom." Was that a tear in my eye, too?

"Do you? Do you really? I know life's been even harder for you ever since your brother came along. But I love you, Davey. I love you so very, very much, and if I could take the thing that hurts you away, I absolutely would."

"I'm not mad at you, Mom."

"You're not?"

"No. Not really." Honestly, I was still a little miffed. That means annoyed, boys and girls. I was annoyed at my mom, but I wouldn't tell her this. Besides, there was someone I could still be truly mad at, and it wasn't either of my parents, nor was it my Grandma Joan, who'd shared my year-old list to Santa without my permission, and that wasn't great, but she probably felt like she *had* to do it once she'd rediscovered it and remembered what was on it.

She probably thought my list was so cute. It's a Grandma thing.

Can you guess who I was mad at, boys and girls? I bet you can. If you guessed Santa himself, then you guessed right.

"I'm still mad at Santa," I admitted to my mom. "All you do is help him. It's not like you or Dad drive the sleigh."

Mom laughed a genuine laugh at this. "No, it's not," she said. And then she walked out of my room and left me to finish my squirrel-plays-baseball picture-book and to play my Nintendo. Which, as a kid of the late 80s and early 90s, I played a lot. Too much, some would say, though I'd disagree. Mostly helping the Mario Brothers in their quest to defeat King Koopa. Of course, I only learned to play the game well when Luke showed me how. What is a best friend when you're a palsied kid if he's not the guy who shows you all the shortcuts and glitches and cheats in your favorite video game?

**

"Form one line, please! That's right, one line, not two! If I see anyone cutting in line, you will be shuttled to the very back … I don't care how bad you need to see Santa; that doesn't give you the right to cut in line, and I will *personally* walk with any of you to the back of the line! So don't do it! No exceptions!"

Even when a mall security guard said there were no exceptions, I always knew there were and that I was one of them. So did my parents, and they were eager to take advantage. The kid with cerebral palsy and his younger brother got to see the big guy first.

It was a palsy-perk; what can I say?

"Santa would love to see you and your little brother first," said the mall's head-elf, looking straight at my wobbly legs and trying to smile but not quite managing it before she looked away.

Santa would love to see you. Sure, he would. So he can apologize to me. He's the one who should apologize, not my mom or my dad or my grandma.

"Alright," I agreed, speaking to the elf. "Brendan and I will go first."

Brendan was so excited to be the first kid to visit with Santa that he was jumping up and down, and Mom had to tell him not to scream. I thought he was gonna pee his pants, and if he hadn't gone to the bathroom right before we left the house, which Dad always told us to do so we didn't need to go while we were in the car on the way somewhere, he might have.

***

This Santa was different from last year's. This one was fatter, and his beard was real, and he laughed harder—a real ho-ho-ho that there was nothing fake about—and he seemed to actually *like* the job. The whole being-Santa thing, I mean. He seemed to like it so much that I almost forgot how a mall-Santa was only Santa's helper, not the real Santa, and that I was steaming mad at the real Santa for not taking away the one thing I didn't want for Christmas, or for any other day anymore.

"Brendan goes first," my mom whispered, and I could feel her breath close to my ear.

Of course he does, I thought. I nodded. I knew how things worked in my family by now. There was no mystery to it. I would tell my mom I wasn't mad at her for picking Brendan as her favorite kid and for paying more attention to him and for choosing him over me because he was just plain *easier*.

Which meant normal.

Brendan was normal.

I would tell my mom I wasn't mad at her because that's what you say as a kid, isn't it? Out of respect for your elders. Regardless of the truth and how it gave you a pain in your belly that Grandma Joan once told you was really a pain in your heart.

***

"Brendan, how wonderful to see you! Ho, ho, ho! I'm pretty sure I saw your name on the Nice List!"

Brendan beamed at the big guy.

"That's right!" Santa continued. "I checked it right before I left The Pole. Since I knew I was gonna be here today, I thought I should refresh my memory! As old as I am, this brain isn't what it used to be, let me tell you!"

Santa's head-elf gave him a skeptical look. *Too much*, it said. *He's a toddler. Reel it in, old man.*

"So, Brendan, what do you want for Christmas?"

Now, I didn't think Brendan would ask for anything earthshattering. He already had his doggy, after all. Lucky would need to be fed when we got home, and I'd be the one to do it. I thought Brendan might want a new Lego set. He wasn't great at building with those little plastic blocks yet—I mean, he was three, it makes sense—but he was too good at leaving them all around the house for Dad to step on when he went to the kitchen for a midnight snack. Dad would swear when he stepped on the Legos, but he swore to me one morning after I told him I'd heard him swearing ... he swore he wasn't swearing, and he never had, and I'd just misheard, which, swearing he hadn't sworn, I thought was kind of funny.

Anyway, I didn't think Brendan was going to ask for anything I'd actually want. Not this year. What do a three-year-old and an eight-year-old have in common, anyway?

Besides love for a black lab named Lucky, that is? What toys would we willingly share? If that kid ever touched my Nintendo, and if I caught him touching it, I always told myself, he'd be lucky to still have arms after.

I thought that back then, but I know now I wouldn't have hurt Brendan. I'd have been mad, though. That was *my* Nintendo, not his.

Instead of answering Santa, Brendan just sat on his lap. Just sat there still, like one of the mannequins in the clothes store at the mall, where Mom liked to shop and where Dad liked to sit in a chair and wait for her to be done shopping.

I can see a couple of you dads and husbands chuckling to yourselves. You get it. You've been there.

I know I was supposed to be the big brother here. I was supposed to be patient and let Brendan take his time, especially since I didn't really have anything to ask Santa for that year. Even so, I began to sense an anxious boredom—if there can be such a thing—prickling at the back of my mind. *Just tell him what you want already so we can get out of here.*

Santa tried again. "You still haven't told me what it is you want for Christmas, young man."

I had to give Santa credit for his gentle prodding. He'd obviously been working at this whole mall-Santa-thing for a while.

When Brendan finally did answer the question, what he said caught me off guard. It surprised Mom, too. I could see it on her face. "Davey normal."

I think Dad was so shocked he looked frozen in place next to Mom, but I knew he'd heard and that he was trying to register what he'd heard.

Santa was doing the same. "I'm sorry," he said. "Can you ... can you repeat that?"

Brendan did, this time with even more force and conviction. "Davey want normal! I want Davey be normal!"

Even a Santa's helper who played such a good Santa, who'd heard so many varied requests ... for toys and games and trips to see Grandma and Grandpa up in heaven ... even he couldn't hide his momentary discomfort.

"I'll look into it," was all he said. "How about if we see what your brother wants for Christmas, okay, Brendan? And then the three of us will take a picture? How does that sound?"

"Picture!" Brendan shouted excitedly. He'd already forgotten how uncomfortable his ask had made our Santa interaction.

"That's right, a picture," Santa said, at the same time beckoning for me to step forward. I did so at my mom's urging—she pushed me forward just slightly. Brendan slid off Santa's lap to stand just a couple feet away while his big brother and the most famous big guy in the kid-world discussed gifts to come. And my lingering anger and resentment—you may not know what resentment is yet, boys and girls, but it's not a good thing. I can say that much. I still had anger and resentment around the one gift I still wanted more than anything, the gift that hadn't come last year.

"What's your name, son?" Santa asked me, trying his best to perform in his well-known jovial tone. He was clearly still shaken by what Brendan had said.

"I'm Davey. Davey Boyd."

Santa's face was blank a moment, as though he wasn't quite with us, as though his mind was somewhere else. And, if it was, I couldn't exactly blame him.

Santa's head-elf saw her boss's mind wandering, and she snapped her fingers at him.

"Ah ... Davey ... yes, Davey Boyd. You were on the Nice List, too, I think. On the same page as your little brother there."

Not wanting to be heard by anyone but him, I moved in close to Santa and whispered, "Did you get my letter last year?"

"Last year ... ho, ho, ho ... I think so."

"Then how come the gift I asked you for never came?" I was proud of myself for keeping my tone of voice even, in spite of how loudly I wanted to scream into his ear. Into his rosy-cheeked face.

"What was it you asked Santa for last year, little Davey?"

I wasn't little anymore, and he knew it.

"The same thing Brendan just asked you for *this* year. I didn't know he was gonna do that, by the way. I didn't *tell* him to say it ... I was born with cerebral palsy. Mom and Dad say the doctor messed up, and that's why I walk the way I do. Slow and unsteady won't win many races, Santa. Trust me, I know. That's why I want to be normal, like Brendan. Like my best friend, Luke. Mom and Dad have told me forever there's nothing they can do to make me normal, and Mom gets sad whenever I ask her about it, so I've stopped asking her about it. Dad barely talks to me, unless it's about sports. Mom says he loves me; he's just really busy with work. And my Grandma Joan has sent my Christmas list to you every year but this one—I didn't make a list this year—but she usually sends my list and that's really all she can do. That means the only person I can ask is you, Santa. But when I did ... when I asked for you to get rid of my palsy last Christmas, you never responded. And I woke up on Christmas morning—after dreaming about how it would feel to have my palsy gone forever—I woke up, and it was still there. What happened, Santa?"

Brendan's Christmas wish had left Mom, Dad, and Santa speechless. My query drained the color from all three of their faces. Only then did I realize how loudly I'd spoken my complaint, justified though it may have been.

"I ... uh ..." Santa swallowed hard.

His head-elf took charge of the situation. "It's picture-time, boys! Brendan, you wanna climb back up onto Santa's lap there? Yes, just like that! Good. Now both of you turn this way and smile and say, 'Merry Christmas!'"

We did. But, at that moment, I didn't feel very merry, and when I look at that picture now I can see just how false our smiles are.

Even Brendan's.

His grin says *I'm just now realizing—for the first time—that something is wrong here.*

***

The drive home from the mall was quiet.

That's not quite right, though. Quiet doesn't get at the volume of this silence in our car. There was absolutely no sound beyond the road whirring by under our minivan wheels. Dad even kept the car radio off, and that wasn't like him at all. He was always playing 1960s music and reliving his youth through those tunes in three-minute, song-aided memory jogs.

"Hey, Davey, did you know I almost saw the Beatles live?" he'd always say to me when a song by The Fab Four came on. And I did know. He'd told the story so often, so many times, I could tell it myself. As a teenager, Dad and some friends walked toward the concert venue, Dad's friend clutching all of their tickets in his right hand, when someone else running the other way snatched the tickets from his grasp. The group could only listen to the show outside, standing in front of a set of wonky P.A. speakers.

But today Dad wasn't saying anything. What could he say? His eldest boy was clearly still crushed by disappointment, and contained within his youngest was the empathy to want to help. To the point where three-year-old Brendan was willing to forfeit his own chat with Santa, his own Christmas wishes if it meant his older brother would get to be what he wanted to be: normal.

Whatever that meant. Whatever that means.

If someone tells you that you need to be normal, boys and girls, they might say you need to conform; that's a big word, I know. What they're really saying is that you're different than they're used to, and they're not sure how to deal with your form of different.

Find someone who knows how to deal with your form of different, and tell those who can't how you've got better things to do than to judge—or be judged by—them.

Dinner that night was KFC, a big bucket of yum that I'd usually have fun helping to devour; except Mom didn't feel much like cooking, which is why the bucket was there in the first place, Dad and I didn't feel much like eating, and Brendan didn't eat much of anything ever without prodding. All three of us went to bed a little hungry and a little more than a little sad that night.

Little did Brendan and I know as we fell asleep in our beds what awaited us that chilly night.

The biggest adventure we could imagine. And, honestly, it was even bigger than that because, before it happened—and as open as a child's imagination can and should be—neither of us would have ever dared imagine it.

CHAPTER 11

Who Are The Beatles?

The Mall

The kids are leaning forward, hanging on my every syllable. Some of the parents look pretty interested, too. And that's when Carrie the Elf steps forward.

"Alright, folks. Time for a break. We gotta give Santa time to eat his lunch."

Forty-five minutes, to be exact. So sayeth the third floor.

When a collective groan goes up, I smile to myself. *I got 'em*, I think. They want to hear the rest. Just like every other group who's ever heard this story every other day. Of course, something I know—Carrie knows, too, but she'd never tell the kids—is that this will be the last day I portray a mall-Santa and, as such, the last day I'll tell this story.

"We'll continue the story in about an hour, boys and girls," I say.

I grin at the adults. "And to you parents and grandparents out there," I add. "Make sure to come back and see me then. If you're leaving before I return, all I can say is I'm sorry. Santa's gotta eat his milk and cookies!"

***

Forty-five minutes flies. You're already familiar with the conversation that was had then between Carrie and me, and I see no need to retread it, other than to remind you how it had to do with Carrie's little niece, Emily, the little girl's love of spaghetti, and my brother and his wife, and how they came over to comfort me with some leftover lasagna. An after-Aubrey lasagna.

I return from my lunch to find today's core story time group of kids and adults largely unchanged, including Celia and Ricky.

"Tell us how the story ends already, so we can sit on your lap, tell you what we want for Christmas, and go home and wait for our presents to come! Some of us have other places to be, you know?" This is Ricky.

Of course it is.

A woman I haven't noticed before—a harried middle-aged blonde with too much make-up and penetrating blue eyes—gives the little bully a dirty look he doesn't miss. *His mother. The poor woman.*

"Do you guys want to hear how my story ends?" I ask. It's a perfunctory question. I know they do. But this is how it goes every time I tell this particular story.

"Yes!" a chorus rings. Celia's may be the loudest voice.

"Okay, good. But first you need to know this: we're not at the end of my story; actually, we're only in the middle yet. The part of the story I like telling the most."

Celia raises her hand.

"Yes?" I say. "Celia."

She grins, at once impressed and happy that Santa's remembered her name. "I just have one question, Santa. Before you go on?"

"Go ahead."

"Who are The Beatles?" the little girl asks me.

I can barely stammer out a reply. And I can't remember what I've said ten seconds after saying it. I've never felt— I've never *been*—so old in all my not-so-many-yet days.

CHAPTER 12

The North Pole

Forty Years and Two Weeks Ago

A thud I couldn't place woke me from a sound sleep.

What was that?

Was it the bump outside my bedroom window that roused me? The scraping on the roof? Or maybe it was the startled "Ho, ho, ho!" following what sounded an awful lot like what I imagined a sleigh landing hard directly below my bedroom window would sound like that got me to jump out of bed. Could it perhaps have been all three of those things combined?

I went quick as I could to my window and looked out, peering down at the snow-covered ground. I can't tell you how many nights in the cold winter months I wished for it to be colder and snowier so that school would get canceled.

If this snow could just stick around 'til Monday, I hoped. There was nothing better than a snow day.

Except maybe on that night when, as I was looking down at nothing but white, a large red-and-gold painted sleigh, the writing on its side reading "Santa: H.Q. North Pole Est. A Long Time Ago," rose into the air and stopped at window level, hovering just outside, just out of my reach, it seemed. A fully suited Santa sat in the sleigh's driver's seat and gave me what I think is the universal sign for *roll down your window*. In this case, all I could do was open mine.

I did.

"That was a rough landing," he said. "Rudolph's having an off night. Of course, it's not Christmas yet; our Christmas trips won't start for a couple days, so I don't think he was expecting me to take him out tonight. The whole team, to a deer, was surprised. We don't usually do many test runs. Honestly, the team doesn't *need* them. If anyone needs them these days, it's me."

Our Christmas trips? I thought. *Isn't Christmas a one-night-a-year thing?*

I was so close to asking about this when something distracted me. Santa looked down at a ledger at his side. Then he looked up at me and said, "You're Davey Boyd, yes?"

I couldn't speak. All I could do was nod, my mouth agape.

"You open your mouth any wider, Davey, and one of the reindeer's liable to fly right into it! Ho, ho, ho!"

I closed my mouth. "Why are you ...?"

"Why am I here, hovering just outside your bedroom?"

Another tiny nod.

"Ho, ho, ho. A fair question. The truth is, that's a bigger question than I can fully answer right now. But one of the reasons is because I couldn't get our visit today out of my mind. I tried. I told Mrs. Claus all about it and how it bothered me, and she tried to feed me my favorite before-Christmas meal, spaghetti and garlic bread with snickerdoodle cookies for dessert. But I couldn't eat. Can you believe that, Davey? Me, Santa Claus himself, I couldn't bring myself to eat."

"I couldn't eat much for dinner, either," I admitted.

"Well, how about that? Ho, ho, ho! We have that in common, then." He paused, and his face lost some of its magical mirth in favor of the seriousness most adults take on when they let go of their childhoods for good. Or when they forget how important it is to laugh every day. (Make sure you laugh every day, boys and girls—you'll live longer.) "I have a question to ask you, Davey Boyd."

"Yes?"

"How would you and your brother like to take a trip with my reindeer and me?"

"A trip? Where to?"

"Why, to the North Pole, of course."

"I'd like to," I said honestly. "But I can't."

"Why not?"

"If our mom or dad wake up in the morning and we're not here, they'll be really upset."

Santa looked crestfallen. "Davey, Davey, Davey ... I know you're just on the edge of still believing in me, maybe leaning into the non-believers' camp, but don't you think I've considered your parents?"

"What do you mean?"

"I'm not here to worry them, Davey. I'm here to talk to you. I *need* to talk to you. And don't you think a guy like me—who's been delivering toys to boys and girls just like you for centuries now—would be more than able to take you on a trip to the North Pole, show you around, say what needs to be said, and then get you and your brother home before your parents ever even knew you'd gone?"

"I *guess?*" I said, uncertainty ruling my tone.

"I need you to stop guessing, Davey. Stop guessing and supposing and start *believing* again."

"Won't Mrs. Claus be upset that you've taken the sleigh out on a day that isn't Christmas? Or Christmas Eve? I mean, what if someone sees you flying through the sky?"

He was risking discovery, maybe even permanent incarceration. That means Santa would go to jail, boys and girls. For *me*? Just because both our tummies had been a little unsettled and not quite as full as usual after our visit?

"Mrs. Claus was all for this trip, actually. Ho, ho, ho. Who do you think told me I should come see you, Davey, that I needed to convince you to come with me back to The Pole? Now, go wake your brother, but be quiet about it. We don't need the whole neighborhood knowing I'm here. Ho, ho, ho!"

***

Brendan was groggy when he first woke. But when I told him Santa himself had come to visit us and that he was outside in the sleigh with the reindeer *right now*, my little brother whooped a three-year-old whoop and jumped from his bed, nearly banging his leg on a little night-table Mom had set up for him. Had he banged his leg on the table, the trip would have gotten scrubbed; his crying would have woken people five neighborhoods away.

"You better put on your shoes," I advised. "And maybe a coat. I think it'll be cold where we're going." Even colder than it was outside our house just then, I meant.

Brendan donned both his most recent pair of shoes—he was running everywhere in those days, as toddlers tend to do once they realize they can, and he went through shoes pretty quickly—and his coat without complaint.

It wasn't his winter coat; Mom kept that in the coat closet in the hallway; this was my brother's favorite coat, the one Brendan kept in his bedroom because it was his favorite coat, and if anyone told him to put on a coat, he'd always choose this one.

We wouldn't be gone long, I reasoned. His favorite coat would do just fine.

The first thing Santa did once Brendan and I were seated in the sleigh—after letting go another round of happy ho-ho-hoes, that is: he introduced us to the reindeer individually.

"Rudolph you know of, I'm sure."

Rudolph's red nose glowed its very own bright shade of crimson, and the reindeer nodded at us. Was he smiling, or was that what Dad would call an optical illusion?

"We do," I confirmed. Brendan didn't say anything, but he clapped his hands and jumped up and down on his bottom. I seat-belted him into the sleigh. If Mom were awake, she'd insist on it.

"Rudy's our guide. He leads us. He's very businesslike, a serious deer. And he takes that as a compliment, don't you, Rudy?"

The famous nose glowed brighter. This must have been Rudolph's way of saying yes without taking either his mind or attention from his task.

"But I'll bet you boys know much less about the other reindeer."

Santa wasn't wrong about this. Other than how they might participate in Reindeer Games, whatever those were, we knew nothing of the other creatures who flew Santa's famous sleigh beyond the names *everyone* knew.

"Would you like to meet them?"

Since the reindeer were standing right there on our lawn—waiting to take off for their home—and they could hear us, it would have been odd and impolite to say no. But then what kid wouldn't want to learn as much as they could about Santa's reindeer, if given the chance? What kid wouldn't want to meet them? "We would," I said.

"Introduce yourselves," Santa told the reindeer. It wasn't an order. More a respectful ask.

Dancer, his black nose glinting in our porch light—they all had black noses, save Rudolph—spoke first. "I'm Dancer," he said. "Santa's second-in-command." His voice was throaty and deep but not unkind or unpleasant. "And this is my wife." He kicked a hoof in the direction of a beautiful white-furred reindeer.

"Hello, Davey, my name is Prancer," she said, her timbre somehow both breathy but not exactly soft. She, too, projected authority.

Dancer continued. "We all—the whole team—live on Rue Reindeer at the North Pole."

"What does that mean?" I asked. "Rue Reindeer?"

"It means we live on Reindeer Street. But we call it 'rue' instead of 'street.' It's a French word."

"I'm Cupid," said another deer. "And I can promise you boys this. We reindeer will never rue living on Rue Reindeer."

"Excuse me?" I didn't understand, so I *knew* Brendan didn't understand, either.

Santa ho-ho-hoed. "Oh, don't mind Cupid. He fancies himself something of a wordsmith."

"He always wins at Scrabble when we play our Reindeer Games. Hello," said another white-tailed reindeer. "I'm Vixen. I'm the daughter of Dancer and Prancer there." She pointed to her parents with her hoof. "Dasher is my brother. He's the fastest of us, so his name was easy for Santa to come up with."

"Does Santa name all of you?" I asked.

"Sure does," said Cupid. "He probably would have given me a name like Diction or Elocution or something word-related. But he named me based on the fact that I'm the one who introduced Dancer to Prancer at one of our reindeer socials. Ever since then, I've been Cupid." He gave a proud snort.

"Reindeer is happy!" Brendan put in, beaming. It was the first thing he'd said since I'd hustled him into the sleigh.

"That's right, buddy, he is," I said.

"I know we're still in the middle of introductions here, everybody," said Santa, his voice booming. "But we really should get moving. Are you all ready?" he asked his team.

They kicked their hooves in unison, and the sleigh moved a good ten feet in a second. Or less.

"Oh," Santa said, jolted. "I get it. You're raring to go." With that, Santa gave the call. You all know it. "On Dasher, on Dancer, on Prancer and Vixen ..." ending with, "Now dash away, dash away, dash away all!"

And so on and so forth, and so we were off.

***

The flight to the North Pole didn't take long at all. No more than ten minutes, if I had to guestimate. The wind blew past us cold and fast; the stars blurred.

About halfway through the flight, a radio on the dash of the sleigh crackled to life. "Big guy, this is Mama. Are you on your way home? Over."

Santa clicked the radio's mic and ho-ho-hoed. "That's a ten-four. On our way home, Mrs. Claus. We'll have visitors for dinner tonight. Over."

"The food'll be ready when you arrive. I hope you're up to eating, big guy. We're having your favorite. I'll be glad to have you home. Over and out."

Other than this one transmission, there was no talking, despite my now knowing the reindeer could talk to us, if needed. They were diligent workers, comfortable and confident in their duty and their ability to do it as the sleigh wormholed its way through the night sky. There wasn't time or space for any communication beyond the basics, and the basics did not require words. When he wanted to turn, Santa would simply yank the reins of the sleigh left or right. When he wished to go straight, which we did for most of the flight, he'd lean into the immense wind-wake created by his vehicle. Anything you travel in is a vehicle, boys and girls, whether it's a car or a truck or a bus or a train or a sleigh. The whole time, the big guy wore an expression that could only be described as intense concentration.

***

Our landing was smooth. Much smoother than the sleigh had managed to come to rest at the Boyds. If they'd landed correctly there and had been quiet about it, I might never have woken up and gone to my window. Then again, Santa probably landed the way he did on purpose to ensure I *would* wake and investigate the clatter.

Where were we? This wasn't Santa's home. It wasn't *anyone's* home. It looked like we'd landed in the middle of a snow-covered street, a street otherwise empty, smack-dab in the center of a small town.

"Home sweet home," said the big guy.

Really? I thought.

"To Rue Reindeer!" Santa went on. "Who's ready to get a little rest before Christmas?"

All nine animals snorted happily. Then, once again, the reindeer jetted forward, the team working as one, and I was thrown back in my seat. Santa saw this and offered a few ho-ho-hoes that I couldn't hear clearly over the roar. But there was no take-off this time. This time, the reindeer moved so sure-footed and swiftly across the icy ground that I could barely take in the snowy landscape surrounding us as it blurred past.

We dropped Dancer and Prancer off first; they lived together and so this was an easy call. With each reindeer that unhooked from the sleigh, our speed decreased. Thankfully, all of the reindeer lived on Rue Reindeer, and when we'd dropped off the last of them—Comet—Santa turned to Brendan and me.

"So, my young friends, who would like to see the workshop?"

What kid would say no to this? Santa might as well have asked if I, long a child obsessed with space, would like to treat the craters of the moon like my own personal sandboxes! Yes, please! ("So you actually watched pictures *from the moon* on your TV, Dad?" I said once, dumbstruck. To which he'd responded, "We sure did, Davey!")

I was so excited about the workshop that any words I might have said caught in my throat, so I merely smiled and nodded.

"To the shop then!" Santa cried.

And so it was that, without his team of reindeer, the two Boyd boys rode leisurely aboard Santa's sleigh through the North Pole streets—from Rue Reindeer to Candy Cane Court to Snowman Circle.

"That's where Frosty lives," said Santa, pointing at an ice-encrusted, white-painted home. "It's always cold enough to snow on Snowman Circle."

On we went through Avalanche Avenue. "There are never any avalanches; Mrs. Claus simply thought it was a clever name for a street, and I agree with her," Santa said.

Of course, we were traveling north the whole way, according to the sleigh's compass, and soon we reached a pleasant but squat redbrick building replete with many wreaths, a building clearly marked as 1224 Elf Drive. Santa parked his sleigh in a spot reserved for "The Boss." Then he turned to Brendan and me.

"We're here, boys," he said, as though I might not have deduced as much from the gigantic sign hung from the building's awning. A sign that read, in big, flowing letters that alternated from red to green: "SANTA'S WORKSHOP."

Underneath this lettering was something that I took to be the slogan of the place, though it was in much finer print. I had to work to make it out. I also wasn't sure what at least one of the words meant. The word "derives," boys and girls, means "comes from." You have to know this to understand the slogan of the workshop. The words read:

"Christmas spirit derives from love. Love is the main ingredient in family, whether that family is found, fractured or fortunate. The heart of Christmas is family."

Underneath this quote was a dash followed by the name of the quote's purveyor. A name I should have guessed. You may have guessed it already yourselves.

"– Santa."

***

As the door above the shop's front entrance jingled to announce our arrival, a myriad of high, but never shrill, elf voices rang out.

"He's back!"

"The big guy!"

"So much work to do still!"

"Do we need to make more rocking horses?!"

"More dolls!"

"More toy soldiers!"

"How long until Christmas?!"

"How long until *next* Christmas?!"

So much hammering and drilling and sawing and cobbling, but somehow it didn't sound discordant at all. The workshop was its own uninterrupted symphony, from percussion to strings and back again, all in service of building the right toy for the right deserving child over and over again. The interior of the place looked not unlike a quaint small-town shop filled with knick-knacks and potential souvenirs of a quick, quiet, coastal weekend vacation. With Brendan at my side (although I'm not sure how much of what we saw he was able to fully comprehend, but he was definitely there; it's a point of pride for him today), I stepped inside a few paces, the big guy in tow, and we turned left. It was the only direction we could go as turning right would have led to a dead end indicated by the sort of tall yet empty metal shelf common to any hardware store. Only after the mandatory left turn did the shop expand, stretch, and widen to fully reveal itself to us.

Our young eyes widened with it.

Santa began conducting a tour. To this day, I don't know how many other kids have ever gotten a tour like that.

Maybe thousands, but I doubt it.

Maybe *a whole* ten. I think that's more likely.

"Ho, ho, ho! It's so good to be home! Everyone, come meet my new friends, Davey and Brendan Boyd!"

Unlike my parents, Santa had put me first just then. And it mattered.

Elves began appearing from every corner of the shop. They emerged from behind walls that folded in on themselves, became flooring they could walk upon, and once the elves had reached the actual floor of the shop, the walls would reform and regain their solidity again, hiding their secret and anyone still working behind them.

My mouth dropped at the sight.

Santa hugged them all in turn, saying things like how he knew they were all working hard and he knew he'd left the shop in good hands, before introducing us to each and every elf. It took a long time, though maybe not as long as you'd think.

There was Craig, the head action-figure elf. Soldiers and action figures were his purview. Frieda, the head of the elves' doll department. A bespectacled elf named Gabrielle was in charge of electronics, which she told us was actually less work for her and her elves now, ever since Santa's workshop began outsourcing so much of their former work to the computer and videogame manufacturers around the world, who were—she hated to admit it—more adept at the broad area of electronics than elves, with only rudimentary training and knowledge in the field. Cameron was the elf in charge of everything fashion. Santa joked that, since coming to work at the shop, Cameron had updated everyone's wardrobe but his.

"Kids expect a certain ... aesthetic ..." Santa explained this to us, at the same time looking at Cameron to see if he'd chosen his words right. Cameron winked at him, and Santa ho-ho-hoed back. "Yes," he continued, "kids and the world at large expect a certain aesthetic from their Santas, their Father Christmases, their Joulupukki."

"Their Joulu-what-y?"

"Joulupukki," Santa corrected me. "It's what I'm called in Finland. I even have a home in Northern Finland, believe it or not, to help Finnish kids with the whole *belief* thing. Not everyone thinks I live in the North Pole, you know."

"But you do, right?"

"For you I do, Davey. For little Brendan I do. But not for everybody."

He took a moment to himself.

Back then, I didn't know, or even think about, why he got quiet then. Now I have my theories. I think Santa was silently reflecting on his own global reach and importance and on how incredibly exhausted he was. Here was a man who loved his job, there was no doubting that, but at the same time he was overworked, underpaid, and overfed, and he had been all three for decades. A not-so-good combination. (Although, to this day, Santa very much enjoys the aspects of his job that involve eating, and don't let him tell you differently.)

"We have many more departments to see within the shop here. Will you boys please follow me?" Santa invited, returning to our current Christmas season and to the tour of the shop at hand.

"Yeah!" I said. "We're coming."

I tapped Brendan on the shoulder. He was standing still, transfixed. His attention had been overtaken by a nutcracker currently undergoing repairs in the workshop's "Broken Toys" department. This particular nutcracker hadn't cracked a nut in several years, that much was clear. An older bearded elf (though not as old as Santa, because *no one's* as old as Santa), Eric the Elf was the head of the Broken Toys department—well, he'd renamed it the Craftsmanship department. A little paper sign with big letters hung over his workbench. I asked Eric what was wrong with the non-nut-cracking nutcracker, and he said the poor guy had run afoul of a family dog a couple Christmases ago after falling from a mantelpiece. Following the incident, and in the dead of a winter night, said former cracker of nuts had been spirited away aboard Santa's otherwise empty sleigh during one of his very few "practice runs" and brought here to the shop to be rescued by a division full of elves who took much pride in their careful work.

"Of course, every department takes pride in their work. And every department is careful. You'd expect that, wouldn't you? But my elves are a little different. They're highly skilled. Master craftsmen, all of them," said Eric.

"Crafts-men, crafts-men, crafts-men, crafts-men," Brendan began to chant. Apparently, my annoying little brother liked the sound of that word (a lot more than I did). Of course, if my parents had been there, they would have thought this repetition cute, and they might have even clapped for him.

Not me, thank you very much. I'll clap for him when he deserves it. "Brendan, can you be quiet please?"

Brendan stopped chanting. I'd asked him nicely—well, the words were nice; my tone was not—but Brendan still looked at me with wounded little-kid eyes. The kind that always made Mom scoop him up into her arms and want to kiss all his owies good-bye or whatever. But I knew I'd spoken out of turn.

"Hm," said Santa mirthlessly. He walked ahead of us now. He knew the layout of his shop much better than we did, after all, in that he knew it *at all*. "No room for any type of fighting or arguing here at the workshop, Davey Boyd."

How had Santa known we were fighting? What did he have, eyes in the back of his head? Did he really know when kids like us were bad and good? Did he see *every time* we were bad and good?

I was pretty quiet for the rest of the tour. Being reprimanded once by Santa Claus himself was enough. I let Brendan keep babbling a word whose meaning he couldn't possibly have known as he resumed chanting about craftsmen, and the three of us rounded another corner that went unseen until we were about to turn it.

"Davey, I've been saving this room. It's the last we'll visit today. Mrs. Claus has dinner waiting for us. She keeps a tight schedule—always has—and I wouldn't want to be late."

"Why have you been saving this room?" I asked as we entered, Santa pushing through a big oaken door as he simultaneously turned its big gold knob. I looked back to make sure Brendan was still with us. He was.

If I lose him, Mom'll kill me, I remember thinking. "Keep up," I mouthed at him, even though I was the one out of the two of us who walked slow and unsteady. I was still the older brother, though. I had no say in whether or not Brendan was born, and if I had, my life would have been completely different. Probably better. But now that he was here ... well, I was gonna make sure he stayed here and that he didn't die or anything.

"You haven't figured it out yet, Davey?" said Santa. "Why I've been saving this room?"

"No," I was slightly embarrassed to admit. Was I *supposed* to figure it out?

"I've been saving this room because it's full to bursting with children's Christmas wishes." For the first time in my presence, Santa's voice broke. He stopped walking, and I almost ran right into the back of him. I would have, if I hadn't veered left at the last possible moment to stand close by his side. *Should I reach up and give him a comforting pat on the belly?* I wondered.

I didn't. I just stood there with him.

Once he was able, Santa continued, his gaze fixed on me as he spoke. "It's full of shelves from the floor to the rafters, each one crammed with Christmas wishes. Wishes I *couldn't* grant. Including your wish, Davey Boyd of Seattle, Washington, United States, who wished last Christmas that he would wake up without his cerebral palsy. That he would wake up *normal*. I wasn't able to do this for you, Davey, and I wanted to tell you that I am so, so sorry."

***

The Room of Ungranted Wishes turned out to be a fairly private—likely intentionally so—frosty white, high-ceilinged snow globe of a place, at whose bottom we entered through that oaken door. The door was brown and gold-knobbed on the outside, a matching frosty white with its handle resembling that of a refrigerator on its inside, snow cascading all around.

It was the frostiest space in a very cold place, even though it was technically indoors. A room filled with shelf after shelf overflowing with every desire ever communicated to the big guy—either via list, letter, thought, or voice—desires which he could not, for whatever reason, follow through on.

As you entered, the Ungranted wishes were both huddled on those shelves as well as all being shouted at once, in all their myriad original kid-voices, meaning most were impossible to hear clearly. Unlike the elves' workshop and their practiced, precise builders' musicality, this freezing room was *too* noisy, with a cacophony that made my stomach want to come out of my throat. If only so the racket would stop!

Santa knew all about his small town. Some folks call places like his North Pole a hamlet, and it does fit the definition (even though there are no princes in it who might have a little trouble getting along with their uncle; that's a little bit of Shakespeare humor for you older folks).

Anyway, Santa knew everything there was to know about the little town's inhabitants, as well as about the children who believed in him, be they lapsed or still devout.

He proved this now as Brendan and I stood shivering. He stepped forward and, with confidence, said, for only Brendan and me to hear, "Boys, we're here looking for shelf 25,009. Each shelf has a number on its bottom, so that's where you'll want to look. From the exact middle of that shelf, we'll move ..." Santa extracted a ledger from his expansive Santa-suit pocket and studied it. "Let's see ... it looks like eight wishes to the left and then we'll need to dig down about twenty wishes deep."

"What are we looking for?" I asked.

"We'll find a wish chronicled in list form. It's about a year old, and the list and the note it came with were written by none other than you yourself, Davey Boyd."

I know what I wrote, I thought. *And so does Santa.* And I knew Santa said no to my wish, so why should I dig for, find, and then read aloud a wish that Santa himself denied? I didn't share this thought, but it definitely rattled around in my brain, and it would not be ignored while the three of us did as he asked and searched that big, frozen room.

As we traversed the many aisles in search of shelf 25,009, an odd number that struck me as a rather *odd* number, Santa sidled up to me and asked, "You don't want us to find that wish, do you, young man?"

I didn't. "I don't," I said.

"And why not?"

He was gonna make me say it out loud, which struck little Davey—little me—as more than a little mean.

"If the answer's no, the answer's no," I told him, repeating a phrase my mom had used recently whenever she'd given a firm negative response more than once to some outlandish request of mine.

You know what I'm talking about, right, boys and girls? Ah, I see you do! One of my favorites was, "Mom, could we make brownies on a school night? With extra chocolate chips in them? And fudge in their middles?" This would mean the best kind of brownie! A kind I'd originally baked with my Papa Dale. (By the way, he was not only my grandfather but also the first Santa's helper on whose lap I ever sat because he was the only Santa for whom I'd sit still long enough to allow a picture when I was Brendan's age. And Papa didn't even need extra padding for excess girth around his middle!) Anyways, my mom wouldn't hear of such a thing ... "Brownies on a school night?!" though I'd ask her the same question about twenty times a month, each time wording the thing a tad differently, each time hoping against hope for a different, more positive response. Each time beyond the original getting, "Davey, please ... if the answer's no, the answer's no."

I don't know why, but I think the stress of being adults makes adults like my mom forget what it was like to be kids who get to bake brownies on school nights, even when both parent and child know they maybe shouldn't. And let me be clear, boys and girls, I'm definitely *not* saying you shouldn't bake brownies on school nights.

Santa smiled, and his belly shook with a laugh. "Ho, ho, ho! When the answer's no, the answer's no?"

"Yeah, that's what my mom says."

"Okay. That's what *she* says. But, Davey, what makes you think I *ever* said no to you?"

With that, Santa enveloped me in a hug. One he brought Brendan into about halfway through it, saying, "You, too, little guy."

Brendan giggled. "I not a guy! I small, I kid!"

I had to give the kid credit. Even then, even with his limited vocabulary—maybe *because* of his limited vocabulary—he'd actually said something almost funny.

Brendan might really be cool someday, I mused. Then, just as quickly, I banished the thought. I'm *not cool. Not even close. So how could Brendan ever be cool?*

"Are you saying you could take away my palsy, Santa?" I mumbled into his belly.

"I'm saying it's a bit more complicated than that, Davey."

At this, I began to cry.

No one timed it. No one would later ask how long the three of us stood huddled in that hug. How long Santa let me cry into his suit. All I know is it lasted a while.

***

"Why is it so cold in here?" I asked Santa. Our hug had broken, and I was again on the verge of shivering, and so was Brendan, even after a warm embrace, even after we'd acclimated somewhat to this enclosed snow-globe environment.

My mom would also kill me if Brendan came home dead. She wouldn't be happy if he got a cold, either. We absolutely could not have him freezing in here.

"I know this is the North Pole," I allowed, "and it's *supposed* to be cold. But it's really, really cold." *Too cold*, I wanted to say but didn't. Who was I to judge Santa's ways or the ways of his magical homeland?

"We keep it cold in this part of the shop, in this part of the room, to better preserve the memories of childhood. Believe it or not, memories can melt."

"Huh? You mean like ... snow melts?"

"Exactly like snow melts, actually, Davey. Have you ever seen an old person who can't remember where they put their glasses?"

"Sure. That happens to my Grandma Joan all the time," I said. "Sometimes, I'll be at her house, or she'll be at mine, and she'll come find me to ask where she put her glasses, and I'll laugh because they're right on top of her head."

"Well, childhood memories are like that. They're the memories that last the longest, Davey. But if we let them, they'd melt away as fast as an ice cream cone on a summer beach."

That was fast!

Now I understood why—and how—most wishes to Santa were preserved. A day at an amusement park with Mom and Dad, or a trip in the motor home I knew so well from my youngest years, or a vacation with Grandma Joan—whose hair was always black and never grayed—and Papa Dale, her silver-haired, short-order cook, workin'-on-the-railroad, glad-to-help-raise-me-for-as-long-as-he-was-here (which wasn't long at all) husband. The two of them were more than happy to take a pint-sized Davey Boyd to a water park in the hottest, most stifling heat of summer when I was small but not *too* small, giving Mom and Dad a much-needed kid-break.

What I didn't understand was why we had come to *this* room. To shelf 25,009, eight memories to the left and about twenty memories deep. Why was my ungranted wish important enough to be revisited now when the wishes of so many others were not?

Once we got to the correct shelf, Santa left the digging to me. I wanted to do it. Brendan wanted to dig, too, but Santa had asked me, I told my little brother. He understood; I'm not sure I would have if our roles were reversed. I came up with the wish we were looking for in less time than it takes for your parents to make their coffee each morning, boys and girls. I was proud of myself as I held the single page limply in my hand.

"Do you remember writing this list, Davey?"

I'd tried to forget this list for most of this past year. But, in trying to forget it, I'd only sharpened the memory. Now, it was a knife.

"Yeah," I said, my voice slicing through the frozen air. "I remember."

Just then, what must have been some sort of alarm—not quite a siren, not quite a buzzer—sounded. Santa looked startled a moment, then he'd regathered his wits and was back to his jolly self.

"That's Mrs. Claus reminding me dinner is ready at home. If it weren't for her, I'd forget to eat," he said. "Are you boys hungry? Mrs. Claus was making something for us, but I can't seem to recall—"

"Spaghetti and garlic bread, with snickerdoodle cookies for dessert. Your favorite," I reminded him.

"Ho, ho, ho! You're a sharp one, aren't you, Davey Boyd? You've got quite the memory on you."

He patted me on the shoulder. I'd been so focused on where we were going and the means by which we were getting there that it was only then that I realized how I barely came up past Santa's belt buckle. In order to hug his belly, I'd stood on my tiptoes without knowing it. Santa wasn't just big around, as we'd all been taught as kids, he was just plain *big.* Tall. Huge. I wondered if Paul Bunyan was a relative. Dad had just told me the story of Paul and his blue ox, Babe, calling it his favorite tall tale and chuckling to himself at something I didn't get.

"Well, what do you say, boys?" Santa went on. "Want to fill your faces with some spaghetti and such?" We both nodded. "Good. And then, after I've filled this belly of mine, too, Davey and I can talk about why some wishes I want so badly to grant I simply can't."

Santa led us back through the labyrinthine workshop. That means it was huge, with twisty and turny corridors. Brendan was holding tight to my hand the whole time, which was only slightly annoying, I decided, since the little guy had a certain charm to him, I guess. I remember telling myself this and trying to believe it. Once we were settled back into the sleigh, the elves—all of them, every single one, it seemed—came out to wave good-bye to us. We were on our way to Santa's house, Brendan and me seated on either side of St. Nick.

"One of the first things we learn when we're kids," I said to Santa as the sleigh trundled along, a carriage ride through a snowy park (considerably quieter and slower without the reindeer attached to give it speed-of-light power), "is our address. The address where we live. You know ours, don't you?" I turned to my brother expectantly, realizing only just then that I'd asked this question to Brendan, not Santa.

"Sure!" Brendan gave an excited squeal. "It's one-five-two—"

"Brendan, you don't need to *say* it right now," I stopped him. My tone was near a scolding, but it didn't quite reach that level. Mostly because Mom had told me Brendan was too young to understand a proper scolding. What he needed, she said, was something called "positive reinforcement." "You can tell Santa later, okay?" That's about as positive as I could get.

"Okay." My little brother was completely unfazed. Whereas at his age I would have taken a light correction as a harsh rebuke, and I wouldn't have forgiven it for months. That's just me.

126

"I wanted to ask Santa what his address was." I said it so the whole sleigh could hear, including Santa. I wasn't loud, didn't need to be. Just ... enthusiastic.

"Oh, ho, ho, ho!" Santa guffawed. "I don't know why you're asking me that, Davey. You know the answer already."

"I do?"

"Of course you do. You *both* do. Believers have always known. Mrs. Claus and I live at 1 Santa Claus Lane."

***

Mrs. Claus can cook.

No great surprise there, I suppose. Even so, I hadn't expected the meal to taste *this* good. Her spaghetti and garlic bread still remain the best I've ever had, and that's a tough bar to reach, let alone to clear. (My Papa Dale was the best cook I ever knew. I knew Papa until I was only five and he was seventy-three, when his cancer decided he couldn't be here with our family anymore. The man who'd raised my father was gone, and my Grandma Joan was alone for the first time in fifty years.)

Carrie the Elf isn't happy with me for this little aside, I see. Some of you parents look a little squirmy, too. Don't worry, my story's getting back on track now.

Like my Papa Dale, the short-order cook who worked on the railroad, Mrs. Claus was talented in something more than just cooking. The fact is, she may well be a world-class baker, too. Her snickerdoodle cookies exploded with flavor in my mouth; Brendan loved his, too, not least because it was the first snickerdoodle he'd ever had. The perfect mix of winter sweetness and spice and chewy goodness.

"Glad you made it home, Nick," said Mrs. Claus. "Not that I had any doubt you would."

Wow, she doesn't call him Santa like we do, I thought, feeling like I was being given a glimpse behind the scenes and fully savoring that glimpse. Was his name really Nick? Or was it something else, like Walter, and she was just using that familiar name because they had company and she knew their company expected it?

"You know I have to make those practice runs, Mother," said Santa. "Work out any kinks with either the sleigh or the team before the big night."

"Yes, I know, but you don't often have passengers. And the sleigh is rather old. We've talked about that."

It is? It hadn't looked old to me. In my child's eyes, the sleigh gleamed, and I would have sworn it wore at least one fresh coat of paint. Maybe its beauty came from Christmas magic? Then again, Santa had basically crash-landed in our backyard.

Perhaps Mrs. Claus had a point, after all.

"You don't need to worry about me, Mother," Santa said.

"It's been one hundred and fifty years, Nick. More than that. I'm going to worry about you. It's what I do. What I've *always* done."

More than one hundred and fifty years? My grandparents had only been married for fifty before Papa Dale had to go.

Now Santa was using a loud whisper. "And what I'm saying is I understand, Mother. But I have to have a talk with Davey here." He draped his big hand over my little-kid shoulder. "A pretty important talk. Do you think you could watch the little guy while we go and do that? His name is Brendan. We shouldn't be too long, but I owe Davey an explanation."

Instead of considering her husband's proposal, it was as if she'd already agreed to the idea. Mrs. Claus immediately brightened, as though they hadn't just been civilly arguing. "Brendan and I will have a blast together, won't we, Brendan?"

Even though he didn't know what fun Mrs. Claus had planned for them to have together, being three years old Brendan was prone to agree with pretty much anything adults said to him, as long as they said whatever it was in a merry manner. Except for when adults said he should eat, go to bed, wake up each morning at a prescribed time, or when they shared an opinion as to how often he should cry in his one-of-a-kind, dramatic way. On that last one, Dad and Mom—and I—would have preferred *never.* Brendan preferred any and all waking hours, and some hours that should not be waking. Anything to focus full attention on him.

"We may even decorate the Christmas tree tonight," Mrs. Claus said. "It's getting to be that time again, isn't it, Nick? Would you like to help with that, Brendan?"

"Twee!" was all Brendan needed to say. He was in.

"Wonderful. Well then, Davey and I should get going," Santa put in.

"You don't have the reindeer with you, do you?" asked his expert-baker wife.

"No. I dropped them off at home to rest for a bit."

"Okay," she said, still looking circumspect. "Well, you two be careful then. And if you have any trouble, you can raise me on the radio." Mrs. Claus looked at a closed door behind which I guessed her own radio lived. "I'll have it on until you get back."

"Yes, Mother," Santa said, clearly ready to get past this preamble. This wasn't the talk he really needed to be having. As to the one we were going to have, I couldn't avoid wearing a good amount of apprehension on my face.

"And Davey must wear something out of our coat closet. It's winter out there, Santa. A North Pole winter, no less."

"Yes, Mother."

I borrowed a coat to wear, a big, puffy one. "Or else you might catch a cold, dear, and we can't have that now, can we?" said Mrs. Claus. "The coats you boys brought are barely sufficient to keep you warm in the summer!"

It wasn't long after this that the two of us made our way out the front door at 1 Santa Claus Lane. You should see the wreath on Santa's front door. No one's ever seen a wreath as big or as green. I noted that when he stepped outside, his doormat changed. The message on it flipped from "The Big Guy Is Home" to "The Big Guy Is Gone."

"Cupid made that doormat for me," Santa explained. (Remember, boys and girls, he's the reindeer who likes to play with words.) "He's fascinated by words that look like they should rhyme but don't, like bone—a bone for your doggy, let's say—and gone, as in, gone fishin'"

We headed in the sleigh away from Santa's house and back toward the workshop and the Room of Ungranted Wishes. We were showered with good-byes and see-you-soons from those we left to decorate the North Pole's most famous Christmas tree, the one belonging to the Boss and his wife.

CHAPTER 13

Santa's Bidding

The Mall

Celia has jumped down from my lap and is now sitting, her legs crossed in front of her, in story time's front row, neatly organized by Carrie the Elf.

"Were you still mad at Santa … Santa?" she asks me. "For not taking away your palsy?"

Carrie the Elf, who's heard this story many times before, knows the answer. I see her out of the corner of my eye, mouthing my well-worn reply, and I have to hide a smile as I offer it again. In time with her mimicry.

"I wouldn't say I was mad anymore, no. But I did want answers from him."

"Answers like what?"

Celia's insistence that I nail down specifics puts me back on that trip, in that so-special Christmas season so long ago. Santa and I rode for the workshop again, this time just the two of us, with the sleigh puttering more than chugging along through what must have been two feet of snow, with eight-foot snowdrifts at either side of what used to be a road.

I wasn't sure what it was I wanted to hear from the world's biggest elf.

I'm lost in thought when Carrie the Elf brings me back to my now. She's stepped in close to me to say, "Santa, there's only an hour 'til we close. If anyone else wants to see you this evening, we need to do that now if you hope to finish your story." She points down at her watch, tapping at its face for emphasis.

"Okay, Carrie. Will do." To her and only her, I say softly, "Thanks for always keeping me on time."

She grins wide before the smile leaves and her eyes go … sad. I don't know how else to describe them. Carrie's eyes suddenly sadden. "You're welcome, Santa. It's my job. You got any plans tonight?"

"Dinner at McDonald's, maybe." What I don't tell her is how this is *the* dinner of the recently single man. Load up on carbs, sink into the sofa, forget your sad life, stream some true crime until I fall asleep. Lather, rinse, repeat for the foreseeable future. "Santa may be an expert at making toys," I continue, my voice still quiet and only for her, "but unfortunately he's not much of an expert at making money."

Carrie laughs her genuine, I-really-did-find-what-you-just-said-funny laugh (as opposed to her I'm-laughing-'cause-they-pay-me-to-laugh laugh, which she smartly reserves for customers who are annoying but well-off).

"As an elf, I feel your pain," she returns. Then she locks right back into her job. Her face is soft, because her face is *always* soft, but otherwise it's expressionless. What she's about to say won't be popular, and she knows it.

"Alright, folks. Santa's gonna call it a night here soon. We've got to get the visits with Santa done. Who still needs to tell Santa what we want for Christmas?" The Victorian we. Carrie often employs it around the kids. Have we had our picture taken with Santa yet? What did Santa say when we asked him for that doggy? It's Santa's lunchtime. Maybe we should eat, too. Ask your parents.

No one moves.

"Come on, guys! Last chance to tell Santa this year. I know some of you haven't seen him yet. Don't be shy."

At last, a few hands rise, a pair wiggling in the air in the universally recognizable sign: *pick me, pick me, pick me!*

Celia doesn't raise her hand. She's already told me what she wants: a new cell phone. Kids are different these days, aren't they? When my parents let me have a telephone in my room, a landline, it was a massive coup for twelve-year-old Davey Boyd. Celia has four years or so before she can be called a tween like I was then.

"But, Santa," the little girl says, her voice near breaking, "your story! You were just about to go back to the workshop, weren't you? Back into that really cold room. You still need answers from ... from Real Santa."

I feel bad. I've told the story I'm so used to telling much more slowly today; usually, a couple story times throughout the course of the day is plenty of time for the whole tale to unfold. Not today, though. Maybe because I'm savoring the telling for the last time. Maybe because, on some level, I don't *want* the story to end. Since, once it ends, a new chapter in my life will begin.

And not a happy chapter.

I was *this close* to a happy ending. But without Aubrey, my happy ending won't be. It can't be.

I'm both anxious and nowhere near prepared for whatever will come next. There's a rumbling in my unsettled gut.

"You're right, Celia, you deserve the end of the story."

She does, but unless I rush through it right now, I won't be able to finish it. And mine isn't a story anyone should rush through.

I think back to another treasured time in my early childhood when I baked Christmas cookies with my Papa Dale, and an idea strikes me. "Those of you who still need to speak to Santa, do you know what you want to ask for?" I say.

Nods all around.

Good, I think. That means I'll be able to finish the story for Celia, and for Ricky if he wants to hear it—and for me—after all.

"Perfect. Everyone who wants to talk to Santa, raise your hands again."

They do. It looks like six kids still need to lobby on their own behalfs.

"Okay. Now, when I point at you, tell me your name and what you want for Christmas. Santa's gonna talk really fast, so you'll need to talk fast, too. Are you ready?"

No movement from the kids. But their hands stay up.

"Alright, then. I take your silence as agreement. I'll move from left to right around the circle. That means we're starting with you. Everyone else, keep your hands up until I get to you. What's your name?" I ask a girl who isn't much older than Brendan was the year he helped decorate the Claus Christmas tree.

"Abby," says the girl.

"And what would you like for Christmas, Abby?"

"A talking dolly. Do you know the one I mean?"

I don't. But *he* will. Santa will. So I say, "I do." I pause. Never promise too much, even if you know the gift they want is a gimmie. "I'll look into it, Abby. Have you been a good girl this year?"

She beams. "I have."

"Good. Merry Christmas, Abby."

Next kid.

"And you?" I say with a smile.

"I'm Travis. I want a new baseball bat. I broke my old one. But you probably know that, Santa."

"Mmhm. Have you been a good boy this year, Travis?"

"Yes."

"Good to hear. A new baseball bat. I'll look into it."

I'm giving off some real auctioneer vibes right about now. My Papa Dale would be proud that I'm remembering a day when I was around five years old. The day my papa told me all about what an "och-shun" was and how he planned to hold one soon for the Christmas cookies we baked. So I'd better have my wallet out and ready. I told him I didn't have a wallet.

And by *we baked,* I mean *we. No Victorian we here, thank you very much.* Though I'd thought I couldn't bake cookies, or anything else, because of my poor coordination. I thought I'd be too messy. Papa told me that day, "Don't you *ever* tell me you're not good enough, Davey." Sometimes, I have to remind myself of his words. They guided me when I was young. They guide me now.

I look over and see that Travis is here with his parents, who stand at the edge of the circle, their eyes on him and a friend who must have come with them. If being best friends with Luke has taught me anything, and it has, I've learned to read the way kids interact with each other, specifically boys about the age we were in those memorable Christmas seasons. I notice Travis is excitedly glancing over at the kid, wanting to share in his good Santa fortune; I'd guess they're best friends and have been for a while.

Travis's friend is next. I do a quick count to myself ... only three kids remaining.

And they go just as quickly as I'd hoped. Travis's friend is Tony, and he wants to make it to the NFL. Santa and his elves are really more about toys and games and childhood than far-fetched life goals, but I tell Tony I'll look into it, anyway, and that the best way to achieve a dream is to identify it—which he has done—and then to work for it. Tony looks at me like I just asked him to recite the number pi to five hundred decimal places. But he knows I'll look into it, so he doesn't push his luck. *Smart, Tony.* Lisa wants a stuffed bear as tall as she is; I tell her, "I'll look into it." Gina wants her parents to get back together. She's got tears tickling her eyes that she won't let fall. Santa tells her how sometimes big people make choices children don't understand at the time, but that he's sure her parents love her very much. Nothing for Santa to look into there. Just a little heart to suture with a friendly, "Two houses means two Christmases. Two Christmases means extra work for my elves and me, Gina, but we're up to it! Ho, ho, ho!"

I hope Gina's parents aren't here right now. I don't think I could handle an irate parent or two just as I'm about to go into the crux of my story for the last time ever. But before any parents can get angry, Gina says, "Two Christmases! That's the best thing I've ever heard of! I love you, Santa!"

"Santa loves you, too," I say reflexively. And he does. I do. Then I ask, "Is that all of you?"

Carrie the Elf confirms, "That's all of them, Santa."

"Carrie, do I have time to finish my story, do you think?"

Carrie makes a show of looking at her green-tinted elf-watch. Every one of my elves has one of these, provided by the mall as a "perk" of this minimum-wage seasonal gig that the elves do because they love it, not because they plan to get rich off of it. And when she looks up at me again, she says what I know she'll say.

"You've got time, Santa."

Since she knows this will be my last day in the big guy's chair, Carrie would have said I had time even if I didn't. The mall can't actually close until its daily cleaning is complete, and that can't start until the last shopper leaves the mall. Which means that, to an extent, anyway, Santa's story time is immune from the mall's closure announcements. They become incessant beginning with fifteen minutes to go, but we're still well clear of such crackling-loudspeaker intrusions yet. I've got half an hour before the customers perusing the various stores here at the mall will turn back into frazzled holiday motorists with kids who still believe in magic and need some decidedly not-magical rides home.

"Alright, where did I leave off? Santa gets confused now and then," I pretend to admit, playing up my supposed senile befuddlement. I look around our North Pole in a put-on daze. Most of the kids buy it. "Celia, I know *you've* been paying close attention."

"You're in Santa's sleigh headed back to the workshop and that really cold room."

"Ho, ho, ho ..." My Santa laugh is a bit forced and nothing like the real one, but Celia buys it. Because she *wants* to buy it; it makes her happy to buy it. Because she still believes. "So I am," I say. "And let me tell you, it's pretty weird to be in Santa's sleigh with just Santa and nothing and no one else. No reindeer, no presents, no Christmas magic. Nothing except the two of us! And ... well ... I wasn't sure I *deserved* such a privilege. I'd convinced myself a ride in the sleigh was something special you got because you'd *earned* it, boys and girls. And I wasn't sure I'd earned it. Not really. But we were already halfway back to the workshop, and soon enough, we'd be talking over a memory I wished hadn't been preserved at all."

I'm still not sure how I feel about it now. But I don't say this to Celia.

CHAPTER 14

The Talk

A Fortnight Shy of Forty Years Ago

There were huge snowdrifts outside the workshop, and I cautioned myself that I couldn't let them swallow me whole like the abominable snowman. There was a little brother I'd better be sure to get back to and bring back home. I'd have to tread carefully.

Santa didn't exactly greet the elves on our return. Not like he had our first time around. That is to say, there was no pageantry to our entrance this time, no re-introductions. The elves had their jobs to do, which went on uninterrupted, and we had ours: *to get to that freezing room where we can both see our breath in the air and explain yourself, old man!* I thought but would never say.

How many times do we think things we'd never say out loud, boys and girls? And to you adults, how many times do we worry about something having nothing whatsoever to do with the current moment? I was so anxious about what Santa had to say that I allowed myself to ponder anything but.

The room full of Ungranted Wishes wasn't nearly as cold the second time Santa and I entered it. Thanks, in part, to Mrs. Claus's forethought. A coat, a *real winter coat*, was a good idea. It also helped that now we knew where the shelf we were looking for was precisely located, shelf 25,009. And we knew the exact position of the wish we were seeking.

Santa retrieved it. "For the sake of time," he said and held it delicately in his giant hand, as one might hold a snowflake just before it fades to shapeless liquid and drips away. Behind and all around us, elves bustled and scurried, as they must have been bustling and scurrying the first time we were here without my noticing. They busied themselves securing memories of the season to be frozen until they might one day be needed, brought to mind in a moment of sentimental reflection.

"We all have a story to tell," said Santa. "That is why we preserve these memories, Davey. Because without childhood memories, lives would be woefully incomplete. And there are so many times when those memories are needed, when it's important to have them near."

As my memory of last Christmas—the Christmas when Santa let me down—was needed now.

I maintained the strong sense that few kids were ever brought to the North Pole as Brendan and I had been. "Is it because of my palsy?" I asked Santa as I stood beside him, looking at the memory, my list and my sadness of its going unfulfilled, fluttering like an unpropped bubble in his big paw.

"Is *what* because of your palsy, Davey?"

"Is my palsy why you brought me here?" *A palsy-perk?* I wondered. "You know how bad last Christmas made me feel, and you feel bad. That's why I'm here, right?"

I knew how life worked when you had cerebral palsy. Kids made fun of you. Bullied you. Excluded you. And too many of them were gleeful when they played their parts. Adults, meanwhile, felt bad for you. For *me*. But not just bad; these adults stewed in how awful my poor, sad life made them feel. So they'd inevitably and invariably do something nice for me. Let me have an extra scoop of ice cream in my cone at the farmer's market, say. Palsy-perk. Let me "play" football, even though everyone knew I couldn't play football; some adult would get the idea, though, that poor, palsied Davey Boyd might like to score a touchdown in an actual game. Hand him the ball and let's all back up into the end zone and cheer when he gets there. When he *finally* gets there. In about thirteen hours. Palsy-perk. Give the kid a good, lasting memory filled to overflowing with magic that rings false even as it's happening, the referee waiting until he crosses the goal line to blow his whistle and put his arms up. Palsy-perk. Then let's craft a memory full of joy and Christmas, with Santa crashing his sleigh on the lawn like a drunk driver who'd had way too much eggnog and talking reindeer who made sure their boss was okay before climbing back up into their harnesses. And flying at speeds so fast they'd make you sick if you ever made the mistake of looking down to try and get your bearings, so I never did, and I told Brendan not to, either. And meeting the elves and Mrs. Claus and seeing the workshop. Palsy-perk?

Was this whole trip one long, drawn-out palsy-perk because Santa felt sorry for me, because he knew how hard an adult life saddled with palsy would be?

"Oh, no, of course not. You have your own way of remembering last Christmas, Davey. You think I let you down."

"You *did* let me down," I made clear to him.

"I'm sure I did. I'm sure you feel that way right now. Follow me, will you please?"

"Where are we going?"

In amongst this large, freezing space, somehow there happened to be ... of all things ... a fireplace. Beside the fireplace sat two red recliners.

"You won't need your coat where we're going," Santa said, heading that way.

"But if we go over there ... I mean, won't my memory of last Christmas get too warm and melt away? Kinda like Frosty the Snowman did in his story?"

"Frosty ...? Oh, yes, you mean Harold, of course. Harold never *melted* away. So dramatic, Harold is. He simply turns into water, which is what happens to all snow when it melts. He becomes a droplet of water that then gets sucked back up into the sky and into a cloud and falls from that cloud as a raindrop the next day. In the winter, and when he's at home here at The Pole, Harold calls himself Frosty. He can call himself whatever he wants; I don't care. But, especially in the winter, in this season, I guess he's Frosty, and we all just kinda play along.

"But, yes," Santa continued, "I suppose it's fair to say that when we go over there and begin talking about what actually happened last Christmas, then your memory will melt away. We want that to happen, though. Once you've confronted the memory that's spent a whole year hurting you, it *should* melt away."

"Why?" I asked. "Why do we want that to happen?" But even as I asked, I was moving closer to the fireplace, shedding my borrowed coat.

"Just as Harold was reconstituted into something else— just as our Christmas magic will reconstitute him whenever needed—your former memory won't exactly melt away to nothing, Davey," Santa said, "but it will be reshaped, and that memory reshaping will change you just a little. I know you're a little too young to understand yet."

"I'm not too young to understand!" I shot back. Santa had struck a nerve. I think he knew he would.

"Oh. Well, good. Ho, ho, ho." His tone said he didn't quite believe me, and his heart wasn't exactly in the perfunctory laugh. "So, can I tell you why I didn't take your palsy away last Christmas? I owe you that much."

I'd wanted the answer to this question from him—and only him; no one else would suffice—for a whole year now. Until tonight, I was pretty sure I'd never get it. Besides, wanting a thing didn't mean I deserved it. How many times had Grandma Joan and Papa Dale drummed that concept into me?

I nodded wordlessly, draped the big, puffy winter coat from deep in the Clauses' coat closet (Cupid would love that wordplay there), a coat that I wouldn't be wearing for a good while—the fire blazing a hot bright orange beside us--over my red recliner. Then I sat. It took considerably more effort for Santa to lower himself down into his seat, and he could not have been comfortable. It was one thing to be big around, as he was, but quite another to be big around and also nearly eight feet tall.

Not ideal. For anyone.

He sighed a heavy sigh that weighed a ton. "Okay, Davey. Where do I start? Let's see," he said, basically to himself, though I could hear him plain. His head rested against the back of his chair, his eyes looking just about straight up into wooden-raftered, no-snow air. The part of the workshop we were occupying now resembled a cozy winter cottage. Or a ski lodge, though I wouldn't have known this reference when I was younger. I'm not known for my skiing ability, shock of shocks. Yet if we walked a hundred feet back the way we'd come, either of us might contract frostbite within minutes (frostbite that could be removed via North Pole magic, of course).

When he looked my way again, lowering his eyes to regard me, Santa's brown eyes were clear, focused, and determined. It was as though, in his moment of uncertainty, Santa had been reminded, by years of experience in his post, how the job was done right when it got hard to do.

"I couldn't take away your palsy, Davey," Santa said.

"You couldn't? Why not? No kid has ever wanted any toy or game or bike or baseball glove or whatever more than I wanted my palsy to be gone so I could ride a new bike and break in a new baseball glove of my own. And I even made it easy on you, Santa. You know I didn't ask for anything else."

I'd learned, from Grandma and Papa mostly but also from my parents—when they weren't focused on Brendan, their new, unbroken child—how being greedy never ends well. "You're owed nothing in this life, Davey," Papa had said to me one day when I was sad because I couldn't run like the other kids ran, and I thought they should slow down and give me a chance to catch up. And, young as I was—this was probably about six months before Papa Dale passed away—I'd never forgotten it. "Palsy or no, you are owed nothing. None of us are. But you should absolutely go out and *get* whatever it is you want. *Earn* it. Prove yourself. I know you can do it, even if you're not sure you can just yet. Your grandma and I both believe in you, and you need to know that." By the same token, being greedy when you're already asking Santa for the biggest gift you'll ever ask Santa for in your whole life is—as Papa might have said, "a pretty bad look on you, Davey."

"Davey, what you were asking me for ... you weren't being greedy," Santa tried to assure me. "I know you were *afraid* you were being greedy, but you weren't."

Santa stopped talking for too long. Gazed toward the ceiling. Finally, I broke the silence.

He can't possibly be done. "Were you going to answer my question?"

"Oh, yes, of course." He guffawed a group of tired ho-ho-hoes. "Sorry, I was in my head. That's happening more and more these days. First, before I answer your question, Davey, I have to ask you a question of my own. Do you know how I became Santa?"

"You were a saint or something, right?" eight-year-old me half-guessed. "That's what my dad told me." In my mind, I did have *some* evidence in Dad's tale, one he'd tell me each Christmas Eve as I drifted off to sleep.

"The *original* Santa was a saint, that's true," said the big guy. "Saint Nicholas."

"The *original* Santa ...? Wait. You're not the original Santa?" In the fireplace, I saw my eyes widen.

"Oh, no. In fact, far from it. I'm the twelfth or thirteenth Santa since the tradition began. Mrs. Claus and I ... we're not entirely sure of the exact number because *no one* is entirely sure. It doesn't really matter, anyway. Not anymore."

"What do you mean it doesn't matter?" My own kid mind expanded to accept the existence of twelve or thirteen former Santas as the current title-holder told his yarn (which means "story" and not "string," by the way, boys and girls). Told it in fleeting but vibrant glimpses, full color but soundless, in which all the Santas who came before introduced themselves to me with their own particular version of a wave, a grin, and a laugh that shook their bellies.

"Davey," Santa went on, "my mind is filled with all *my* Christmases. The Christmases I've spent as Santa, the holidays I've spent on the job, and the holidays I have left to work. There aren't many, in the broad scheme of things."

"You're almost done?" I asked in wonder.

"I am indeed." He grinned, his tone approaching relief. "And I'm joyful, let me tell you. Mrs. Claus and I are ready for a rest. And we're ready to go home. Back to the home we used to know in England. The home we want to know again."

"England? But you don't sound English, Santa," I pointed out.

"No, I don't. I wouldn't. Not to you, anyway. As Santa, my voice sounds however each child on my list imagines it sounding. So, for you, it's deep and it sounds a little like your Papa Dale's voice used to. Speaking of Papa Dale, I heard he played one of my helpers a couple times."

"He did! More than a couple times," I said, unable to disguise my excitement. Santa knew about Papa and how he'd been my first Santa before I knew the real Santa!

"That's good. I can always use more help. I've got a pretty big job, you know?"

I hadn't known. Not until Santa took the time to show me around a little. But I'd definitely assumed or suspected.

"Were you always so tall?" I asked.

"No, not at all." He chuckled at his rhyme, clearly unintentional. "I mean, I was never a *small* man. But this ..." Santa rose from his chair to his full height before sitting again. "All of this comes with the job, Davey. As does the house ... and the workshop ... and the town. I'm the mayor, you know? By default, I suppose."

I didn't know. And I never would have guessed the current Santa was English. It would never have even crossed my eight-year-old mind that this could be possible. Santa was big and jolly and liked not just a plateful of cookies with milk but chocolate, too, and cooking and baking.

"Where do you live, Santa? I mean, where *did* you live before ... you know? London?" This was the only city in England I'd heard anything about. They had a big clock, an eye, and a thing they called the tube that was also a subway or something. But my mom said they probably didn't sell sandwiches there, which little me thought was weird. Why wouldn't they sell sandwiches there? Then Dad said they might but that Mom hadn't been to England and neither had he so they weren't authorities on the subject, whatever that meant.

"Ho, ho, ho. No, not London. Mrs. Claus and I lived on the coast. Right by the sea, in fact. In a little cottage we both loved. And we'll love it again. Just as much as we love it here."

"But aren't you, like, super old? I mean, when you're finished being Santa, won't you just ... die or something?"

"Santa's don't 'pass on'—we don't say die; we say 'pass on'—until they're ready to go. Same with anyone who has ever held the title of Mrs. Claus. It's the one bit of Santa magic any former Santa retains once the job is through."

"So you and Mrs. Claus could live forever?" At age eight, forever meant, I don't know ... ten years or something.

"We *could.* But we won't. We'll decide together when our time has come. Right now, we're excited to get back to our original home."

I scooted up in my chair, which had swallowed me whole without my noticing in the gentle way that only a large, comfortable chair or couch can. "If you loved your home so much, Santa, why did you leave it?"

"Because I said I would. I promised. I made an agreement myself ... And now I need to choose another to take over from me, make a new agreement, if you will."

Santa paused again and cleared his throat, adjusting himself in his own chair. "Does that sound good?"

I didn't jump up and down on my bottom at this the way Brendan might have. Truth be told, I didn't do much of anything besides look confused. I mean, Santa wanted me to, what? Help out ...? Help find a new big guy to take over? That might be cool.

"I guess," I said.

"Good, good. Well, let's get back to you, shall we, Davey Boyd of Seattle, Washington, United States? I still owe you an answer, don't I?"

***

Someone else had said that to me once. That they owed me an answer, that we needed to make an agreement. About three years before I sat with Santa in what was both the warmest and the coldest room I'd ever been in.

"I owe you an answer, Davey," my Papa Dale said right before he was gone forever and I couldn't go over to his house anymore to eat his cookies or even talk to him on the phone.

Grandma Joan was always sad now, and Dad said we couldn't blame her for being sad; it wouldn't be fair to her. We were all sad to lose Papa.

Losing a person, I learned then, was nothing like losing a favorite toy or a set of car keys. Mom was forever "misplacing," never losing, her keys—she always found them. Once you lost a person, you couldn't ever get them back or find them again. They weren't hiding with the loose change in the couch cushions, and you couldn't go and buy a replacement for them at the store. No. People who were lost were ... just *gone*.

Forever.

I leaned forward in the uncomfortable plastic chair Dad made sure I was in.

"So you don't have to stand the whole time we're gone; I know how much standing in one place hurts you, Davey, so why don't you sit right here?" he'd said, indicating the little plastic thing before he left Papa's hospital room with Mom. Grandma went with them, claiming she needed some caffeine.

"Are you awake, Papa?" I said once the door shut behind Dad.

Papa Dale's eyes weren't exactly closed, but they weren't open, either.

"Yeah ..." His voice was all breath. But he wasn't whispering.

"Grandma says you've lost a lot of weight, Papa." Five-year-old me dreaded being in his not-great-smelling hospital room, but if this was the only place I could see him ... well then ...

I wanted to talk to him, to one of my best friends in the whole world. He even used to record himself reading my favorite books on tapes for me to listen to at night. He'd do all the voices: his bears were deep-voiced, his pigs southern, his sheep stutterers like me, and his kangaroos, fittingly, he said, came from Australia and they'd kinda "hop around" from topic to topic when they talked.

I wanted to talk to Papa, but he looked different than he usually looked, which scared me. His face was hollow, and his normally Santa-sized gut had flattened like one of the pancakes he liked to make for me at breakfast time.

"Grandma's right," he said. "I have lost *some* weight." He added the qualifier, attempting to make a scary situation less so for his young grandson.

"Are you gonna get it back?"

He shook his head. "I don't think so, kid, no."

"Why not?"

In that why not, there was so much more than two innocent words. I was really saying, I know I'm young, Pop. Heck, some people still think I'm a little kid, my parents especially. But unlike Brendan—who was too young to come here with us to the hospital to see you so Mom and Dad left him with a babysitter for the day—they brought me to see you, Papa. "To say good-bye," my dad had said. Three words I hadn't understood. Not fully. Until this point.

"Why not?" He scooted up onto his elbows in his hospital bed. He got as near its rails as he could and said, "I owe you an answer, don't I, Davey? A 'why not'?"

I nodded weakly.

"We need to make an agreement, you and me, ok?"

"An agreement?" I said, uncertainty leaking into my tone.

"Yeah. I need you to agree to listen good when I tell you what I'm about to say. You might not like it," he warned.

I was pretty sure I *wouldn't* like it, that Papa knew best. "That's okay," I lied. "I'll agree, Pop. Tell me."

He said it quickly. "I'm dying, Davey."

"D ... dy ..." My attempt at the word trailed off. I couldn't get my tongue around it. "What does that mean?"

"It means this is probably the last day we'll see each other for a while."

"How long is a while?"

"Until you get really old like me."

"That *long*?"

Papa wasn't talking about "a while." He was talking about *forever*. I wouldn't be as old as him for forever.

"Is there anything I can do, Pop?"

"Ah, well. You can tell me you love me."

"I do!" I meant it more than I'd ever meant anything in all my half-decade.

"Then say it."

"I did."

"Say it again. Please."

"I love you, Pop."

"Good. Knowing that will help me with what I have to do today."

"What's that?" I asked.

"Leave," he said, adding nothing else. A single tear trekked its way from his left eye to the middle of his bony cheek.

And Papa was right. He did leave that day. He left right after my parents and Grandma returned with their Styrofoam cups of coffee. He left, and he never came back, and I wished I'd never agreed to listen to what he needed to tell me.

***

I've never told the part of the story I just told all of you—a few of you parents are wiping your eyes, I see; sorry about that. I should have warned you. I didn't tell that story to Santa.

I think he already knew it and that his quoting of Papa had been intentional, meaning to bring the memory to my mind.

Only after he saw he'd been successful in doing this did Santa actually answer my question. Finally.

Why couldn't Santa take away my palsy?

"Just like you couldn't stop your Papa Dale from leaving when he left for good, I couldn't take away your palsy, Davey. At the workshop, we make toys better than anyone else in the world makes toys. A proven fact, if I do say so myself. It's what we're famous for, as you well know. And sometimes—if I have enough notice, mind you—I can get the elves to make a bike special for someone, or I can find a new puppy who needs a home and pair him with the little boy or girl best suited for him. As a kid, you might call this magic. I call it resourcefulness. Santa is resourceful."

"What does that mean?" I asked.

"It means Santa knows many people who are good at many different things. But I couldn't really call anyone to get rid of your palsy, Davey. I don't know anybody who's good at that."

He joined his two hands, as though he was about to clap them together, rested them on his prodigious lap, and looked straight at me.

"Besides, wanting to be rid of something that helps make you who you are isn't a good idea. There are lots of people in the world who don't like certain things about themselves. Certain things about their bodies. About their minds. Certain things they have to deal with each day."

"Like what?" I broke in, sure there was nothing worse than my palsy. Than the constant bullying it allowed and almost invited. The school days at the end of which my legs were spent and screaming with an ache no one—and no medicine—could effectively relieve.

"Well, for example," Santa replied, "your Grandma Joan lives with arthritis in her fingers."

"Oh. Is that why they look all crooked like an old witch's fingers?"

"Indeed. And it's why she can't open jars, or sometimes even doors, and she has to ask for help. Has she ever asked you for help, Davey?"

"Mmhm. But Grandma takes pills to make her hands better. I've seen them. I can't take pills for my palsy." *Not the same thing*, I thought, proud of myself for besting him.

"Okay. I'll grant you that," Santa allowed. "There are no pills to make you feel better. Not permanently, anyway."

"Which is why I came to you," I shot back, accusatory. "Before last year, I'd gotten every present I'd ever asked for from you. So my best friend, Luke—you know him, don't you, Santa?—he and I decided I'd ask you for the one thing I've always wanted. I figured you were good at time travel. You *had* to be, with all the deliveries you have to make. And I figured you could time travel to the delivery room where my parents told me an old doctor made a big mistake and a baby—a baby who was me—got hurt. I just *knew* you could fix it. Fix me. Take away my palsy."

"But you weren't really asking for your palsy to be gone, were you, Davey?"

That's *all* I'd asked for. No wonder Santa was retiring soon. His memory must have been failing him fast.

"You weren't asking for your palsy to leave you. You were asking me to grant you a "normal" life. The kind of life Luke has. The kind Charlie Cage has. And your parents and your grandparents and everyone else you know."

I couldn't deny it, but I didn't want to admit he was right, either. "Maybe," I said. "I was so disappointed, Santa. It was like losing Papa all over again."

Another elf appeared with a big plate of cookies, enough for both of us to fill our tummies twice—though I knew I wouldn't be allowed to do that—and set it down before us. My favorite cookies, thanks to Papa: chewy chocolate chip.

"These are my favorite of all the cookies we make here in the North Pole."

Santa and I had *the same* favorite cookie!

"Take one," he suggested before returning to the subject at hand, his mouth full, talking through cookie crumbles. "We all have to learn disappointment sometime, Davey. I understand this was your first time, but—"

"But this wasn't my first time being diss ... dissa ..." I couldn't make the word come out.

"Disappointed," repeated Santa helpfully. He tapped the plate. "Cookie?"

I still hadn't taken one, but I finally reached down, grabbed one, and popped it into my mouth.

"Yeah, that. This isn't my first time being … that."

"Oh, what was your first time being disappointed then, Davey?"

"The day my brother, Brendan, was born. Before that … I mean, I'd get bullied by Charlie Cage and his mean friends, sure. We all have. Pretty much every kid in my class. Since kindergarten. But I have Luke to help me talk my way outta trouble with Charlie.

"Before Brendan, my parents didn't have anyone else to pay attention to. They cared about me before Brendan. Now I've been taken out of my bedroom, I've ridden in your sleigh all the way to the North Pole, and they haven't even noticed."

Santa leveled his gaze at me, the same way Papa Dale would look at me over his glasses when I'd misplaced one of life's puzzle pieces, told a clear fib, or flat-out misread a situation. When he was gone, Grandma Joan carried on this tradition. They called it "setting me straight."

These days, with me Santa-ing at the mall, and both of my grandparents high up in the sky, I know it as the best kind of love they could have given me. Back then, though, I saw it as intrusive and not all that helpful. And I didn't like to be told I was wrong. What kid does?

"Did you forget that Brendan came here with you tonight, Davey?" Santa half-asked and half-reminded me.

My cheeks reddened suddenly. And, this time, they weren't coloring because of the flame in the fireplace. I was embarrassed I'd forgotten, but Brendan was having his own North Pole experience with Mrs. Claus and a Christmas tree right now. Not that he'd remember any of it when we returned to the real world. He was too young to remember much of anything, Mom had told me when Brendan first came home from the hospital. I told myself, as I sat in that room with Santa, Brendan was still too young years later. And yet, it was wrong of me to deny my little brother's involvement tonight. Mrs. Claus, in particular, seemed to like him.

Why?

Who knew?

"Well, Brendan is kind of forgettable, isn't he?" I dared. "Maybe that's why I forgot." An attempt at humor that landed like his sleigh on my lawn.

"Young man!" Santa didn't exactly yell; he didn't have to yell. "It's comments like that one just now that get children like you placed at the top of my Naughty List!"

Okay, he wasn't pleased.

Santa indicated a group of green-clad elves I hadn't noticed before who were not unlike those who'd brought our cookies and, I noticed just then, cups of cocoa with which to wash them down, "I was going to have those elves bring us both double-chocolate brownies next, Davey. But after what you just said about your little brother, I don't think we need the brownies."

"I'm sorry," I said.

And I was. But was I sorry because I was *genuinely* sorry, or was I only remorseful because someone I admired had called me out on my bad behavior and now I wouldn't be enjoying a double-chocolate brownie I hadn't known I wanted until I knew I couldn't have it?

"We all make mistakes, Davey. But there are consequences to those mistakes." Santa's voice had evened, and I was grateful for this. Anger did not suit him. It did not fit him as well as his suit. "Now, let's see ... where did we leave off?"

155

"My grandma takes pills for her arthritis, but I can't take pills for my palsy. That's where you left off, Santa."

"Ah, right! Thank you, Davey. So, since you can't take pills for your palsy, you thought you'd try the surest method you'd ever known to get what you want, and the surest method you've ever known is your Christmas list. The one you write to me and that your Grandma Joan sends in a bedazzled envelope every year, besides this one, because she loves crafting and she's convinced you that your bedazzled envelope will surely get noticed and opened before any of the others I get."

"Uh-huh."

Santa could be a detective, I thought.

***

Sitting there with Santa in both the warmest and the coldest room I'd ever occupied, I remembered—for the first time in what felt like forever—the first piece of mail Grandma and I ever sent to Santa. Remembering that letter wasn't difficult because we'd sent it right after my papa died.

Who here loves their grandparents? Raise those hands up high if you do! Ah, that's good! It's unanimous, I see!

Anyway, back then, I only wanted one present from Santa. For him to bring my Papa Dale back. Without his cancer, that is. Of course, Grandma talked me out of putting that wish at number one on my list.

"We all want Papa back," she'd said. She pointed at herself, wearing the kind of floral-print shirt only grandmas wear. "Especially me. If I could get your grandfather back by asking Santa for him, believe me I would have asked six months ago when he left. We can't ask Santa for *everything* we want. It's unfair to him and it's unfair to us because doing that will only lead to disappointment."

My first real disappointment.

Grandma advised me to modify my first Christmas list. What took the place of my papa's possible return? A bunch of toys whose names I can't recall now. And we went down to the local craft store and got all sorts of supplies to decorate the envelope to make sure my letter would stand out. "Santa won't miss Davey Boyd's list this year," Grandma promised.

She was right. He didn't. I must have gotten most, if not all, of the presents I *could* ask for. Santa hadn't let me down.

But, for the first time ever, life had.

Somehow, I'd forgotten to call upon this life experience when Luke suggested I ask Santa to get rid of my palsy, and I forgot to do it again when I woke Christmas morning and the palsy I'd wished banished with all my little heart was still with me to stay.

"How come Grandma didn't stop me from asking you to get rid of my palsy like she'd stopped me from asking you to bring Papa back?" I asked Santa.

"You never told her getting rid of your palsy was what you wanted. You kept that between you and Luke."

Santa was right. I had. On purpose. Somewhere deep down, I knew what would happen if I shared my plan with anyone besides Luke.

"Your grandma sent your list to me last year, just as she said she would. She did not read it before she sent it. I know a part of you thinks she did, but what she told your parents was the truth. Your grandma only read last year's list *this* year.

"Maybe she *should* have read it before she made a copy of it she would keep, before she sent it off, but she didn't. I understand why you stayed quiet, Davey." The big guy leaned forward towards me, gazing upon me with kind eyes. "Your parents were focused on Brendan. You wanted to surprise them, didn't you?"

I nodded, this time quite vigorously.

"Yes, of course you did! You thought you'd wake up on Christmas morning, discover your palsy was at last gone for good, and then you'd run downstairs—actually *run* downstairs, which you'd never done before, and then what?"

"And then I could help Mom and Dad with Brendan and I could be the big brother I've always wanted to be instead of the broken brother I was. Getting rid of my palsy wasn't just so I could play sports with Luke."

"I didn't think it was," Santa said, his tenor matching his eyes.

Could I say the same? Just as my parents were focused on their newest child—as parents *must* be sometimes—I'd been focused on me.

Only then did it hit me ... I didn't hate my younger brother. Far from it. If I'd really hated him, Santa would not have shown up on our lawn to remind me how much I didn't hate the little guy. How much I *loved* him.

No, I only hated how I'd never get to be his older brother in the strong, wise, protective way most older brothers got to be older brothers. There was the old car my parents wouldn't give me upon my high school graduation, that they'd never ask me to drive him around in because I'd never drive—the state wouldn't let me; it's a hand-eye coordination thing. Then there was the brotherly advice Brendan would never ask me for, since our childhoods would be so different and he wouldn't be able to relate to me. I thought it unfair to him, how I'd be kept out of that job by parents who were cautious to a fault and not altogether sure how to raise two kids, one with special needs and one without. How all of the chores I should be asked to do would instead be Brendan's.

For life.

Would Brendan hate me because of the extra work his life would entail, all because of me? I hadn't even considered how worried about this I was until our North Pole trip. After all, my little brother hadn't asked for the work. Who would *ask* for the work that comes with a disabled big brother? My parents might even insist he travel with me on long trips. Or medium trips. Short trips, too. Or that he push me in a wheelchair whenever the two of us were supposed to be walking long distances, at amusement parks like Disneyland or at the state fairs our family enjoyed attending together.

Just then, just as I was about to cry, to begin mourning for the big brother I'd never get to be, the door to the Room of Ungranted Wishes burst open. Through it slowly sidled a ... drop of water? Once he hit the cold part of the room, though, Harold the Raindrop instantly became Frosty the Snowman. The elves around us barely batted an eye. I did, though. Both eyes.

Seeing as we were in the one part of the room that would have surely melted him in an instant, Harold—I mean Frosty—stayed where he was, just inside the door. From there, he called out, "Santa, you're wanted at the town square. It's time for the Christmas tree lighting!"

Christmas tree lighting? Santa hadn't said anything about a Christmas tree lighting, had he? Was this just Harold the Raindrop being a little ... let's call it eccentric?

Apparently not, boys and girls, because, upon hearing he was needed in the town square—a summons he may well have been expecting—Santa sprang to his feet in a way I hadn't thought him capable of springing.

"Come with me, Davey," Santa said over his shoulder, already making his way toward the door. "We'll finish our chat in the sleigh. Come meet Harold ... I mean Frosty."

I rose from my chair. Thankfully, I didn't forget the borrowed coat. I put it back on and said another silent thank you to Mrs. Claus. Santa called her Mother, and letting me have that coat so I didn't freeze solid was quite motherly indeed.

***

"I didn't mean to interrupt you, Santa sir," said Frosty. By then, we were outside the shop, conversing in front of the sleigh. "I knew you were in the middle of something very important with Davey here. But the others sent me as a messenger. They knew if you saw a raindrop squeezing through the door, it would get your attention."

"That it did, Frosty," said the big guy. "That it did." Santa turned to me. Still speaking to Frosty, he said, "I'd like you to meet a fine young man and a very good friend of mine, the famous Davey Boyd of Seattle, Washington."

"United States," I added, out of habit.

"Is he the one with the pals ...?" Frosty's whisper was too loud. As a raindrop, he didn't speak at all. He couldn't. So whenever he took solid form, Mrs. Claus had explained—Frosty being one of the many topics we'd touched on over our long spaghetti dinner— he needed to quickly relearn how to talk. And how to not be rude, apparently. He wasn't *trying* to be a bully like Charlie Cage. But what Frosty said hit me in the same way one of Charlie's insults would.

"Davey is our *guest*," Santa explained, "as is his little brother, Brendan."

"Ah, yes," said Frosty. "I met Brendan. Mrs. Claus brought him by my place for a quick visit. Brendan and I built a snowman. Only took a few moments. They were on their way to the tree."

"Speaking of which, we should get moving. Do you want to come with us, Frosty?"

"Oh, no thank you, sir. I know the reindeer aren't with you tonight, and I wouldn't want to make you late for the lighting."

"Alright, thanks for coming to get us." To me, Santa said quietly, "He likes to ride in the sleigh with me at least once or twice each year. He stays frozen the whole time because it's so cold up there, and he loves it. It's just as well he's not coming with us tonight, though. I still have more I need to tell you, Davey, and Frosty—while well-meaning—would definitely monopolize the conversation. Since he can't talk as a raindrop, he really makes up for it when he solidifies! We'd both be lucky if we got to say three words in a row."

When the two of us were back in the sleigh again, and after I'd stopped asking what Brendan got to do with Mrs. Claus that I'd missed out on—besides building a snowman with Frosty the Snowman, of which I was jealous but I couldn't bring myself to say so—Santa asked me something I hadn't thought about until then.

"Davey, when do you think childhood ends?"

I gave the most honest reply I could. "Um, never really thought about it, Santa."

"Where you live, childhood supposedly ends at eighteen. That's when children suddenly become adults. With the flip of a few calendar pages and the crossing off of this date or that one. I've never liked that definition of adulthood myself."

"Why not?"

"The way we figure it here in the North Pole ... no matter how old you are, no matter how old you get, childhood can only end when you let it."

I've never been able to chase this thought from somewhere deep in my mind ever since.

CHAPTER 15

Fifteen Minutes

The Mall

Is Carrie the Elf crying?

I've never seen her cry. I immediately want to get out of the big chair and comfort her. It's what I *should* do. But I know it isn't my job right now.

Sure, Carrie's heard me tell a version of this story several times. But I'm fairly certain I've always ended the previous section with Frosty's jovial refusal to join us in the sleigh, followed by Santa's gratitude that we'd get to commute alone.

I don't think I've ever added what Santa said to me next.

Probably because I've spent my whole life up to this day trying to understand it and hoping there was truth in it.

Childhood only ends when you let it.

I say nothing of the tears I see streaming down Carrie's face, nothing of the tissue she's using to futilely combat them. Some things don't require comment, and my friend's raw emotions are, for certain, a non-comment sort of thing.

And yet ... Carrie looks like she needs a hug. I should probably go give her one.

"All shoppers, the mall will be closing in fifteen minutes. Please plan accordingly. Thank you. And happy holidays."

What the pleasant-voiced lady is really saying is this: "Move it along, Santa. You're working against the clock now. Wrap your story up already."

You can give the woman a hug in fifteen minutes. Assuming she'd *want* you to give her a hug. And that's one big assumption, considering all that's ever gone on between you is some friendly banter and one tiny, chaste kiss.

CHAPTER 16

The Tree-Lighting

A Fortnight Shy of Forty Years Ago

"In order for magic to happen, Davey," said Santa as we neared the center of his hamlet-home so that we were at last in a position where I could just begin to see the lights that illuminated the town square awaiting Santa's arrival, "in order for *our kind of magic* to happen, that is, first, you must believe magic *can* happen. This requires a child's perspective.

"There are some exceptions, of course. But, by and large, children believe in magic. In its possibility, in the anything-can-happen-ness of it. Early on in a child's life, such beliefs are reinforced. By those the child loves. Through stories of me and my benevolent kindness."

"Ben-ev ... I don't know what that means."

"Never mind, Davey. I'm getting ahead of myself. Brace yourself, kiddo. We're coming in for a landing."

I braced myself, holding onto my sleigh-seat with both hands, lowering my head, and preparing for a crash. What little I knew about Santa's ability to land his sleigh did not paint him as an expert pilot.

Our landing was surprisingly soft. The sleigh came to rest on a grassy knoll only steps from the North Pole's Christmas tree, which sat—unlit—in front of a building marked "City Hall." The town's residents—all of them, it looked like—lined the sidewalk three or four deep for a mile or so, each trying to crane their neck to get the best view they possibly could of that year's tree, soon to come to electric life. I even spotted Dancer, Prancer, Comet, and Cupid among the crowd. Unlike the rest of us, those members of Santa's sleigh-team attending the tree-lighting did not require coats. Well, additional coats, anyways.

"Why aren't *all* the reindeer here?" I asked Santa.

"It's the Reindeer Games tonight. For those reindeer who get eliminated, their consolation prize, if you will, is getting to come and see the tree light up!"

Santa surveyed the scene with the eye of a proud but exhausted grandparent who'd just spent a full fortnight with a full-of-energy toddler. I'd seen that same look on Grandma Joan's face after she'd spend time with Brendan and me. In that fleeting moment, I could see—really for the first time—how much he loved the job of Santa, how he relished it, and how much he longed to not give it up but pass it on.

I still wasn't sure how I could help him, but I was sure going to try.

"But the rest of the team will be here very soon. We all have work to do. Come on, Davey. It's time we make our entrance," Santa finished, holding out his hand to me.

I took it.

***

"Ho, ho, ho! It's so wonderful to see all of you here!"

"We here, too!" screeched a high-pitched voice that could only be Brendan's. He and Mrs. Claus stood closest to the tree, near a big red button that announced: "PRESS TO LIGHT."

"Yes, I see that," said Santa. He didn't need a microphone. If needed, he could project his voice for continents or quiet it to be heard by the lucky child on his lap, a talent that came with his position. "Have you all met this year's Christmas tree lighter, Brendan Boyd?"

Brendan smiled unabashedly. His smile turned full-grown adults into puddles. They just had to kiss him all over his little face. Grandma liked to use those exact words. If anyone did, Brendan knew how to be the unchallenged center of attention. Ever since he was born. And yet, this time around, when I saw my brother enjoying the spotlight his cuteness afforded him, I enjoyed it with him.

The crowd gave a cheer and moved, as one, a foot or two closer to my little brother and Mrs. Claus. Somehow, most of them, including Frosty—whom I also spotted, still in snowman form (thanks to the freezing North Pole temperature, he wouldn't become Harold the Raindrop again for at least a few days)—most of them knew who Brendan was.

"And everyone here," Santa went on, "with the exception of our guests, of course, knows what happens immediately after the tree-lighting, right?"

"YEAH!" A booming cheer went up.

"Tell me what happens!" Santa knew how to work the crowd.

"CHRISTMAS!"

Christmas? I thought. *That can't be. We've still got a whole two weeks before Christmas, and I should know.*

When you're a kid, waiting on Christmas to finally show up at the end of the year is both the pleasure and the pain of the occasion. You'd agree with me, wouldn't you, kids? I see Celia's nodding. You understand what I'm saying, don't you, Celia?

Anyway, now—as you might expect—I had even more questions for Santa, though I was afraid he wouldn't answer this batch. Since they weren't exactly fully baked. Instead, they were about the mechanics of what he did and how he managed to do it. Trade secrets I figured I needed to know before I could ever hope to be helpful in his Santa search. But I shouldn't have worried because, as it turned out, Brendan and I would be coming along for the biggest sleigh ride of the season!

***

The townspeople were eager to help Brendan, Mrs. Claus, and me with the tree-lighting countdown. Their entire town was built around a holiday founded to bring mirth. Eagerness, in its myriad forms, was somehow a defining characteristic of everyone Brendan and I met while visiting that place.

"Three ... two ... *one!*"

"*Now!*" shouted Mrs. Claus.

Brendan did his part. He pressed the big red button, and more unbridled joy reached for a sky warning of yet another round of snow.

Talk about eager! Frosty was beside himself for the frozen precipitation that kept him solid. He liked to joke, "If I'm ever beside myself, someone should come along and build me already!"

Once the tree was lit, and not a second after, I heard Santa say to Mrs. Claus, "We best be going, Mother. It'll be the Boyd boys and me this year."

"Are you sure?" For the first time since our meeting, Mrs. Claus's eyes flirted with a wary concern.

"I am."

She exhaled a big breath. "Alright. You know how to reach me when you're up there. Call in at every one of our checkpoints. And you be safe, you hear me? It isn't just you and Frosty and the reindeer up there this time. This year, you'll be transporting some very precious cargo."

"Yes, Mother." This was their we-do-this-every-year-one-way-or-another dance, and each played their role well, probably because they'd played them for so long and both looked a little worse for all the wear they'd taken on for what you and I would call forever.

I couldn't help but wonder if the exhaustion the Claus couple exhibited was part of how every Santa knew when the end of his tenure in the post—while not yet upon him—drew near.

CHAPTER 17

Fraught Night: Carrie Stops the Story

The Mall

"You're saying you rode in Santa's sleigh, and you were there when he made deliveries on Christmas?" This is not one of the children, nor is it one of their parents or grandparents piping up. This is Carrie the Elf herself.

Of course it is.

She's concerned. Whenever I've told this story before—so many times before—it has always ended where I chose to end it; with the tree-lighting. Brendan pressed the big red button, and Brendan and I hugged and made up as though we were starring in a very special episode of some late-80s/early-90s family sitcom that was never all that funny but had enough syrupy goodness to it to sustain a whole industry for a decade or so, followed by a long, lucrative run in syndication. The kids on those shows never stayed mad at each other for long.

I look up at my head-elf. "I'm saying precisely that, Carrie. Yes."

Now Carrie is stomping towards me in her pointed elf shoes.

Uh-oh. She's mad, and she's not even trying to hide it.

"You know," she says in a hoarse anger meant only for me, "it's one thing to tell the kids stories. Heck, I'm the one who suggested we start story time in the first place because, without it ... well, without it our North Pole was a little boring, *is* a little boring, not gonna lie. And one break in eight or nine hours just isn't enough for you. But, Santa, you've gone too far this time."

"I ... How's that?"

"You know how! Gosh darn it, Santa!" She's near tears. "I want what you're saying to be true. I swear I do! And I let your story run long tonight because ... well, because it's our last day here together, probably the last day we'll see each other ... ever, and I know you and Aubrey finally broke up—which you weren't gonna tell me; what is that? Pride? But I knew it, anyway, and it was a long time coming, by the way. I've barely heard one word about her this whole season. When I asked to meet her last season, do you remember what you said she said?" I didn't, so I shook my head. "She told you, 'Why do I need to meet her? She's just some girl you work with. We probably won't have anything in common.' I'll give Aubrey credit. She was right about that one thing. She and I have not a thing in common. And, besides, when you do mention her, even if she's nowhere near you when you're doing the mentioning, your heart is in your throat every time, you tense up, and you're scared to death you're going to say or do something to upset her. That isn't a healthy way to live, Santa.

"Anyway, I wasn't going to stop you telling your story tonight because I wanted to finally hear for myself how it ended. Do you realize you've never *actually* gotten to the end of this story before? Not in over fifty retellings. The tree-lighting *cannot* be the end of this story. I've never once stopped this story, Santa!"

I did mention earlier, dear reader, how Carrie can be a tad chatty, did I not? Also, apparently, she'd realized Aubrey and I were now done. Good for her, I guess.

And, evidently, Carrie has had thoughts on thoughts about the dissolution of my relationship, which she'd kept to herself until now. Never once in all our shared lunches had my uber-chatty, let's-make-small-talk-about-literally-anything head-elf ever said a thing against Aubrey. It wasn't her place, and we both understood that.

"But now?" I say, sensing where my head-elf is going.

"Well, now I absolutely *have* to stop you, Santa. I don't want to, but I have to."

"Why?"

"Because you're about to tell us how Santa delivers all his toys in one night. Which I'm fine pretending for the sake of the little ones," she hiss-whispers at me; no believers heard her words, "but which is—and hear me real good when I say this—a physical impossibility."

"Well, you see, Carrie, right there, you're making an assumption that isn't true."

"What assumption?"

"The whole one-night thing. Do you remember how much time there was prior to Christmas on the night that Santa came to visit Brendan and me and then took us back to the North Pole with him? Do you remember how many days there were before Christmas? Because it was more than one."

"I don't think this is relevant."

"As an elf, you should *never* stop believing in magic. Of all my elves," there are about ten who'll rotate in and out, doing various jobs, from sweeping The Pole at the end of each day to picture-duty—Carrie's favorite job—to clean-up-the-little-kid-pee, "what I like most about you, Carrie, is how you've always been open to the idea of magic. Aubrey—and her parents, her whole family, really—they weren't."

Boy, wasn't that the truth?

To my former fiancée and, especially, to her unimaginative parents and sister, practicality was God. The be-all-and-end-all for a successful life, if not a happy life. When I tried to tell them how I loved to write and why— how the writing of stories and the telling of stories, in some cases the very *purging* of stories, allowed me to feel like I mattered, and when I tried with all I had in me to communicate the joy and love and reward (that was, unfortunately, in no way monetary) that I experienced in the work, Aubrey's parents bristled. They didn't just bristle; in fact, they openly scoffed.

"What kind of money do you make doing that?" they demanded without demanding. I heard the demand in their speech, even if it wasn't there. "Nothing? You make nothing?" Then, passion be damned, my work was nothing more than a hobby, they ruled. For the first time in five years, as I thought again of two people I'd never see again, I recognized relief within myself. That I wouldn't constantly have to be proving myself to people to whom I could never be proven worthy.

"Now, first of all," I continue, still speaking only to Carrie in what has gone from a well-intentioned, whisper-screamed argument to one of our patented and well-practiced two-person huddles, "if Santa were to deliver all his packages in one night, that would be magic, would it not? As an elf who's spent two seasons with me, you believe in magic, don't you? In the *possibility* of magic?"

"I do," Carrie concedes. "I think I *have* to."

"Good. We agree on that." The smile I offer her is tight but real. "But what if I told you Santa doesn't do all that delivering in one night. No one can do that. Not even Santa with the help of all of his Christmas magic. He delivers all of his packages over the course of a fortnight, Carrie."

"A fraught night ...?"

"No, I mean he gives himself two weeks. Santa goes around the world in two weeks and makes it *look* like all that mail gets parceled out in just one night. Of course, within that two-week period, Santa's constantly making time-travel-aided return trips home to refill his big sack. He only has one sack, you know?"

"I didn't," she says, and I see now how my explanation has rocked her back onto the heels of her elf shoes, an elf's awe returning to her tone. Disarmed.

"Uh-huh. Those trips back home are a necessity."

"Two weeks?" Carrie repeats.

"Yeah, a fortnight," I say again.

"Not one night."

"Not one fraught night, no."

"Then why does everyone say it all happens in one night?"

"I don't know. Probably because they think it sounds better. More romantic or something." I take a deep, needed breath. *Calm yourself, Davey,* my Grandma Joan, who left long ago to be with her beloved husband, my Papa Dale, says in my mind. "They wouldn't say that, though, if they'd ever seen Santa and his reindeer time travel like Brendan and I have. It's crazy. They hitch up the reindeer right after the tree-lighting—Blitzen won the Reindeer Games that year, by the way. Did you know reindeer can do the shotput?" She shakes her head. Her face says *What? How?* "I didn't, either," I say. "Anyway, Santa will do one region, then he'll hit the sleigh's red "Return Repeat" button, and that takes him back to The Pole and the tree-lighting. Always back to that specific point in time. He picks up more toys from the workshop, where a few elves, the only ones *not* at the tree-lighting, a skeleton crew, await him to help him load up for the next section of the world, the next section of believers. Both Brendan and I got to press the big green "Deliver Repeat," button during our multiple trips, and now off we went once more.

"Every now and then—I couldn't figure the logic of *when*, but there must have been some logic that only they knew—Santa would call Mrs. Claus on the radio and note a series of coordinates. Likely his global position, I realize now. And, each time he called in, he'd shout over the roar of the reindeer-assisted sleigh what number trip we were all on."

Who was the chatty one? Me or Carrie? You could argue I'm making a play for the title at this moment.

"Now, can I finish my story? It's almost done. And tonight I promise you'll actually get to hear how it ends, Carrie."

"You better end it tonight. Especially since this is it for both of us."

"What? Why would you leave, Carrie? You love this job."

"I love *certain aspects* of this job. If you're leaving the mall, I'm leaving, too. It won't be any fun for me without you."

"The kids will really miss you," I say.

"The *kids* will?"

"Uh-huh."

"Thank you." She backs away from me just slightly. Then, turning toward the story time circle and speaking loud enough for everyone to hear, in her best head-elf voice, Carrie the Elf says: "Alright! Tell us how the story ends, Santa."

As I prepare to do this, clearing my throat, the mall's loudspeaker clears its own throat and crackles to life once again: "Ladies and gentlemen, the mall is closing in five minutes! Five minutes, ladies and gentlemen." Repeating a phrase like that would get it stuck and revolving in a lazy shopper's mind. I knew how Calvin Grigsby thought.

"Please finish all purchases now and begin making your way toward the nearest exit!"

While shoppers loaded with full bags bustle toward the doors around us, those listening for the conclusion of my story stay right where they are. *I've got them.* They dare not move a muscle for fear some magic spell my story has cast them under might be broken with even the slightest twitch from any one of them.

CHAPTER 18

All In One Night Sounds Good, But ...

A Fortnight Shy of Forty Years Ago

Santa commanded the team with his usual monologue, now familiar to Brendan and me. Gentle but firm, and ending with, "Now dash away, dash away, dash away all!"

Almost immediately, we traveled at a dizzying, disorienting clip that was at least twice as fast as the previous night when Santa brought us to the North Pole.

"Don't look down!" Cupid, the wordsmith reindeer, now clearly in work mode, advised with a shout back at me as he and the rest of the team powered the sleigh. "Motion sickness is a real thing! You don't want to test it!"

I acknowledged Cupid's warning with a quick wave of my hand in his direction. *Got it*, I meant to convey.

The trips and present deliveries—and then the subsequent time-hops and relaunches—continued apace until trip fifteen of what Santa said would eventually number twenty-three brought Brendan and me back to our very own neighborhood. As the sleigh slowed and Rudolph and Santa together began to seek safe landing spots, the big guy pointed out our house.

"Look there! It's the Boyd castle!"

Then he pointed out Charlie Cage's house. I hadn't known my bully lived so close by, only about five blocks away. It made sense that he lived so close, of course, since we attended the same school. But little-kid logic is such that you don't always connect where one of your peers lives with where he's educated. In Charlie's case, he was clearly educated against his will.

"How come you're always writing on your computer, Davey?" Charlie once sneered at me.

"It's how I communicate, Charlie," I said, thinking the answer obvious.

"It's how I communicate," he repeated, mocking me. "Everyone says you like to read books," he added.

"Everyone's right."

"You're so lame! I hope you brought enough lunch money today. It's chicken sandwich day, Davey, and I'm *real* hungry."

I wasn't worried. I knew that if Charlie did steal my lunch money, as was his routine, Luke would share his bagged lunch with me. His mom, Corrinne, always made an extra half-sandwich in anticipation. Luke said he'd asked his mom to do this.

Now that's a true friend. And a good mom.

"What did Charlie Cage ask for this year?" I asked Santa, once we were settled on the ground and he was lugging his sack out of the sleigh, preparing to go down the nearest chimney, hoping there wasn't a fire burning inside it. He always touched his hand to the chimney's base before he took "the slide." If it was too hot, he'd look for alternate means of stealth entry. If worse came to worse, he magicked the situation. Though he didn't *like* to do it that way. He could temporarily enlarge a home's mail slot or doggy door so that he could slip the contents of his sack meant for this home or that into the right house. Then he'd direct the gifts to take shelter under the home's Christmas tree.

The presents wouldn't think of disobeying. They were presents, after all; they couldn't think.

Santa consulted the portion of his list detailing the wishes of the kids in our area. "It looks like young Mr. Cage asked for a new television."

"He shouldn't get it," I protested.

"He won't. Charlie's on The Naughty List. All I've got for him is this lump of coal." Santa held the thing out to me. "Here, you can see for yourself, Davey."

"Lump o' coal!" Brendan shouted next to me, right in my ear.

"Ah, buddy, inside voice," I counseled.

"But we not inside. We outside! With toys! And lump o' coal!"

"I don't mind the enthusiasm," said Santa, the hint of a smile playing on his whiskered lips. "We're initiating another true believer in Brendan. I can feel it."

Following a flurry of activity, magic and otherwise, our entire neighborhood was spoken for, with presents delivered and Santa's sack almost empty. Since I hadn't written a letter to Santa for my eighth Christmas, I didn't think there'd be any sort of gift in his sack for Davey Boyd of Seattle, Washington, United States. There shouldn't have been. And yet ...

"Brendan, you'll get your big gift when you and Davey celebrate Christmas with your family."

"Okay!" Brendan said, enthusiastic beyond measure because what else was he going to say, and how else was he going to say it?

"But Davey's gift ... it's ... well, it's a little unique, to say the least, so I wanted to give it to you now, Davey. If you don't mind?"

"I don't mind!" I couldn't help bouncing in my seat. You could argue I'd taken lessons in how to behave as a guest from Brendan Boyd himself. "What is it?"

I expected Santa would pull something amazing from his sack of diminishing returns. We'd need to head back to the North Pole soon to replenish it. But the big man did not grab for the big bag, its big, gaping mouth lolling left with its emptiness.

Instead, he looked me dead in the face; I didn't know why then, but now I think I do. I think it was to emphasize how what he was going to say was no laughing matter, even though he was about to let go a hearty laugh. "Ho, ho, ho! You're very smart, Davey. You might have guessed what your Christmas gift is already!"

I hadn't. I must not have been *that* smart.

"It's our agreement, Davey."

I was befuddled. I furrowed my brow, before I ever knew what furrowing my brow meant. "Our what?"

I didn't have to wait long for an explanation. As we prepared to lift off from my own neighborhood, Santa said it was time that we get back to what he called "The Pole."

"Are we gonna hit the button again?" I asked.

"I can push!" Brendan chimed in.

"No, not this time, little guy," Santa said. "Although you are quite the button-pusher, that's for sure."

He sure used to push my buttons! I didn't say out loud.

Santa tousled Brendan's hair in the way only old people are allowed, and my brother reached up and touched Santa's beard in the way only young people are allowed.

"It's real!" Brendan crowed, pulling lightly at that most famous beard.

"Ho, ho, ho. Yes, it is. And ... *ouch!*" Santa feigned minor injury. "I've been growing this beard for too many years to count!

"Now that today's deliveries are done, we're going to drop you off at my house, Brendan—Mrs. Claus knows you're coming, and she can't wait to see you again—and then Davey and I have one more trip we need to take in the sleigh."

"Where are we going this time, Santa?" I asked.

"To talk about our agreement, Davey."

Oh, good. I'll finally figure out what it is I'm supposed to do, I thought.

We didn't verbalize it, but both Brendan and I could sense our time at the North Pole was coming to a close. (I've talked to Brendan many times since about this shared, unspoken awareness, and he's told me he's retained as one of his first solid memories in life his last few hours up north with Santa and Mrs. Claus.)

Once the reindeer were deposited in their respective homes on Rue Reindeer—as was routine now—and the sleigh was again parked at 1 Santa Claus Lane, and maybe even before it had come to a complete stop, Mrs. Claus had the wreathed front door open. Unlike the last time we'd been there, now the entire outside of the home was ringed with Christmas lights and what I'd call a proper Christmas display, including a plastic Frosty and a properly glowing plastic Rudolph, who wore an all-mouth smile the genuine animal would never wear. I was sure the home's matriarch had had elf help to put it all up. But there was one thing I thought was missing from the Clauses' display: no depiction of Santa in his sleigh with the reindeer hitched to it good and tight.

Santa was a lot of things. Big and tall. A surprise to me. Jolly, as reported. But he was no narcissist.

Speaking quite broadly, boys and girls, a narcissist is someone with an inflated opinion of themselves. This would certainly not describe the Santa you all know. It would describe many a politician, however. The adults who're chuckling right now agree with me!

"You're home!" Mrs. Claus called to us.

"We are," Santa called back.

"To stay?"

"For a while, Mother. I've got a couple of trips left, but the reindeer need to rest, and we can make them over the next few days. We won't need much help. Maybe Frosty will want to come with us. Right now, Davey and I are going to chat."

A curious expression crossed Mrs. Claus's face then. I couldn't read it, but as the years have gone on, I now recognize that expression as a mixture made up of equal parts sadness, joy, and relief.

"Did you tell Davey what his big present is this year?" she asked, knowing the answer already.

"I did, Mother."

"Okay then! Well, Brendan and I will be here when you two are done, won't we, Brendan?"

Brendan shrieked in the affirmative, leaping from his seat in the sleigh to the snowy ground. Somehow, Mrs. Claus made it from her front porch to the snow just outside the sleigh—a distance of at least thirty feet—in seconds. However she managed it, Mrs. Claus was there to scoop my little brother out of the cold, fluffy whiteness and into her arms.

"Can we build snowmen with Frosty?" Brendan asked her.

"Of course we can! I'll just call him and let him know you're back, and he'll be over in a jiffy! Let's go inside, shall we? It's a little nippy out here, and I've got gloves and snowshoes we'll put you in."

They retreated into the house, waving to us as Mrs. Claus shut the door against the constant cold she seemed both glad and sad to be leaving behind soon.

As I'd soon discover, *soon*—in this instance—was a relative term.

CHAPTER 19

A Minute 'Til Closing

The Mall

I can see most of you parents know what "relative term" means. That's good. Explain it to your little ones sometime that isn't right now, if you would; I don't have time tonight.

I look at my watch: Santa joyously sleighing his way around a snow-white clockface with easy-to-read black numbers, and I see it'll be in precisely one minute, at six p.m. on the dot—that the mall closes.

All I will say is that "soon" meant something very different to the two Clauses than it means to you and your children. Something different than it meant to me. To the joy-filled, elderly couple my brother and I had come to know, soon meant: *We'll see you in forty years.*

Let me explain.

CHAPTER 20

He Sees You When ...

A Fortnight Shy of Forty Years Ago

Once we got moving in the direction of the workshop, there was no need for Santa to tell me where we were headed. Which was good because it seemed he was preparing to impart so much to me. I could see the weight of what he still had to say—whatever it was—in the way Santa carried himself. How what he knew weighed him down, his shoulders sagging under a burden that wasn't just his own considerable, Christmas-is-coming-soon, in-season, thanks-to-Mrs.-Claus bulk.

His usual heft.

This was about our agreement, whatever that agreement was—I still didn't know—and his present to me that year.

After Santa parked the sleigh out in front of the workshop, the two of us entered, again with no fanfare or preamble. We were two elves come to work, and we took our seats before Santa's favorite fire in the otherwise freezing Room of Ungranted Wishes.

An unspeaking red-haired elf, whose nametag read Gordon in green lettering that matched his "uniform," as it were, brought each of us a cup of hot cocoa, for which we hadn't asked, but as mine was placed with little ceremony—only a slight nod from the elf—into my waiting hand, I realized how much I wanted that cup of cocoa.

"Thanks, Gordon," I said, almost without thinking. He offered a deeper nod in acknowledgment of my gratitude but still no words. Language was not Gordon's forte; hot, sweet beverages were.

I hope Brendan's having his own cup of hot chocolate or cocoa with Mrs. Claus, I thought. (In our family, we use both names for the drink.) The little guy was going to need it to warm him up after spending as much time as he could stand out in the snow with Frosty the Snowman. Who was really a raindrop named Harold, one who grew eccentric and fun—and a little too talkative—when he froze, but who even kept track of these things besides me? Come to think of it: Carrie the Elf, you'd get along with Frosty pretty well.

The cocoa went down easily, as cocoa will do. Mine without marshmallows; Brendan's cup would have surely included them. (The big guy, for what it's worth, was in my non-marshmallow camp.) And, though we seemed to be in something of a time-crunch I didn't quite understand, Santa waited until both he and I had finished our drinks before he spoke. Once we'd set both our drained cups on Christmas coasters on the large Christmas-lit coffee table before us, Santa started in.

"Okay, Davey Boyd of Seattle, Washington." He put intentional formality into his words for the first time between us. "There are a couple of things you need to know."

"Like what?"

"Like the fact that your cerebral palsy isn't what brought you here. This visit is *not* a palsy-perk, young man."

"It's not?"

"No. You're here because I admire your belief."

"Thank you," I said, "I guess," I added, as I knew his compliment was misdirected. Since, by the start of my eighth Christmas season, I'd given up believing.

"Oh, sure," Santa allowed, "I let you down, and you told yourself you'd stopped believing in me. That was just about the saddest thing I'd ever read on the Nice List. How little Davey Boyd's belief was at risk. I talked it over with Mrs. Claus, and she said I should meet with you sooner rather than later."

"Why?"

"Well, first so that I could convince you I was real, of course. But even more so I could convince you of the *job* of Santa. It's a year-round vocation, make no mistake."

"The job?"

"Yes. I've already told you how I've been doing this job forever. Or as close to forever as time kept by humans can approximate. Well, before I can leave the post, it's up to me to find a suitable replacement. That's how it's termed in the agreement all Santas sign. 'Before any Santa may vacate his post, he must first find a suitable replacement.'"

Right, I thought. *So this* is *what our agreement's about. Santa wants me to assist him in finding a new Santa.* "So you want me to help?"

"That's right, Davey. I do."

"Okay," I said, although I had no idea how I'd be able to help him in his search. But I kept my lack of ideas to myself.

"And ... well, after much consideration, after seeing and watching over several potential candidates when they were sleeping, as well as while they were awake, and after reviewing all that the Room of Ungranted Wishes has to say about all the Ungranted Wishes ever wished onto Santa's list on my watch, and considering who amongst my believers could serve as a worthy successor ... I've made my choice."

"Already?" I exclaimed. "I thought I was gonna help you." I was kind of looking forward to more trips in the sleigh because surely, to help Santa choose a new big guy for the Santa job, I'd have to come back a few times. And drink hot cocoa, of course.

"You are going to help. I've chosen *you*, Davey Boyd of Seattle, Washington, United States. *You* will be the next Santa Claus."

What??! Without thinking, I blurted out, "I can't do that!"

"And why not? I certainly think you can, my boy."

In answer to his question, I stood. It took a moment or two for me to get my feet underneath me—as it always does, as it always *has*—to know beyond a doubt that I wouldn't fall straight back into my chair or, worse, straight forward and onto my face if I tried to use my legs before they were ready to be used.

I took five small paces—these were my normal steps, but they would have been small to anyone else, and to you, boys and girls—away from Santa in the direction of the room's bitter-cold climate change. With my hands, I indicated Santa should pay close attention to my lower half—the legs that didn't work right, the feet that couldn't do much beyond slowly wobbling from one place to another in an out-of-alignment gait; heck, my right foot was turned its usual half-backwards, a frequent cause of the falls that made my bully, Charlie Cage, guffaw. (That's a funny way of saying laugh, in case you're wondering.)

"It's hard enough getting older kids to believe in you, in Santa," I said. Slowly, too slowly for my liking, I made my way back to my seat. "Imagine if the Santa kids were asked to believe in ... wasn't like them."

"I'm not like them," Santa pointed out. "I'm much older than the little ones who put their faith in me every year and who wait for my deliveries every Christmas."

"Not what I mean, Santa!"

"What do you mean, Davey?"

He was going to make me say it. *Fine, I'll say it then.* "Kids won't accept a Santa who isn't ... normal, like them."

"Are you not normal, Davey?" Maybe the more appropriate question would have been, *Is anyone normal?* But that's not what Santa asked.

"Charlie Cage doesn't think I am," I answered. I couldn't help it ... a couple tears rolled down my cheeks then.

"And what do you think? That's what's important. Do you agree with Charlie Cage?"

"Well ... no. I don't ... think so." I wasn't *supposed* to agree with my bully. So I wouldn't.

Easy enough.

"Ho, ho, ho." These hos were free of any jollity. He'd done that a couple times now around me, laughed his iconic laugh without laughing at all. It was jarring. "I sense some hesitation," Santa said, his voice rising to emphasize the sentence's final word. "Where does that come from, Davey?"

Now, I can tell all of you, with confidence, that my hesitation came out of a lack of trust in myself. How do I know this? You're about to find out. But back then I could say no such thing. I wouldn't have known how.

Instead, I said, "Normal kids can play sports. They can jump rope and climb trees and walk like everyone else walks, and they can help their parents with their little brothers. I can't do any of that."

"You can't?"

"You *know* I can't, Santa. You've watched me every day."

"Yes, I have watched you every day. And, as such, I know many things about you, young Davey Boyd. Would you like to see how I watch you and every other believer in the world? If you do end up as the new Santa one day, if our agreement is struck and works out as I hope it will, then you'll spend much of your time there."

I shrugged my shoulders. Words weren't necessary. *Lead the way*, I said without saying it, and Santa took my cue, unenthusiastic though it was. We got up from our comfy chairs, and he beckoned for me to follow after him.

***

The next room we visited was considerably smaller. Any room would have been considerably smaller than the space occupied by all the wishes Santa couldn't grant. But this one was really just a converted broom closet now used for … what? Watching those who believed in Santa via a collection of televisions, it looked like. And not *good* televisions, either. The old kind your parents knew when they were kids, the ones that are as deep as they are wide.

"I'm not watching all the time," Santa said to me as we settled into considerably less comfortable seats in this former janitor's headquarters. (I didn't know then just how much time I'd spend in broom closets in my life.)

"You're not?"

He shook his head. "Couldn't possibly do that, no. But I am able to review any incident relevant to either of my lists, Naughty or Nice. Let me show you."

With that, Santa *did* show me. He showed me first my most recent interaction with Mom. The night before Brendan and I visited the big guy at the mall, she'd made a meatloaf I hadn't eaten; I'd even openly hated it, trying not to gag while I put tiny bites into my mouth. She noticed— my mom always noticed those sorts of things—and she was instantly hurt, even though she wouldn't say so. She would *never* say so. When my mom got hurt like that, she got all mopey. It was no fun for anyone around her.

"Meatloaf again?" was all I said.

She got up and left the table wordlessly. When I realized I'd hurt my mom, I immediately began shoveling meatloaf into my mouth in a silent plea for her to return. *Make her happy again, Davey,* I thought. *You're the reason she's sad.*

"Davey, slow down," Dad warned, loud enough for me to hear him but not for Mom in the kitchen checking on a dessert she'd checked on ten minutes before and probably didn't need to check again.

Brendan sat in his seat, from which my little brother could see Mom, and he said the most obvious thing anyone had ever said. Ever: "Mommy sad."

Thanks for that.

Dad didn't pipe up often; the most he might say to us on any given weekday was, "How was your day, Davey?" I'd tell him it was good. "And how was yours, honey?" Mom would say the same, maybe that hers was fine. He never asked Brendan, figuring the little guy didn't have the kind of days needing recaps. So when Dad said more than this, we knew it meant something, and I sure listened.

I listened then.

"You have to be judicious about this thing." *Whatever that means,* I thought. "If you shovel the entire meatloaf into your mouth, your mom will know why. Because you felt you *had* to, to make her happy. She's really sensitive, your mom. Push your food around your plate a little." I did what Dad asked the best I could. "Yes. Good. Like that. And take smaller bites. That's the right way to do it."

I took his advice. Mom came back to the table a few minutes later, neither of us mentioning my dislike for our dinner. But only while reviewing it all with Santa did I get to see Mom's point of view. While Dad and I worked together to carefully craft and construct the look of my plate—the loaf somewhat diminished through supposed eating but mostly thanks to an optical illusion, while I filled up on the starch that was the meat loaf's dinner partner, mashed potatoes (which I didn't like much, either)—while all this was happening, Mom sat in her bedroom, on her side of the bed she shared with Dad, taking deep breaths and giving herself time to calm down. Every ten minutes or so, she'd emerge from the bedroom and check the progress of our dessert.

"He's just a boy," she said to herself more than once during her alone time. "He's not *trying* to hurt me."

"Who else do you watch besides me?" I asked Santa. I was fully over this Davey-watches-Davey trick. I wasn't all that entertaining. He *had* to watch kids who weren't me.

"I focus on the kids who are somewhere in between my lists. Not exactly nice, but not full-fledged naughty, either. To tell you the truth, I watch a lot of your classmate, Charlie Cage."

"He's a bully," I stated. This was a *fact*. To call Charlie Cage my classmate was to give him far too much credit. His brain was rarely set to "learn." Rather, its default setting had to be "beat the palsied kid 'til he cries. It's easy 'cause he can't defend himself."

If Luke hadn't been there to stand up for me, the beatings I received from Charlie would have been even worse.

"How do you think a bully learns to bully?" Santa asked me.

"I don't know. Some sort of bully school? It's probably the only school Charlie Cage is any good at."

"Bullies learn to bully from their bullies, Davey. In Charlie's case, his own father."

With that, I saw Mr. Cage—a medium-built man with light hair who thought himself an imposing giant around his son—in action. There was a lot of yelling, a lot of crying, and a leather belt. I didn't need to see much more than that before I told Santa I'd seen enough. Charlie Cage and I would never be friends; that ship was long out of port. However, I was grateful to understand him better from that moment forward.

***

When the tiny room was at last quiet again—no more meatloaf incident revisited, no more Charlie Cage and his not-great upbringing, no elves bringing us desserts, no Frosty the Snowman barging through the door—that's when Santa finally asked me the question he maybe should have asked at the beginning of this trip.

"Davey, it's only just now dawning on me, my boy ... and I'm sorry for this ... I'd decided I wanted you to be the next Santa because of the strength of your belief in me and your love for the magic that makes Christmas what it is for children all around the world. But I haven't properly *asked* you if becoming the next Santa was something you'd even want to do! So now I will ask, and I hope you'll be honest with me: Would you like to be the next Santa Claus, Davey Boyd of Seattle, Washington, United States?"

I was conflicted. Could there possibly be a cooler job in the world than being Santa Claus? But, from my glimpse into the work tonight, I'd seen it was a hard job. The big guy got *busy*. "Yes ... and no," I said.

"Thank you for that ringing endorsement of my work!" he quipped, reaching over and playfully tousling my hair. "Ho, ho, ho."

"It's not about you, Santa," I assured him.

"I know that, Davey. It's about *you*. There are two things that must happen before you can take over this job. That is, if you want it. I've done far too much assuming up to now. Lucky for you, you've got plenty of time to achieve these goals. Forty years, to be exact."

What's he talking about? I stared at him, my face blank.

"First and foremost, you will need to accept your cerebral palsy as a part of yourself. It's a part of you, but it's not your *whole* self. Do you understand the difference, my boy? It's a very important distinction."

"I think so," I said, apprehensive.

I did not think so. Acceptance of the thing that made me not normal? I didn't know one thing as to how to go about that.

Again with the hesitation, Davey, I scolded myself. *Not what Santa wants to see or hear.*

Santa—have I mentioned, by the way, that I never saw him out of the full Santa suit, not even for a spaghetti dinner with the missus?—rose to his full Paul Bunyan-esque height. In this tiny room, I hadn't even been sure he could do this, figuring he'd hurt himself, crack his head real good on the ceiling if he tried.

How did he avoid injury? I had my answer when Santa rose and, with him, so did the room's apparently pliable ceiling. As I watched this happen, wonderment wrote a novel—before I knew what a novel was, let alone how to write one—across my agog face.

"Then, of course, there's the thing every Santa needs before he can become Santa: a good Mrs. Claus."

"You mean a *girl*?" My face got hot and my stomach started to churn. *I might throw up ... Don't throw up in front of Santa!* I couldn't do that. But what I could do was say, "Ewwww!" with feeling.

"You say 'ewww' to the idea of girls now, Davey," Santa replied, "but I'll bet you'll feel differently in a few years."

"You think so?"

"Sure. You'll come around on girls. And you'll come around on the whole being-Santa idea, too. I know you will, Davey. I *believe* in you."

I deeply doubted Santa, but I also doubted my doubt mattered to him. He knew I'd honor our agreement. And now I finally knew what that agreement meant.

CHAPTER 21

New Endings Begin

The Mall

I won't go to my locker to pack up tonight like I'd always planned to do on this last day. My stuff will be boxed up and mailed back to me. I'm not worried about it.

Meanwhile, Calvin Grigsby, the man who will remain my boss for about the next thirty seconds, according to my watch, has just rushed into our North Pole from on high, up on the third floor, to interrupt my story and tell me and everyone still gathered to hear the end of my tale (apparently, the crowd is not dwindling at a rate Calvin can appreciate) that—regardless of what Carrie the Elf says—story time is over and done.

"Attention, shoppers," the mall's loudspeakers crackle. "It is six p.m." On the dot. These announcements are nothing if not punctual. "All customers currently in line may complete their purchases. To all other customers: We. Are. Closed."

"Move along, folks. You heard the lady," says Calvin. "Come back tomorrow. We'll be open and more than happy to see all of you then."

All of you and all of your wallets, Calvin doesn't need to say. He shoos them with wild hand gestures towards the nearest set of automatic doors. I've never seen Calvin this eager to be rid of potential customers, what he calls "fresh money," but then my stories have never kept him after closing before. Other than greenlighting story time a year ago and his whole lunch-must-be-precisely-forty-five-minutes thing, Calvin Grigsby has pretty much left our little corner of the mall—our slice of the holiday season—alone.

"But this is the real Santa!" a passionate Celia pleads. *You tell him, kid.* "And we don't even know who the new Mrs. Claus is yet!"

"What the hell is she talking about, Boyd?" Cal says, looking slightly bemused but mostly pissed.

Good point, Celia, I think. *I don't know who my Mrs. Claus is yet, either.*

Which may—which should—constitute a problem. Without a Mrs. Claus, my new job offer, which is quite an old job offer if you really think about it, will likely be rescinded. A dream taken away.

No Mrs. Claus, no residing at 1 Santa Claus Lane for you, Davey Boyd.

Had this been the real reason I was so sad to lose Aubrey? After all, it couldn't possibly have been the relationship itself that kept me tied to her for half a decade.

***

About five years ago, I thought I'd found my Mrs. Claus. I was all but certain of it. Not that I was looking, exactly. For a girlfriend, yes; for a life partner, maybe. However, both Brendan and I—in our own minds—had, at some unnamed point in our collective past, marked down our time at the North Pole as the most vivid of dreams. The most florid of nightscapes. It was only after we rediscovered how it was a *shared* dream, a rediscovery that took place following Grandma Joan's funeral—when

Brendan was eighteen—at the funeral reception, held at an IHOP, Grandma Joan's favorite breakfast place.

"Brendan, did you know Grandma was the one who sent all my letters to Santa?"

"I didn't," said my brother.

"Did you know Papa Dale played Santa?"

"I didn't," said my brother. "I was probably too young to remember that stuff."

"I had a dream about Santa once," I said. "He came in his sleigh, and he and the reindeer took me to the North Pole."

"I remember *that*," said Brendan. "I think we might have had the same dream. My favorite reindeer was Cupid."

"Mine, too," I agreed.

Only then—over eggs over-easy and strawberry waffles and crisp bacon—did we at last compare notes and realize that shared dream was some sort of unexplainable, heightened reality. That was when I began to wonder if there might actually be truth in it. Truth in my imagined agreement with Santa Claus. And in my need to find a Mrs. Claus. And not just any Mrs. Claus, mind you, but *the right* Mrs. Claus.

But we'll get back to that.

For now, let me just repeat something I'm not ashamed to say I picked up in counseling. Relationships that end badly start out just as wonderful as those destined to last fifty years and beyond. A relationship's ultimate demise isn't in the big fights; by then, the thing is all but over already. Relationships fail when communication repeatedly fails. As happened with Aubrey and me.

Our communication failures started innocently enough. With the occasional: "Oh, I forgot to tell you ... I'll be hanging with Susan and the boys tomorrow!"

"But I thought we were gonna hang out at home tomorrow? Have a lazy Sunday together. Weren't we gonna watch *Up*?"

Both Aubrey and I loved Disney—their theme parks, their sweet and lovable characters, and their movies. Beyond these obvious draws, for a handicapped kid growing up in the late-80s and early-90s, being handicapped wasn't a plus anywhere but Disneyland. Where you didn't have to wait in line for any rides. Simply rent a wheelchair and enter any ride through its exit, said the unwritten park rules, since the park was built before 1990 and the Americans with Disabilities Act (Disney wasn't about to redesign a decades-old repository of fun. *We'll get you—and five of your closest friends—on any ride you'd like, just as long as you're in a wheelchair.*) If we bonded over anything and, looking back, that's debatable, then Aubrey and I bonded over a little company founded by Walter Elias Disney of Marceline, Missouri, and how, when we visited Disneyland in California, Aubrey was less depressed, even happy, and I was instantly considered more human by the woman I loved.

"I know we were gonna do that, David. A movie would have been nice," Aubrey had said. "But we're engaged. We've got plenty of time to rewatch a movie we've both seen a hundred times." Did we? "Susan needs me to help her take care of the boys since their dad is out of town this weekend."

"I understand," I'd said.

"Family comes first," Papa Dale had always said, and when he was gone Grandma Joan and Mom and Dad echoed this sentiment. "If your family needs you," they'd all drummed into me, "real friends can and will wait."

"Have fun," I'd told Aubrey.

"Thank you, David." The phrase completely devoid of thanks.

Where was the person I'd fallen in love with? The person I'd lost and had been trying to find again for too many years? The person who said she'd always love me for who I was, regardless of what her family thought of me? All of this before I met her family; her practical parents who didn't—and never would—understand anyone who lived a life different from theirs. How could that possibly be? Someone who valued art over utility? *You can't eat art. It won't sustain you. So why do it?* Those people couldn't comprehend anyone who put happiness and contentment over cash compensation.

Aubrey went to her sister's for the weekend. She had fun. She had so much fun, in fact, that I barely saw her after that.

Aubrey barely reacted when I told her over the phone how I'd taken a seasonal Santa job at the mall. "You could do *so* much better, but okay, David. If that's what makes you happy." Her tone was depressed chic. I say this because Aubrey tried on depression, and then she never took it off. It never left her.

It never left me, either. Until she did.

I'd hoped the new Santa gig would make me happy ... because it sure didn't make Aubrey happy.

The beginning of the end for us went on longer than it should have. We languished in it because we knew each other so well we hadn't known where else to go. I think because, in my mind, the relationship we were in and had built together was *something*, and if I let the something I had go, how could I know there'd be something, someone, anything, or anyone to come after it?

I couldn't.

Aubrey didn't so much leave me—she'd already physically left, of course—as she and her sister, Susan, worked hard to force the issue. To engineer our end.

Originally, we talked by phone every night at nine p.m. This was the sliver of night we'd agreed to carve out for us. This was until we moved in with each other. Which Aubrey said she wanted, and I wanted it because she said she wanted it, and I'd been taught—by Papa and Grandma and my parents—to want what people I loved wanted.

And then Aubrey donned her depression, thick and woolen and massive, and she couldn't take it off like the giant fur coat I imagined her mental illness to be, just like I can't take my cerebral palsy off like a coat, either.

Then she left.

She didn't move out exactly. She left for her sister's. But I thought the tradition of the nine p.m. phone call would— *should*—stand. I'm not sure why. Likely because I liked it.

As it turned out, Aubrey did not. I probably should have known this, but we weren't communicating well by then. She'd answer my calls, but she wasn't happy to do it anymore, and when she answered, she wasn't even really there.

"What?" It wasn't quite the pleasant hello I'd expected. At least she hadn't hit "ignore" and sent me straight to voicemail.

"Hi, sweet," I said. I started calling Aubrey "sweet" at the beginning. She liked it, she'd said. At first. Now I wasn't so sure. "Just wanted to see how your day was." *And if I still matter to you. If I ever did. But, yes, let's start with how your day was.*

"Fine. How was yours?" she answered, in a way that told me her day was only fine because I hadn't been in it and her sister and her nephews had. But, hey, at least she was talking to me. Right then, that was the best I could hope for.

"Good, actually. We had this sweet little family in the North Pole today. A boy and a girl. The boy was probably three and the girl was about nine. It reminded me of my brother and me and how we were at those ages once."

"Why do you always talk about the Santa Claus thing?"

"Because it's what I do. Isn't that how these calls go? We talk about what we did during the day?"

"You talk a lot more than I do, David."

"That feels like a personal choice you're making. I'd love it if you talked more. I was going to ask you what you wanted for Christmas. Could you tell me?"

"We've been dating for years," Aubrey pointed out. As if I hadn't known. "You should know what I want for Christmas."

"Well, I mean, I have a couple ideas of what I might get you, but you don't like surprises."

Aubrey always insisted I tell her what I was *going* to get her for her birthday or for Christmas. Any sort of gifts, really. They all had to be revealed before they were officially revealed. That way, she could get her head around receiving whatever gift she'd receive. And if by chance she'd be opening that gift in front of my family or hers, she could prepare herself to look properly surprised. It was the weirdest bit of stagecraft I'd ever heard of in my life, and I play a mall-Santa. We're all about stagecraft.

"You remembered that. Good for you. But I don't just not like surprises, David. I *hate* surprises."

"Why?"

I was treading on ice far too thin to ever cover the North Pole. Aubrey had told me the why of her dislike for surprises before, but as someone who loves to both surprise and to be surprised by those he loves, the explanation never quite took with me. It hadn't fallen on deaf ears or anything, just unbelieving ears. I mean, I've been to the real North Pole, after all; no surprise could surpass that, but I like to see people try. I give them high marks for the effort.

"Surprises make me anxious, David! You know that!"

I suppose I did. "Sorry," I said.

"Why are you always apologizing?"

"Well, that time, I felt like I needed to," I said.

"Why?"

"Because you seem upset, Aubrey. I don't like it when the person I love is upset."

"Why am I the person you love, David?"

This felt like the most fundamental of questions. A question whose answer, after half a decade, I should have a good, firm grip on. And yet ...

"Well, we're engaged, aren't we?" I said.

"We've *been* engaged for two years."

It was true. And we had our wedding venue secured via a non-refundable deposit. Though we'd moved the ceremony's date twice already. From November to April. From April to indeterminate.

That last move hurt me.

To an extent, though, I sensed it had freed Aubrey from some undefined prison. From some bond she hadn't wanted, she'd slipped back into a bond she knew. Her sister, Susan, had paid her emotional bail. Hence, Aubrey was both there and not there with me that night on the phone. Like every night in those days.

"Tell me about your day?" I probed, tired of talking about myself, tired of thinking about what about us wasn't working. About Aubrey's anxiety, about topics that might get me into deep trouble—like surprises and Santa and things I liked that helped make me who I was.

"You know what?" she finally said after a long pause. "No."

"Excuse me?"

"I need to go, David. I need to get off the phone." Now her voice shook, a clear sign of the anxiety with which she struggled day-to-day. Lately, minute-to-minute.

"Are you okay?" I asked, knowing the answer before she screamed it.

"No! I'm not okay! Why would you ask me that?"

"Because I'm worried about you."

"I need to go!"

"I just want to make sure you're okay first."

"God. I can't take this, David," Aubrey cried.

"Take what?"

"You want to know what happened today? Do you really want to know?"

"Sure."

"My sister said you were mean!"

"Susan?"

"Yes, Susan. Who else did you think I meant?"

"Why would she say I was mea—"

"Because you *are*. She's not wrong."

"I'm not mean to you. I've never been mean to you. I'm just trying to figure out ... the right way to love you, Aubrey. That's all."

"Well, if you don't know the right way to love me by now, I don't think you ever will, David." She paused. I felt its weight, heavier even than the mall insisted my version of Santa appear. (There was so much padding in that Santa suit.) Then Aubrey delivered the end to a chapter of my life. "I think we need to be over, David."

"What?" My voice shook then, too.

"If not now, when? I'm not happy; you're not happy."

"Of course I'm happy, Aubrey."

209

"No, David. You're not. We haven't been happy for years. We don't work. I'm practical, and I always have been. Because it's how my parents are. You believe in magic that isn't real."

"In order for magic to happen, first you must believe magic *could* happen," I argued, without arguing.

"Why should you believe in magic? If magic were real, it would take away your palsy, like you've always wanted. And it never has. What does that tell you?"

It took Aubrey saying this for the entire breadth of our unworkable relationship to come into stark focus. I wanted to cry, and I would later, but the lump in my throat was too big to allow tears just then.

"It tells me you don't believe in magic. Or in us. Okay," I said. "We're over."

I hung up. She arrived in what felt like seconds to get the rest of her stuff. We sat in her car and cried together one last time, and immediately after she left I dialed Brendan.

Between him and Luke, they share best-friend duties these days. With Luke, I'll reminisce about the old days, when our biggest worry in all the world was Charlie Cage, who now works as an insurance adjuster in Cleveland. (Or so I've heard. Not that I care.) With Brendan, it's about life here and now. If anyone would know what to do as my fairytale relationship that was no fairytale crumbled, it would be him.

Brendan, who, to this day, steadfastly believes in magic because he's seen it in action.

***

"Boyd! Earth to Boyd! Jesus, are you ever gonna answer me? What are you, in some kinda trance or something?

What the hell is this kid going on about? And you better have some idea, or I'll ... Oh, wait. I can't fire you, can I?"

"Today's my last day," I confirm. So whatever Cal was about to threaten, he can shove it.

"Damn good thing because I don't know what the hell this stunt of yours is meant to accomplish! Keeping these kids and their parents past closing time. Keeping *me* past closing time."

This was the real wrong I'd committed.

"Don't you want to go home, Boyd?"

At this point, not really. If it's true that home is where the heart is, then I didn't have a home to return to tonight. Or, at least, I didn't know where I would next reside. If anywhere.

"It's no stunt, Cal. I was telling them a story."

"First of all, I'm Mr. Grigsby to you. And second, I know all about your story. Everyone here knows about that story you tell every year, the story that never ends."

"It's ending tonight," I attempt to assure him and everyone standing near me.

"When tonight? Midnight?!"

As Brendan and his wife arrive in their red, we-haven't-had-kids-yet hatchback, pulling into the mall's parking lot, I say, "Cal, the end of my story begins now. Everyone, follow me." All of us—there's still a group of about thirty of us, kids and adults alike—move toward the nearest exit.

As I move outside into the parking lot, Brendan gets out of the driver's-side of the hatchback and takes hold of me by the shoulders. Jess follows her husband out of the car. Standing there, we begin a hushed conference for three. No one else hears a word of it, and that's on purpose.

"Tonight's the night, brother?"

"Tonight's the night." I nod. "Or ... it's supposed to be."

"Are you ready, Davey?"

"No." Could anyone ever be ready for what is about to happen to me? What might not happen if my inability to fulfill a Claus clause is noted?

"I think you're ready," Brendan says.

"We both think you are," my sister-in-law chimes in. "You got this, Davey."

"But you guys know the rules. You remember what the agreement says ..."

"We do," Jess says.

"So then you know I didn't hold up my end of the bargain. I'm gonna let Santa down. I'm gonna let all these kids and their parents down. I probably already have. Just like I let you down, Brendan."

"When did I ever say you let me down, Davey?"

"Come on. You don't have to say it."

"I'm more than fairly sure I never said anything like that, brother. And I never would. What you just told me is something you've made up for yourself."

"Why would I do that?" I ask my brother.

"I don't know. Why the heck would you insist on a rule that no kids waiting to see Santa can ever see him walk around the North Pole where he lives? Think about that for two seconds, Davey."

"I can't have the way I walk—the way I move—busting their illusion, Brendan. You know that."

"You just walked out here followed by thirty believers. The children you're so afraid to disappoint. And not one of them called you out for not being a good enough Santa because some doctor screwed up so many years ago and you walk a little different. They don't think your palsy is a problem, Davey. Why do you?"

CHAPTER 22

The Heart of Christmas

Forty Years and Two Weeks Ago

Saying good-bye has never been easy for me.

The first set of *real* good-byes Brendan and I ever had to say—aside from my own solo good-bye to Papa Dale—was a shared experience. Saying good-bye to the North Pole, the Clauses, our favorite snowman-slash-raindrop, the elves, and all the reindeer.

We sat in the Claus house, comfortable and warm, the fireplace blazing, snow falling outside the big living room window. The scene outside was postcard perfect, and our stomachs were full but not yet to bursting. We'd enjoyed a brownie dessert after a dinner of chicken tenders, mashed potatoes I actually liked this time, and warm, buttered dinner rolls. A dinner I'd requested that Brendan seconded with an enthusiastic, "Yeah! That! I want that!"

And here's the best part.

It took a little while for the brownies to appear, piping-hot, out of the oven because Mrs. Claus is a truly great baker—no magic needed for these brownies that I somehow knew, without being told, would have chocolate chips and fudge in their middles. But dinner itself took no time at all. Mrs. Claus simply magicked the main course, side dish, and rolls onto the table! That was something Brendan and I hadn't seen for ourselves on the first night we were guests here, the night of our spaghetti dinner, since the food was already on the table when we arrived at the Claus home.

"Alright," said Santa, his mouth full of brownie. I'm pretty sure there were myriad brownie crumbs in his beard, but I wasn't going to be the one to tell him. *Leave that to Mrs. Claus*, I thought. "Before we start the good-byes and before I take you both back home, I want to make certain you're clear, Davey, that *we're* clear—and feel free to remind Davey if he forgets, Brendan—that Mrs. Claus and I will see you both in forty years."

"I'll be forty-eight." I did some quick, probably unnecessary arithmetic.

"Not me," said Brendan, even more unnecessarily.

Santa ho-ho-hoed. "That's right, boys."

The big man had explained to us over dinner just how, at forty-eight, I would have a job as a mall-Santa. "Let's call it practice for the real thing, shall we?" he said. His rosy cheeks seemed to twinkle at this. A twinkle that matched the one in his eyes.

"How can you be sure that will happen the way you want it to, Santa?" I asked through a bite of chicken tender. If my parents were here, I'd have gotten the whole "Don't-talk-with-your-mouth-full" lecture.

"Believe it or not," Santa replied, "I know some people. A hundred and fifty years'll getcha some pull. Now ... the whole learning to accept your palsy bit, Davey—learning to accept who you are and how to cohabitate (that means to live with) your palsy—well, I'm afraid that'll be on you, young sir. No one else. It always has been your responsibility alone. I can't help with that bit, just like I couldn't take away one of the tentpoles of your life that helps make you who you are. You are a boy—and you will be a man—with cerebral palsy. How you see yourself beyond that will have so much—I daresay, *everything*—to do with how others perceive you.

"If you think you aren't worthy of other people's time and attention, Davey, then *presto!* they'll be more than happy to agree with you. It'll be easy for them. Don't *ever* make it easy for them. I understand how it will be hard for you, but you must believe in yourself."

I wasn't eating anymore. I was panicking internally. "But how?"

Santa pointed at Brendan. "He'll help you."

"I help!" Brendan yelled, hoisting the hand holding his fork, reaching high toward the ceiling, Statue-of-Liberty-style.

"How can he help?" I scoffed. "Don't you see how little he is?"

Brendan went from hyper-happy to sadder than Mom when she found out someone—usually Dad, with a baseball game he couldn't watch live because he had to work—had taped over her favorite soap opera.

"Ho, ho, ho. Yes, I do," said Santa. "But he won't be this little for long. When you two grow up, you'll be best friends."

"My best friend is *Luke*," I argued.

"You can have more than one best friend, you know." Santa buttered the last of the warm dinner rolls and then chomped into it. "You're allowed to have more than one."

"I don't *want* more than one."

"You say that, Davey. But you don't mean it. Do you remember why you really wanted me to get rid of your palsy?"

"So I could play sports with Luke." *Everyone knows that*, I thought. Well, everyone who was Luke and me knew that.

"Yes. That's true. But there was another reason, too, wasn't there? What was the other reason? You know the answer, Davey. Remember."

My mind was blank for a long moment before it came to me. The dream I'd had the previous Christmas. The dream I'd done all I could to erase from my memory because it was a fiction I couldn't allow myself to wish for any longer.

The false Christmas morning.

The excitement of a body that worked right for the first time ever. The stretching and "limbering up" that I imagined people did every morning of their lives if their bodies worked right.

Running—actually running—to the top of the stairs. Getting to the bottom stair and standing there, triumphant. "I can be a big brother now!" Everyone rushing to hug the boy they'd always wanted.

And I genuinely *thought* I could be that big brother, be that boy they'd always wanted. Until life's cruel sleep-clock decided my sleep was done and that reality should intercede, intrude, bust through any illusion, even if it might be the most pleasant illusion I'd ever had in seven whole years.

"I remember the other reason," I said.

"What was it?"

"I wanted to be Brendan's big brother."

"You sure did, Davey Boyd of Seattle, Washington, United States. And, let me tell you, from one Santa to—hopefully—a future Santa, I found that pretty darn admirable, if I do say so myself. Ho, ho, ho!"

"You did?"

"Sure. After all, if there's one thing I know—besides toys and candy and candy canes and gingerbread and mistletoe and the usual Christmas staples—and I hope you've learned it after being here for a while yourselves, boys—it is that the heart of Christmas, the *very heart*, is family. Without family to help you celebrate the holiday, why, Christmas would merely be ... what do you always say Christmas would be without family, Mother?"

Mrs. Claus, who was done with her dinner, picked up a slab of steaming brownie, which she'd just brought from the kitchen, and began to peck at it. "Just another cold day in December," she answered. Somehow, she managed to say this with cheer in her voice. "Oh, and don't forget to remind Davey he'll need his own Mrs. Claus."

"Oh, yes. We can't forget to cover the Mrs. Claus of it all," said Santa. "As much as I'd love for you to be the next Santa, Davey my boy, if you haven't found your Mrs. Claus by the date when I'll hand over the job—two days before your forty-eighth Christmas, to be exact—if there's no Mrs. Claus in your life by then, well ... then there simply won't be a job waiting for you. The job would need to go to someone else, one of our alternate choices, and Mrs. Claus and I won't show up that night with the sleigh and the reindeer to welcome you to the work. We'd be somewhere else entirely."

I swallowed hard. This Mrs. Claus thing mattered, clearly. And the prospect of finding a girl who'd want to be *my* Mrs. Claus seemed even more unrealistic than accepting my palsy as a *part* of me and not the *whole* me.

***

When the brownies were eaten and the pan was bereft of crumbs, we walked out the front door towards the sleigh parked in the deep snow.

"The sleigh looks pretty buried," I noted. "Will we be able to get it out of there so you can take us home?"

"With a little Christmas magic, sure thing," said Santa.

217

And yet again, he was right. I was getting used to that by now. As we lifted off for home, flying for the first time without the reindeer, every resident of the North Pole we'd met—and some we hadn't—waved farewell.

When the sleigh landed on our lawn—landed without incident this time, might I add—Brendan and I were instantly transported from outside the house in the sleigh back underneath our bedcovers. At the exact same time when we'd left what felt like a week ago.

Some more Santa magic, I thought, before I was back asleep again.

***

I wouldn't wake until it was nearly noon; Brendan slept even longer, 'til past two. Which my mom didn't mind one iota, she told me as she made me a tuna fish sandwich and potato chips lunch. (Well, she didn't *make* the potato chips; she bought them because I liked them.)

That's when I asked her, "Mom, which one of us is your favorite kid?"

"What?" Alarmed, Mom came to the table and took a seat next to me.

"Me or Brendan. Which of us is your favorite?" She'll say Brendan because she doesn't like to lie and because my palsy makes it hard for me to be anyone's favorite anything.

"I don't have favorites. And neither does your father. What on earth brought on a question like that?"

I see no reason not to tell her. "Brendan and I have been gone for ... maybe a week?" It felt like a week, anyway.

She relaxed. "Oh, you have?"

I nodded.

"Where did you two go?"

"The North Pole. To see Santa and Mrs. Claus and Rudolph and Frosty the Snowman, whose name is really Harold the Raindrop."

She smiled. "You have quite the imagination, Davey. You're gonna be a writer someday, just like my dad was. Just like your dad is, when he has the time. My son the future writer. You love making up stories, don't you?"

I did, but ... "I'm not making this one up, Mom. Santa says I'm going to be the next Santa in about forty years. He felt bad that he couldn't take my palsy away like I'd wanted last year. Then he and Mrs. Claus did some research. That really just means they looked at the lists—you know, the Naughty and Nice Lists—and they watched me and found out who I really was. And Santa decided I should be the next Santa. Then Santa came in his sleigh and took Brendan and me to the North Pole for a visit."

"Yep, my son the future writer," Mom repeated in reply.

"What I'm saying," I said, through the crunching of a potato chip, "is that Brendan and I weren't here for most of last night. It's why I slept so long, and it's why he's still sleeping. I asked who's your favorite because ... because I knew you'd say Brendan. He's your favorite because he's less work than I am. He's less work for you and Dad than my palsy makes me."

Mom put an end to the conversation right there. "Davey, that's simply *not* true. And if I ever hear you saying anything like that again, your dad and I will take all your Christmas presents back. Every single one. Is it hard having kids? You bet it is. Is it hard having kids because *you* specifically have palsy? Not for a second. It's just *hard*, Davey. Being a parent ... you never quite know if you're doing the right or the wrong thing from moment to moment. The whole time you're doing it, the best you can do is to *hope* you're doing it right. You won't find out for years, and maybe not even then. But you hope."

Mom reached over and took a bite of my tuna fish sandwich without asking me whether she could. A very *parent* thing to do.

"Davey, you are my firstborn. Not my favorite, because *I don't have* favorites, but my firstborn. And you'll always be the first little baby I ever held. The first I ever fed, although I had to feed you differently than I fed Brendan to start because your little mouth ... you couldn't latch onto me. It made me sad.

"But I don't ever want you to think that if you got lost or hurt, your dad and I wouldn't care, for some reason. Because you think we care about Brendan more or whatever. We don't, and we never will. Do you understand me, Davey Boyd?"

"Of Seattle, Washington, United States," I said under my breath.

"What was that?" Mom was near tears. "You need to learn to speak up, Davey. You're quite the mumbler."

"I understand, Mom. That's all I said. I was telling you I understand."

And I did.

CHAPTER 23

Santa Claus Is in Town

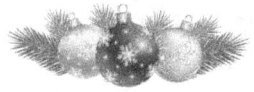

The Mall Parking Lot

My sister-in-law, Jess, is petite and brown-haired. She's beautiful, and after telling me how I "got this," she stands beside my brother now, her left arm slung around his back. She's wearing the kind of Christmas sweater you can only get away with if you're one hundred percent committed to it. Snowmen are raining—snowing is probably the more appropriate word—down onto a backdrop of red and white.

"Brendan's right, you know? These kids adore you, Davey."

I look at Calvin Grigsby, red-faced and seething far enough away from me that I can't feel the flames of his simmering anger, but I can see they're blazing hot. "Yeah, well ... *he* doesn't."

"That's your boss Calvin, right?"

"Yeah."

"Didn't you say he hates everyone?" says Jess.

I did tell them that. Dinner at Brendan and Jess's house is a bi-weekly event for me. One they insist upon, for which Brendan will pick me up every other Saturday night. And I couldn't help but discuss work. I never *wanted* to discuss work, but if someone asks, "How was your day, Davey?" and someone always does, work inevitably comes up.

Aubrey had never come to these dinners. She'd been invited, but she'd never taken my brother up on the invitation, instead making herself scarce on those Saturday nights. Each time she gave an excuse or five as to why she wouldn't be joining us yet again, I'd been hurt anew, Aubrey's refusal to break bread with my family cutting deep at the bond I'd thought we'd had.

Now I was glad for her refusals.

"I did say that, yeah."

"The guy probably hates his own kids!" Brendan jokes.

They laugh. As opposed to Brendan's little-kid laugh, which was shrill and annoying to my not-allowed-to-be-a-big-brother ears, now it's hearty, from down deep in his gut. (His gut is not nearly as expansive as my own, by the way. But then ... I'm in training. And I don't mean personal training.)

Just then, something appears far-off in the sky. At first, it's just a bright glimmer. A star, perhaps. A super-nova? Or some optical illusion caused by residue from the streetlight pollution that makes it hard—almost impossible—to view the stars out here? As the glimmer draws quickly closer, though, there's no mistaking it. Here comes Santa's sleigh. The kids, and even most of the parents standing with them, "Ooooh!" and "Awwww!" in quiet reverence.

"So Cal didn't accept you, and Aubrey didn't, either. We accept you, brother," Brendan says. "But you can't be constantly hoping for external validation, anyway. That will only end in disappointment."

"You sound like my therapist, Brendan."

"Maybe that's what you need me to be right now."

"And what do you need me to be?" I ask him.

"Just my big brother, which you've *always been*, Davey. No one else can ever be the big brother you are to me."

"I've always been your big brother?" I'm not sure I believe him.

"Sure you have."

"I didn't know that."

"Of course you didn't. Because you don't see yourself that way. You see yourself as my palsied burden of a brother who thinks that's all he is and all he'll ever be, and it eats at him. At you. And you let it. Don't let it eat at you anymore, Davey. Accept who you are! Not some doctor's ... mistake. Not just some huge accident. You're *you* ... the caring, amazing human being you've become."

"I think I *have* accepted my palsy," I tell him. *Finally.* My voice is infused with the word, though I don't use it. "I don't think I could have told my whole story today like I did if I hadn't accepted my palsy first. I think that's why I'd never gotten to the end of it before. It wasn't about time constraints or anything, it was about acceptance. And now I've accepted who I am. Something's clicked."

"You *finished* your story?"

"I did."

"The one you're always telling? The one about us?" says Jess.

"Yep. And what do you know? Once I'd finished it ... click."

"What clicked, brother?" Brendan asks.

"When you were little, and you asked Santa to get rid of my palsy for *your* Christmas present ... you didn't do that because *you* thought I needed to get rid of my palsy. You did it because you knew that's what *I* wanted."

"Yeah," Brendan confirms.

"You were being a good brother to me. Even then, I knew that on some level. But on another ... Aubrey broke me. And I went right along with it, thinking it was just part of becoming a *real man* because I thought it was what I deserved. For the last five years, that fire that used to burn inside my kid-self, that fire left me. I *hate* admitting this. Aubrey snuffed it out, and I let her smother my dream. She didn't want me to be who I was. Who I *am*. She wanted the man she saw me as. A man who could get rid of his palsy by simply *thinking* it gone. I tried to be that man for her. For me. For way too long. I really tried."

"But you couldn't," Jess says.

"No, I couldn't. It's funny how we can *know* things as a kid. Beyond any doubt. Then we grow up and forget."

"What do you mean?" says Brendan.

"After our North Pole trip, when we came home, I knew I was who I needed to be, and I didn't need to be anything or anyone else. I *knew* I was enough. Because I was enough of a big brother for you. And, as it turned out, I was—and I'd always been—enough for our parents, too. Then I grew up, and Aubrey's lack of faith in me was so easy to overlook at first. Everyone has lacked faith in me when they first met me. That was nothing new; my palsy looks worse than it is. I told myself Aubrey and I loved each other and that I'd show her how good a man I was over time. Our love would conquer her doubts. Her parents' doubts. Her family's doubts, all of them. Then ... it didn't. Aubrey and I probably *broke up*, whatever that meant to us, about ten times."

"That many?" says Brendan.

"Yeah."

"We never knew," says Jess.

"Because I didn't *want* you to know. And each time we'd be over, my heart would break, and I would cry. And then my heart would scar over. Again and again and again. Until last night."

"What happened last night?" Brendan asks.

"You came right over when I called, like I knew you would. I was sitting at my kitchen table, eating your wonderful lasagna, and I thought about how not everyone's going to accept me. Even people I love will let me down. That's how life works. So the person whose acceptance I need most is my own."

Jess nods. "You're right, Davey. And that's true for all of us."

"Yeah, it is. Accepting my palsy, though, was only one hurdle. Right now, tonight, it's not the biggest one."

I can't make out Brendan's expression. Has he forgotten the obstacle that will keep me from ever driving Santa's sleigh?

"I don't have a Mrs. Claus. I thought I'd found her, but ... well, you know how that story ended, and I've talked about her too much. Now they're gonna give the job to someone else. They'll have to. All because I made the wrong choice five years ago."

"Brendan said you'd be all hung up on the no-Mrs.-Claus thing," Jess scoffs.

"Well, he was right."

"You hadn't found her," says Brendan. "Aubrey wasn't your Mrs. Claus, brother. We knew it before you did. Hell, *everyone* knew it. But we couldn't *tell* you. You had to find it out before you could see it, before you could know it for yourself. We were in no position to tell you anything."

"Aubrey liked a version of you that only lived in her head, Davey," Jess adds. "That version of you wasn't living in the real world."

"And her expectations of me, the whole, 'If you're gonna be a writer, you better write best-sellers or else why try?' They were ..."

"Her parents' expectations. Her family's. And they were unreasonable. Besides which, they were expectations of the man in Aubrey's mind, Davey, not of *you*. They have absolutely nothing to do with the man Brendan and I know."

Brendan reaches out and pats me on the shoulder. He points up at the enlarging sleigh. "Looks like it's time," he says, grinning.

**

Santa's sleigh, including the entire team of all nine reindeer, the two Clauses, and an excited and very frozen Frosty the Snowman—who, if he's not careful, could morph into Harold the Raindrop before our eyes in the temperate climate of Western Washington state—lands between the parking lot's two rows of cars about five feet from where I stand with Brendan and Jess.

The big guy has come. Just as he said he would.

Tonight was, in fact, the night. *Is* the night. Forty years in the making ... Forty years in the waiting.

Yet, even if I've accepted my palsy, there's no debating how I have no Mrs. Claus to present. Santa won't be happy: my failure means he'll need to stay on another Christmas. Or two, if he's unlucky, depending on how long it takes to search out his true successor. Another Christmas or two away from the long-ago home they loved, the quaint English coastal cottage to which the current Clauses long to return.

As the sleigh lands, I glance back at the too-quiet crowd. I mean, they've gone completely silent. Not a peep from Ms. Celia or Ricky the antagonist. *Not the right reaction for what's happening right now.* And that's when I see it.

The bubble.

Contained in the bubble are Celia and Ricky and all the kids who sat listening to my story. All who climbed into my lap and told me their wishes today. All the adults who stand with them, too. They're all frozen in place, including the appropriately red-faced Calvin Grigsby. Only my loved ones, Brendan and Jess, are spared. And Carrie the Elf, I now notice. Carrie the Elf, who smiles at me.

What's going on here? my eyes ask of her.

I'm distracted by the change in the light as the sleigh descends and lands, the reindeer snorting and coming to a stop. Santa emerges from his sleigh in the full Santa get-up. I'm not sure he ever wears anything else.

"Davey, my boy!" We hug. The hug is somewhat perfunctory but still feels like something I hadn't known I'd missed for forty years.

"Santa ... Good to see you." *You'll have to find someone else to do the job, though, because no woman wants the Mrs. Claus job. It isn't the job that scared them away; it's me.*

"We're glad to be here, Davey. It's a big night."

Yeah. It would have been, I think. I have to ask about the bubble. There's no one but Santa himself who could have magicked it. "What's with that bubble over there?"

Good. Very tactful.

"Oh, I had to freeze time," Santa says. "But just for a while."

"Why?"

"I know you wanted to give everyone a proper ending to your story, Davey."

"Well, sure I did. They've been listening to me tell it all day."

"They have their ending."

"What do you mean? They don't get to meet you or Mrs. Claus or Rudolph or Frosty? That's better than any ending I could ever come up with. Can't you let them have that?"

"Alas, no. Think about it. When a child says they want to know who the *real* Santa is, do they *really* want to know?"

Santa is talking with his hands, gesturing far and wide, and I step back so as not to be inadvertently struck.

"Well, I ..."

"No, Davey, they don't. If you find out how the magic works, how the strings are pulled, then the magic stops being magic. So we can't let that happen. We *won't*. The crowd will stay frozen for now. Once we've left and are on our way home to The Pole with your dear Mrs. Claus, then that bubble will burst, and everyone in the crowd who doesn't need to know what's really going on tonight will head home, thinking all the way there of the wonderful story you told them. But ... maybe we can let them see the sleigh fly off across the sky and you nowhere to be seen ... The perfect cliffhanger. Let them join the dots for themselves. Certainty kills the magic, after all."

Santa looks at everyone surrounding me, the ambulatory and unfrozen.

"Now, won't you introduce us to everyone, Davey my boy?"

"Oh, of course," I say, trying to will the shake out of my vocal chords. Trying isn't *doing*, however. The shake remains.

Santa helps Mrs. Claus down off the sleigh. "I've got you, Mother," he says, turning suddenly somber. "We're about to meet all of Davey's friends!"

The phrase "all of Davey's friends" would imply, incorrectly, that Davey has a great number of friends, which I don't. And why did Santa just get all ... well, there's no other way to say it, even though the emotion doesn't fit him in the least. Why is Santa suddenly so sad? Does he know I've failed him? That there's no Mrs. Claus here for him and his beloved to meet?

He *must* know.

I move first to my brother and Jess, who stand at the front of the bubbled crowd.

"You remember Brendan, Santa," I say.

"So I do!"

"We remember you, too, Brendan," says Mrs. Claus. She looks up at the sleigh. Frosty is still seated up there, in what Santa always called his "place of honor."

"Frosty would come down and say hi," Mrs. Claus adds, "but he needs to stay frozen, and the only way he can do that is if he stays in the sleigh. It's—"

"The magic, I know," says Brendan. He steps aside to reveal who's standing behind him and says, "Mr. and Mrs. Claus, this is Jess."

Now Mrs. Claus is back to her smiling, cheerful self. It's as though the fleeting sadness she and her husband both just displayed was nothing but a minor blip in an otherwise fantastical moment.

"A pleasure to meet you, dear," says Mrs. Claus, and the two women shake hands, which morphs into an embrace. When they part, Mrs. Claus says, "You wouldn't happen to be our new Mrs. Claus, would you?"

"No, ma'am," Jess answers, her smile tight. "I'm sorry, but I'm Brendan's wife."

"Yes, of course you are, dear. Your Brendan. Such a sweet boy. Forgive me. I'm a very old woman these days, and the mind doesn't work as fast as it used to, I'm afraid."

We're getting closer and closer. Soon ... very soon ... they'll ask to meet my Mrs. Claus. If Santa and his Mrs. Claus are experiencing sporadic moments of deep sadness now, just wait.

"Who else is here for you, Davey Boyd?" Santa asks me.

"Who else? I don't think there is anyone el—"

Before I can finish, Brendan jumps in. "Davey's best friend, Luke, is here. He's right over there. See him waving, Santa? And there's Luke's wife, Colleen."

"Wonderful to see you both!" Santa says to Luke and his wife. Then, to me, "Are you excited, Davey?" the question all but rhetorical. "It's time for a new Santa, and you're it."

No, I'm not, I think. "No, I'm not," I say.

Not without a Mrs. Claus. I knew the rules, and I couldn't follow them. I didn't. Surely someone else—a better candidate so far overlooked—had crossed all their "t"s and dotted every one of their "i"s.

"What's the matter, Davey?"

"I don't have a Mrs. Claus." I say the words low, so low they're almost inaudible.

"Ho, ho, ho! What was that?"

He was gonna make me say it out loud. At least this time I understood *why* I needed to say it out loud, for everyone listening. To let them in on what should be a joyous occasion. The minute I say what I need to say, though, the occasion will no longer be joyous.

"Now, what was it you were trying to say, Davey? Could you repeat it please?"

I will. I don't want to, but I will.

Just imagine you're ripping off a Band-Aid. That's all this is, Davey. "I don't have a Mrs. Claus, Santa," I say.

Mrs. Claus lets out a surprised gasp; she tries to hide it but can't.

"Excuse me?" Santa says.

He isn't sure he heard me right. I can see this in the way his posture kind of slumps, and I can't blame Santa for slumping. I'm sure that, when he took over the job all those tens of decades back, he'd never dreamed of attending the hand-off—a deal made forty years previously—without a future Mrs. Claus present.

This wasn't how things worked.

When next he speaks, Santa seems to re-inflate. (He reminds me of a rescued Macey's Thanksgiving Day Parade balloon. Saved from the certain doom of a high-rise or live power lines. Somehow, the balloon has steered clear of danger, its former glory resuscitated.)

"I understand," Santa says. He reaches out, pats my shoulder.

"You ... do?"

"Ho, ho, ho! Of course I do," he says, calm and collected. The words of a friend, not a judge looking to hand down a guilty verdict. "Believe me, I do!"

How? I think. "How?" I ask him, genuinely perplexed.

"Well, you must remember, Davey, there was a time way, way back that none of the living can still remember — a time before I myself was Santa."

Of course there was.

"I served as the apprentice to a fine Santa Claus. He did not do the job exactly the way I do it. Every new Claus must put his own stamp on the suit, his own stamp on the workshop and the job."

"And you did that?" I say, without saying much of anything. Just to let him know I'm listening.

"I did. When it was my turn to do it. Before then, I prepared. He said I should work to get rid of my shyness, or at least that I should *try*, and I knew I needed to work the shyness out of me. At least when I was in public. At home, I could be the introvert I was and had always been before anyone ever called me Santa."

"I can't be rid of my palsy, Santa," I say, trying to keep my voice even.

"No, you can't. And I wouldn't *want* you to be rid of it. Remember what I asked you to do, as part of our agreement, Davey? I didn't say you should get rid of your palsy. I said you should—"

"Accept it," I finish for him.

"Precisely. And I know you have done this. And Mrs. Claus and I are so proud of you for it. We know it can't have been a simple thing. Acceptance of oneself never is."

"How do you know I've done this?"

"If you had not achieved the acceptance I asked of you by tonight, Davey," Santa explains, "then the fact of the matter is, the sleigh would never have lifted off the ground. If you hadn't achieved all that I'd asked of you, neither I nor Mrs. Claus nor Frosty nor Rudolph, let alone his whole team, would even be here right now. This is a time for great celebration, Davey my boy! Why aren't you celebrating?"

Firstly, because Mrs. Claus had seemed so sad climbing down from the sleigh. Seeing this, I thought a celebration inappropriate.

"Why is Mrs. Claus so sad?" I say.

"I'm not sad, Davey," Mrs. Claus says.

"You're not?"

"It's just that being the Claus family for all the children we serve and being perpetually full of cheer for over two centuries ... well, the obligations have worn on me, in a way I could never show anyone up at The Pole. But I'm still sad to be leaving our posts, and I suppose that's probably what you saw, Davey. I'm so glad to know that the house at 1 Santa Claus Lane, and the workshop at 1224 Elf Drive that comes with it, will be well taken care of by you and yours, young Davey."

I haven't been called young by anyone in at least ten years. My parents will still refer to me as their kid, and to Brendan and me collectively as the kids, the inference being that we are and will always be young in their eyes, but that's not the same thing. Hearing this from Mrs. Claus's mouth lightens my heart.

"We just have one more question for you," says Santa. "Mrs. Claus and I have yet to meet *the future* Mrs. Claus! We'd really like to. Will you please introduce us?"

My stomach flips and tumbles. *This is when they find out you're a fake, Davey.*

Accept my palsy? Sure, I can, finally, do that. To a point. Over many years. I walked out here the way I walk (what some call the broken way I walk). Brendan's right, that is acceptance. But now ... now they want to know who the new Mrs. Claus will be, and the fact is ... I got nothing.

"I don't ... I don't know," I answer honestly. There has never been less confidence in my timbre.

"Ho, ho, ho. Why, of course you do, Davey," Santa shoots back, too sure of himself.

"I don't, and I've been worried about it ever since you showed up, Santa. Well before, actually. The fact is, I'm in the midst of a breakup. I'm about as far from knowing who my Mrs. Claus would be as anyone could get."

"Davey, we know all about your breakup. And, if you want the truth, had you *not* ended your relationship with Ms. Aubrey Hargrove, we wouldn't be here right now."

"What are you saying, Santa?"

Mrs. Claus is standing at my side, beaming.

Her husband answers with a bemused look on his face. "I'm saying that if there wasn't a Mrs. Claus out there for you—and if she weren't somewhere in the immediate vicinity right now—my sleigh, which is soon to be your sleigh, would never have lifted off the ground. I'd still be stuck at the workshop trying to figure out what went wrong ... So, would you mind letting us in on the big secret after all this time? Who is the next Mrs. Claus, Davey Boyd of Seattle, Washington, United States?"

"I ... I have no clue," I say, defeated.

***

She looks not unlike an elfin apparition. Carrie the Elf, still in full uniform—which makes sense; when would she have had time to change?—floats towards me, and then she's in my arms.

"Carrie?" I say. Nothing else will come.

"I think they might be talking about me," she says.

"What? Why ...?"

"Davey, you're a *great* Santa. The kids love you. There's no denying that. But, I have to say—and hear me when I tell you this—when it comes to women, you're pretty oblivious."

"I am?"

Carrie smiles. "I don't take my lunches with just anyone, you know?"

"Well, sure, but that's just lunch, Carrie. It doesn't mean anything."

"Oh, Davey! You've been so in your head!"

"What?"

"You've been in your head, trying to save a relationship that there was absolutely no saving. We all knew it, but how could we say it? It wasn't our place."

The next person to speak isn't me. And it isn't Santa or Mrs. Claus, either. Brendan comes up behind me and puts his arm around my shoulder. Jess stands with him.

"She's right," my brother says. "And you know it."

"I ..." I can't help but get choked up. Luke and Coleen approach, and they aren't alone, I only now notice—Carrie was right, I really have been in my head—how my childhood best friend and his wife are standing next to two elderly people I hadn't thought would be here at all. Robert and Sylvia Boyd, formerly of Seattle, Washington, United States, and now proud residents of the Shady Grove Senior Center, Renton, Washington, United States. I haven't seen them since a low-key Thanksgiving we spent out at a restaurant called The Gobbler. ("Don't want to cook your turkey? Your Thanksgiving dinner?" their slogan went. "We get it! Let us do the cooking for you!")

"Mom? Dad?" I manage.

Mom and Dad stand off to the side, away from their kids but near enough to be noticed. Besides our Thanksgiving afternoon get-together, which Brendan organized, I haven't seen my parents since Dad's eighty-second birthday five months ago at their new not-home home. Another "party" Brendan organized. That's just how life can get away from you as an adult. Sometimes, the people you should see, you don't, and the people in whom you shouldn't invest time or energy, you do.

In the hopes that they'll do the same for you.

"Well, yeah. Mom and Dad are here. Of course they are. I called them," Brendan says. "Luke and Colleen, too. Luke said he'd pick them up so Jess and I could come straight here. For you, Davey. We're all here for you."

I hadn't known my brother knew how to contact Luke. Then again, social media allows anyone to be in contact with anyone else these days.

"This is a big night, brother." Brendan squeezes my shoulder. "We all wanted to be here."

"You ... they ..." At a complete loss for words, I turn back to Carrie and attempt to explain myself to her and Brendan and Jess and Luke and Colleen and my parents and everyone who cares about me much more than I'd ever let myself think they cared.

"You want to be my ...? I mean, Carrie, I never even thought you liked me like ... I thought you were just friendly with me because you're ... well, friendly."

"It's a good thing I'm the chatty one," Carrie says, chuckling. "You can't say a complete sentence right now to save your life, can you, Santa?"

At this, I give no argument. When someone's as right as Carrie is here and now, what can be said?

She comes closer and whispers, for only me to hear, "I like you, Davey. I've liked you for a while now. I'm not sure you've ever noticed, but I do. Will we work? I don't know. I *can't* know that because your heart has been someone else's for so long."

"You like me? But what about the palsy?"

"Is your palsy all you are?" Carrie asks.

"Well, no."

"Then why do you talk like it is? You seem to be forgetting, Davey ... it's always been my dream to marry Santa."

I'm embarrassed to nod in admission that I *had* forgotten this about my former head-elf. *And future Mrs. Claus?*

"Let's you and I go to the North Pole together, Davey. Tonight."

"Right now?"

"You have something better to do right now?"

I shake my head.

"Then, yes, right now. Let's go to The Pole, and you can show me around. I hear you've been there before. I'll get to know the real place, and we can get to know each other in a *real* way. I think we might be good together, if you're open to the possibility."

"I am!" I say breathlessly, amazed at this turn of karma. I turn to everyone gathered around us. "Santa," I say, "my Mrs. Claus is my former head-elf, Carrie Clark!"

"Very good," Santa replies. "Then, before you go, I just have one more piece of advice to bestow upon you both. May you remember it as long as you carry on in the job and beyond. Don't let other people, especially those who don't like you for you and who you are, those who insist you change to suit them … don't let those people decide how your life should go. And, since time is the only capital you'll ever be sure to have any sort of control over, try hard to only spend your time, romantic or otherwise, with or around people who want something real with you. Make sure they're around you because of who *you* are, quirks and all, and that they won't wade into life's pool with you halfway. Because life is an all-or-nothing proposition. And you want someone who looks at you and says, 'Let's do it all!' with gusto!"

When Santa has finished, I thank him and say good-bye to Brendan and Jess and Mom and Dad and Luke and Colleen.

Then Carrie says, "Let's do it all!" as we climb aboard the sleigh, with Frosty the Snowman in his magical spot, the reindeer hitched up in their proper order, and the two outgoing Clauses for the short, time-bending trip to our new home.

The now-former Santa and his elves—my … *our* elves— have already done all the work needed for this Christmas to come. So Carrie and I will have a solid year to become familiar with the job

And with each other.

***

For so long now, though I hated to admit it, I've thought myself a dismal, palsied failure. Emphasis on palsied. Emphasis on failure. I took my breakup with Aubrey as not just solid but incontrovertible proof and confirmation of this. But tonight, as I advise the beautiful Carrie not to look down—unless she wants to witness the world speeding by us underneath the sleigh at motion-sickening speeds— after I've at last made it to the end of my story, and as I let myself realize, for the first time, how much I care about Carrie, tonight as so many people have shown they cared about me, I am content in my own skin.

In my own body.

And I like how it feels.

The fact that my body is palsied and that I couldn't take my palsy away—not even with the Christmas magic I believe in wholeheartedly, Christmas magic I now control— that's okay.

Truly it is.

Because I've learned I am not merely one thing, or even two. My identity is multi-faceted. If I'm not feeling great about still having my palsy one day, I'll wake and look to my right and see Carrie sleeping by my side to quell any fear of failure I might entertain. And when Carrie and I are so busy that we'll sometimes forget how important we are to one another, perhaps I'll get a letter from a little girl or boy telling me to tell Mrs. Claus I love her.

And I will.

Having allowed myself to be defined by my palsy for so long, *too* long—learning that I'm so much more than the thing I, admittedly, like least about myself—is not an easy lesson to grasp. I don't think it ever is, for anyone, and it's a daily grind. It's worth it, though. I've also come to understand that before anyone else could like me, could even really get to know me—before I could let them in—I had to be happy with who I was.

And I am. Finally. Remarkably.

And who am I?

Well, it turns out I am many things: Carrie's future other half, Brendan's big brother, as well as the most famous former saint who never was a saint in all the world. But, for the purposes of this story, I'm Davey Boyd, formerly of Seattle, Washington, United States. I will now answer to the names Santa, St. Nick, Father Christmas, Joulupukki, and a number of others, and I'm on the way to residing with my future Mrs. Claus at the North Pole. We'll remodel our new home to our specifications (which means no stairs, many ramps, and a kitchen bigger and wider than any I've seen before) and live in a comfortable house, which you can find at 1 Santa Claus Lane in a little hamlet called the North Pole.

EPILOGUE

Christmas at The Pole: A Letter

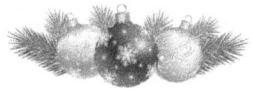

Five Years Later

Dear reader:

Looking back now on all that had to happen to get us here, even I—Santa Claus himself—am amazed. And I'm not easily amazed.

Upon getting to our new home, Carrie and I signed on the dotted lines of the Santa Claus agreement, and we both took to our respective roles quickly. Carrie especially. She isn't just the new Mrs. Claus and, hence, the best baker in town; she is now the head-elf (of course!) in the workshop, a position that hadn't existed in any of the previous Santa administrations. She shows up to work half an hour after me each day (she insists on taking care of "home stuff" each morning before she heads to work). There are many days she stays at the shop later than I do because Carrie loves it there as much as she loves me, and we wouldn't have it any other way.

I thought the shop was efficient before, when I saw it as a kid, but with Carrie cheerfully cracking the candy whip, productivity is actually up from its previous high of off the charts.

"The mall and a man named Calvin Grigsby trained me," she said to me on one of our earliest days at our new jobs. "He showed me both what to do and, more importantly, what *not* to do. Now I get to implement everything I know."

Carrie initiated shop-wide meetings the day after we first arrived. She led the initial meeting while I sat at "Santa's Workbench" eating gingerbread and listening to her do her Carrie thing.

"The thing is, you guys," she said to the elves, "here in the North Pole, we're never gonna stop learning ..."

Just like Carrie herself, I mused.

"Now, in my opinion, the action-figure department should consult with the doll department at least once a week. Your wares are so similar, and if there's a house with a brother and a sister of believer age, chances are you'll both be dropping something into the sack. Those things should be well coordinated. So, we'll have shop-wide meetings like this once a week. Twice a week once October hits, until we reach trip-time. You all know when that is, I'm sure. As with previous Santas, tree-lighting night is the critical time for us, and it'd be great if, on the big day itself, we could all sit back and enjoy some well-earned apple cider, Christmas cookies, eggnog, and conversation."

This got murmurs of happy agreement.

"I'm talking a lot now, I know," Carrie continued. "But I won't be the only one talking! I expect each and every one of you to contribute, always. I ... *we*," she said, looking at me with a smile, "want to learn about your families, your favorite Christmas memories, your favorite desserts so I can make and bake them for you. We're all family now, and Santa and I want to get to know *you* for who you are. Who's with me?!"

The answer: Every. Single. Elf.

Carrie's a Christmas-focused general; the elves are her worthy, well-trained foot soldiers.

I'm so proud of her.

Beyond this, my cheery, chatty wife makes friends easily, and her newest—but certainly not her only—best friend is none other than Cupid, the wordsmith reindeer, who—to commemorate a new Santa, he said—made me a new doormat for 1 Santa Claus Lane. When I'm home, it says: *His palsy is only a part of him, and if you'd like to talk, he's in!* with my smiling face below the message. If I'm at the shop, the mat will read: *He's working hard toward the holiday. If you want to see him, you'll have to go this-a-way!* with an arrow pointing shopward.

Of course, I'm not always at the shop working. So this other side of the mat could also read, *Santa and the missus are sharing some date-night kisses. And spaghetti. Mostly spaghetti. At a restaurant. Not behind this door. Sorry.*

Cupid admits this particular message, as he puts it, "... needs some work."

It turns out Carrie's a heck of a baker, too. A talent the outgoing Claus couple ensured us did not come with the Mrs. Claus role, although an aptitude for confection creation can be enhanced by it.

"You need to have some talent for baking in the first place, dear," said the former Mrs. Claus. "If you do, *then* this house and this oven ..." she pointed at the range as we walked through the kitchen, "they will do the rest."

She told us, as she was giving us a tour of our new home, to call her Carol, her original name from way back. We tried to do this, to honor her request, but it was really hard for both of us.

***

Changing the subject, let's talk beverages, shall we? I don't drink coffee with cream and two sugars anymore. I figured, now that I'm working and living at the North Pole, I should do as the locals do. Their beverage of choice is hot cocoa, so I've adopted this custom, too. Carrie has a steaming cup ready for me every morning to go with my breakfast of eggs and toast and a Boston cream donut.

I don't cut quite the Bunyan-esque figure my predecessor once did, but I'm close. And, just like they did for him, the ceilings in any building I occupy will rise to accommodate me. It's rather convenient.

Carrie and I make sure to go on a date twice a month—just us, no distractions. We can go anywhere in the world, thanks to the reindeer and the sleigh. Carrie loves Italy. But in the interest of not being spotted by the wrong pair of impressionable young eyes glancing up toward the night sky at the wrong moment, or some nosy passerby finding our transport parked somewhere and then alerting the local authorities, we usually stay right here at home. Our favorite restaurant calls itself The Icicle Inn. It makes my favorite steak in all the world—medium-rare, thank you very much. Carrie goes for their spaghetti and meatballs.

She always orders extra garlic bread, and we'll share it.

We've not had any kids of our own, a source of some sadness for me, although Carrie says this doesn't bother her; we've got a world full of them. I'm slowly coming around to this view.

Besides, Brendan and Jess and their two kids spend Christmas with us every year. Their towheaded daughter, Avery, is four and their son, Davey (the poor kid is named after me!), is two, the same age Brendan was when this whole story got started. (And the little guy's got his dad's black hair.)

Having Santa for an uncle is a pretty big deal, Avery tells me, although I'm not her favorite person at The Pole. Avery seems to like Eric the elf best. Eric says she'll be quite the craftswoman one day, and she likes it when he shows her how a tenon joint fits perfectly into a mortise. (That's a little craftsman talk for you, as Eric would say.) Little Davey is best friends with Frosty the Snowman. Taking after his dad yet again.

I can't forget about Carrie's niece, Emily. She comes by now and then, too. Usually on her school breaks. When she pops in, she'll do so unannounced and work as an extra elf for the day, or the week, and we're always so happy to see her.

There's something a tad poetic about all this, I think.

I should also tell you, in the interest of completeness, that my mom and dad, Robert and Sylvia Boyd, are gone now. It's been a while. They passed six months apart. Dad went first, cancer, and Mom followed. The doctors said her heart just gave out.

I think it was broken.

I never really understood them, not in the full way I would have liked to understand them, but they understood each other. And they knew, at least in an abstract sense, what Carrie and I were up to up here, and they were proud of me.

My parents were proud of me.

There was a time when I thought this impossible. A time when, if I let myself dwell on my disappointment for a life I was never given, sadness would routinely overtake me. Now, if I'm sad about anything, it isn't that they're gone; wherever Mom and Dad are, I am comforted by my unshakable confidence that they're there together.

No. If I'm sad about anything, it is only that I spent so much of my life worried about what other people— including my parents and Aubrey and Aubrey's parents and her sister, Susan, and others—thought of me. I didn't spend nearly enough time figuring out what *I* thought of me.

That's more important, isn't it?

Believing in oneself is partly about believing something until it becomes true. But it's also partly about the people with whom you choose to surround yourself.

Like Brendan. Like Luke. Like Carrie.

Carrie and I took our time before marrying: two years. Two years in the job. Brendan was the officiant at our wedding, after which the title of Mrs. Claus was no longer honorary. Our anniversary is two days before Christmas, December 23, which itself was the anniversary of our arrival at the North Pole.

Each and every Christmas, in the center of town, right after the annual Christmas tree lighting but before I begin a tiring, time-hopping journey around the globe, I re-tell this story—complete with its proper ending, no cliffhanger this time. To remind myself of who I once was, who I'll always be, and who I became. And to remind others of the potential they possess to be great, whatever *great* means to them. How everyone can and should endeavor to become great, even while living as the imperfect but beautiful people they were born to be.

My wish for you—beyond a merry, festive respite from repetitive regularity—is this, dear reader: if you haven't already, may you discover the person you were born to be, at whatever time is best for you to make that discovery. Only one person can travel the specific life-path meant for you, and it's *you*. Many can—and will—criticize your choices.

Criticism is easy. Living is not.

Remember that.

And may you spend great swaths of time with your family—whether found, fractured, or fortunate—laughing and hugging and making memories with them.

Spend every day you can surrounded by *your* heart of Christmas.

I do.

I wish you a Merry Christmas (whether you're a believer or not).

Sincerely yours,

Santa Claus
1 Santa Claus Lane, the North Pole
Formerly, Davey Boyd, Seattle, Washington, United States

AFTERWORD

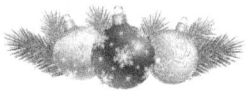

In 2021, I happily contributed two short stories to two wonderful anthologies. First came *13 by 11*, in which I included the story *What Eternity Taught Eve*, which was a seven-thousand-word revisiting of a character I love, Terrence McDonald, from my award-winning novel, *What Death Taught Terrence* (2020).

After *Terrence*, a writing journey that came from the heart (and honestly almost broke me), those who know me well—and a small but loyal contingent of readers—clamored for me to write another novel.

"What's next?" my dad wondered aloud just after he threw me a wonderful surprise book-release party right before the pandemic changed the world forever and locked us all away.

I often joked that what was next for me after writing *Terrence* was "a long and well-deserved nap."

I did not see another novel in the offing. At least, not so soon.

Then came Christmas 2021. I was asked to contribute a Christmas-themed (shock of shocks!) short story to a book called *The Bells of Christmas II*. I came up with a sentimental, ghostly little tale called *The Last Christmas Gift*. Its main characters were versions of me and my deceased grandfather, Richard Dale Kenbok, having one last conversation aboard a ferry on a rainy Seattle Christmas Eve. (Papa Dale in this story you read is again modeled after him, because if I'm going to model my characters after anyone, I want it to be Papa. And so it is.)

The Last Christmas Gift was highlighted by readers as a favorite in the collection. Some months later, I was asked to write another Christmas short story, to be published in the next holiday season. I was happy to do this, and I quickly got to work.

Then the story ballooned.

It mushroomed.

It novelized.

It did all of this right before my eyes.

"This isn't a short story," I told my editor, Jay.

He said not to worry and not to limit the scope of the tale, and that is how I wrote a second novel I didn't know I'd write. Yet, when I told my friends in The Fearless Writers Writing Club that there'd soon be a new Christmas novel from me, to a man and woman they said they'd always known I'd write another book, that I had more to say.

Were he alive today, my papa would tell you I *always* have more to say. Then he'd grin, the smile wide, only half-joking, conspiratorial.

I hope you enjoyed my Christmas story, dear reader, and that you'll consider it a worthy effort. I'm pretty proud of it myself.

Derek McFadden

Redmond, Washington, USA

July 2022

BONUS FEATURE

Deleted Scene

Writing is about many things, one of which is pace. I originally wrote a scene based on an event in my childhood, which, sadly, the "evil editor" (just kidding, Mr. Lewis) persuaded me we should cut in order to help keep up the pacing in the middle of the book. We didn't want to take you, dear reader, out of the narrative structure too much. This block comes from Chapter 13, originally entitled "What is an Och-shun?" I'll always like the scene—any scene that features my papa means a great deal to me—and so we thought you might like to see the scene that was written but couldn't be fitted in.

Enjoy!

Derek

"What is an Oc-shun?"

My Grandma Joan used to love garage sales. They were one of her greatest pleasures in life. The chance to rescue a still-great something someone else no longer needed or wanted and make it a part of your life. Grandma had found many a purse at a garage sale; of course, she'd always make certain the purse wasn't broken before taking it home, since some less-than-scrupulous folks sometimes tried to get one over on an unsuspecting-but-happy-to-dig-for-treasure public. If it wasn't a purse Grandma was taking with her back to the car, in which Papa Dale waited patiently doing his crossword puzzle, then it was a throw pillow or a homemade afghan or a painting she liked that Papa would tell us kids for years was "Creepy as all heck. Why do you think it's in the front room and not our bedroom? I'm not sleeping under that thing. I won't do it." This particular painting depicted a dead-eyed blonde girl, no older than ten, on a simple black background that, when I would touch it as a child, had what I thought was the texture of felt. I wasn't versed enough in art to know if my guess was correct. What I did know was that the blonde girl in the painting haunted my dreams whenever I was over at Grandma and Papa's and made the mistake of making eye contact with her before bed

"I'm not a garage-sale guy," Papa told me one day when he was baking cookies. I sat in what was his kitchen—Grandma did not cook anything besides a pretty decent clam chowder; in our family, she was the one who fixed cars and boats and things that went varoom. We were at the kitchen's green Formica island watching the confections get golden brown in Papa's oven. "You know what I like much better than garage sales, Davey?"

"Chocolate chip cookies?" I guessed.

"No. I mean, I do like chocolate chip cookies. Who doesn't? But ... no, I like auctions. I *love* auctions."

I was only five—and Pop only had a year to live. The cancer in his lungs had advanced to stage four, but none of us knew this yet, and I'm glad we didn't. All I knew was that, being so young, I didn't know what an auction was. So I asked Papa, sounding out the word.

"What is an oc-shun?"

He winked. "An auction is when an auctioneer—he's a guy who talks really fast on purpose—lets people bid on stuff; that means they make a sign they want to buy something. Those folks that want to sell their things hire the auctioneer to help them."

"Have you ever been an auctioneer, Pop?"

"No, but I could show you how it's done if you want?"

I *did* want.

When the cookies I couldn't wait for were done minutes later, Pop introduced me to the fine art of auctioneering.

"Folks, we've got a beautiful batch of chocolate chip cookies here, each cookie to be sold separately. I will start the bidding on the first of these delectable delights ..." I looked at Papa like he was nuts. Though I was glad he hadn't put any nuts in those cookies. *What did he just say?* "I'll start the bidding on each of these cookies right here at a dollar. If you would like to bid, you'll need to raise your hand. I can't read your minds, ladies and gentlemen. So get those hands up nice and high, okay?"

I didn't move. Was I supposed to say something?

"Okay?" he repeated, glancing at me.

Now I nodded.

"Good. Alright. Here we go." Papa picked up a cookie that I could tell was still hot to the touch; he bounced it from hand to hand as he spoke in a staccato fashion. "One dollar! One dollar! One dollar! Do I hear one dollar for this fine cookie here?!"

I raised my hand high.

"One dollar! Thank you, sir! One-fiddy, one-fiddy, one-fiddy! One fifty! Thank you to the lady in the leopard-print dress!"

I looked behind me at the space where Papa's eyes were focused, but there was no lady in a leopard-print dress.

There wasn't anybody in the room but us. Who was he talking about?

"Two dollars, sir! Will you go two for this cookie here? You know you want it!"

I did, but I was five. I didn't have any money. It looked like the invisible woman in the invisible leopard-print dress was getting a fresh-baked cookie.

"Remember, if you're interested, raise your hands, ladies and gents! I won't know you want the cookie unless you *tell* me! And if you don't tell me ... well then, someone else might get to enjoy it! So don't be shy out there!"

Regardless of my lack of financial resources, I was gonna get that cookie. I raised my hand high again.

"Glad to see you've come back in, sir. Two dollars, do I hear two-fiddy! Two-fiddy is all you need to make this cookie yours, ma'am! No? Are you sure? Alright, then. Two dollars going once, twice, last and final call ... and SOLD to the young man in the kitchen for two dollars! You got yourself a bargain, sir!"

I had never heard anyone talk faster than Papa had talked just then. And I'd never wanted to win anything more than I'd wanted to win that cookie. Though I have to say ... I think the fix was in. Pop might have *let* me win. Knowing him, he'd never admit it.

"I don't have any money," I told Papa, half-afraid the not-real auction house for which he worked would come after me for a not-real unpaid debt.

"It's alright. I'm not really an auctioneer." He gave a close-lipped smile that made his silver mustache dance on his face. "That was just a demonstration. That said, you won the cookie fair and square. Here you go."

I didn't believe it, but I was getting that cookie. He slid it across the counter to me. By then, it was no longer hot, only warm—the perfect temperature for eating.

"Thanks, Pop," I said.

"Hey, you want me to teach you how to bake these?" Pop asked, sweeping both his hands above the newest batch—he had made two others, already at home in his cookie jar—of what he called: "Chocolate-chip heaven."

"No, that's okay," I answered. "I don't want to make a mess."

"It's *baking*, Davey. If you ask me, you're *supposed* to make a mess while baking. That's part of the fun."

"I can't bake like you can," I told him, finishing my second cookie in as many minutes.

"Well, no, not yet. You don't know how yet."

"I can't bake at all. The doctor told Mom and Dad I don't have good hand and I orbitation."

"Coordination," Pop corrected, laughing almost to himself.

"Yeah, that. Mom says that my bad ... cordi-whata is because of my palsy."

"I bet she's right."

"Yeah, so you don't need to teach me to bake cookies, Papa, because my hands and my eyes can't do it. They're not good enough. *I'm* not good enough." I lowered my head to stare at the green countertop.

For as long as I live, I'll remember—though I haven't always believed—what Papa said next.

"Davey," he insisted, "I don't want to hear that from you *ever* again. Don't you *ever* tell me you're not good enough. You were good enough the day you were born, when the doctors told all of us who were waiting for you to be born there was something wrong, you're good enough today, and if you want to learn how to make these cookies, there's absolutely nothing and no one stopping you. And, I'm telling you, grandson, you're good enough now. Just like you'll be good enough in forty years."

"Where will you be in forty years, Pop?" Little me was starting cookie three.

Pop tapped the counter three times. It sounded like he was knocking on a door. "Last cookie, okay?" he said. "You don't want to ruin your dinner. Where will I be in forty years?" He took a long moment to think this over. Then he said, "I'll be in the ether somewhere, probably. I don't know."

"Pop, will you take me to an auction someday? I wanna meet one of those auctioneer guys."

"Sure, kid, I'll take you. We'll make a day of it. A Davey and Papa day."

We never did get to go meet an auctioneer. Pop was gone before he could arrange it. Yet I am grateful that, deep in one of the alcoves of my mind, the story of Pop's love for auctions—and his knowledge of auctioneers—still comfortably resides so that I could call on it now.

***

Seated in my employer's sad and—let's be honest, shall we?—their woefully inaccurate depiction of the North Pole (there aren't even any plastic reindeer, and forget about any houses for the reindeer; who can talk in real life, by the way), I think again of Papa's auctioneer story. Which I haven't thought of in decades. But it could be useful tonight.

I say, "Those of you who still need to speak to Santa, do you know what you want to ask for?"

Nods all around.

Good, I think. That means I'll be able to finish the story for Celia, and for Ricky if he wants to hear it—and for me— after all.

...

AUTHOR BIO

Derek McFadden is an author, a poet, a podcast presenter, a radio enthusiast, an unapologetic fan of the Seattle Mariners, and a former March of Dimes ambassador.

He lives with a mild version of cerebral palsy, and his eyes aren't great at being eyes.

Derek's acclaimed novel *What Death Taught Terrence* was a **Next Generation Indie Book Award Finalist 2021** and the **Best Adult Fiction Winner** at **The Wishing Shelf Awards 2021**. The audiobook version, read by the acclaimed BJ Harrison, was a **Best Adult Audio Book Finalist** at **The Wishing Shelf Awards, 2021**.

ALSO AVAILABLE

What Death Taught Terrence

The TV is on, and I'm on the couch, leaning as far back as I can. My heavy, indecisive brown eyes—their lenses blurred ever since my tumultuous, too-soon entrance into the world—flutter between open and shut. I am half-watching, half-listening to a football game on a Sunday afternoon. Was that the doorbell?

"Who is it?" I call out, expecting to hear my daughter, Megan's, voice. These days, she is the one person who visits me. The only person who knows I'm making my home in this little oasis fashioned from wood felled by my own hand.

"Terry, it's Mom. I'm here to help you move."

My mom? That's not possible. She's …

Wait. To help me move? Oh, God.

I rise from the couch and glance back at my lifeless body.

Life is a journey. So is the afterlife.

At the end of his life, Terrence McDonald must discover its meaning, or he'll be banned from the afterlife forever, and his soul will cease to exist. Join Terrence—and those who love him—on a poignant and unforgettable journey through a life at once wonderful and harrowing. Learn what Terrence learns. See what Terrence sees. By this provocative story's end, readers may even learn a thing or two about themselves.

Winner, The Wishing Shelf Awards, 2021
- Best Adult Fiction

Finalist, The Wishing Shelf Awards, 2021
- Best Adult Audio Book

Finalist, Indie Next Generation Book Awards, 2021

Find at all good booksellers in
hardback, paperback, and e-book

Praise for *What Death Taught Terrence*

"What Death Taught Terrence offers a powerful, painful, and poignant look at the life of a man rarely encountered in fiction. Derek McFadden's writes with an insight few can match."
— T.F. ALLEN, author of *The Night Janitor and The Keeper*

"A good story allows the reader to experience life as another person, and McFadden made me do so on a deeply personal level. If you like the works of Mitch Albom, I think you'll find What Death Taught Terrence a worthy addition to your library and the reading of it a life-affirming journey."

— BRADLEY HARPER, Edgar-Award Finalist and author of *A Knife In The Fog* and *Queen's Gambit*

"In What Death Taught Terrence, Derek McFadden builds a world that satisfies both our desire for imagination and our need for personal introspection. I found this (story) immediately immersive, and it stuck with me long after I finished. McFadden is doing something rare in today's fiction—exploring the limits of what we will believe to form a better understanding of who we are."

— ALEX DOLAN, author of *The Euthanist* and *The Empress of Tempera*

13 by 11

13 short stories by 11
award-winning and up-and-coming authors

"*13 by 11* excels in strong images and depictions that
provide much food for thought."

– D. Donovan, senior reviewer *Midwest Book Review*

- features Derek McFadden's *What Eternity Taught Eve* -
(a loose sequel story to *What Death Taught Terrence*)

In part ONE, we encounter life both within and outside of
the earthly realm. Stories by Vincent Czyz and **Derek
McFadden** ask us to consider the ties that bind and define

us in our earthly existence, with tragic, yet hopeful, tales of loss and love.

In part TWO, we visit characters at different stages of life: childhood, early adulthood, and parenthood. Jeffrey Kahrs's charming vignette journeys back to a childhood incident and its effects—both immediate and lasting—on family dynamics, while Caroline Scott introduces us to two teens embarking on adulthood while coping with the pressure of their pasts. Erol Engin warns us how the first child—and Steve Jobs—can change a marriage, leading to competition and vicarious coping, shall we say.

Be careful what you wish for in part THREE, where enticing temptation meets delicious pleasure, but at what cost? Your life? Your soul? Bradley Harper's dark, tantalizing poems wrap around Lilla Glass's unfurling tale of hunter and prey ... and hunter, before Harper spins a whodunit, with a dash of whimsy and perhaps time travel, if the detective's client is to be believed.

Part FOUR takes us to other spaces. Harriet James shows us the futility of resisting the spark of attraction in a charged love-across-the-divides spec-fiction story. Carla Rehse whisks us off to outer space, where we find two partners, divided in a way we could never imagine, fleeing from a Church determined to part them. Will Knight's dialogue-driven diary tale looks for smiles as it touches on hope vs. reality, even as we wonder what the space of that reality is.

The anthology concludes in part FIVE by considering loss. Bradley Harper's short passage here is a true story, looking at loss of life, while Greg Gerke brings the collection to a close on a pensive note as he describes a gradual loss of self, finding that travel does not necessarily enrich the soul.

Enjoy this delightful mix of award-winning and up-and-coming authors. Together, they blend literary, historical, speculative, mystery, and romantic fiction with a dash of light sci-fi thrown in ... but all centering on connection to others—in life, in death, in school, in families, in space, in cyberspace. Even in France.

Find **13 by 11**

at Amazon
in paperback, on Kindle
and *free* on
Kindle Unlimited

"An eclectic, genre-busting gathering that will appeal to a wide audience."

– D. Donovan, senior reviewer *Midwest Book Review*

The Bells of Christmas II

Eight Stories of Christmas Hope

- features Derek McFadden's *The Last Christmas Gift* -

Featuring an all-star cast, including:

The Bells, Santa Claus, Mrs. Claus, the Ghost of Pops, Young Maria, Old Bear, and even *Sugar Plum* (yes, the fae).
Guest starring the *Soul of Tintoretto*

"Roll up, roll up, folks! Hear ye, read ye these eight—yes *eight*—stupendous stories we have for you upon this year's yuletide. Come one, come all for tidings of Christmas hope! Savor these dainty dramas and delight in delicious darkness fantastical, with all sure to enchant readers aplenty this holiday season!

"Come, good gentlefolk, as we alight gently on December 24th, the last sleep before Christmas! In Bradley Harper's *The Bells of Christmas* the midnight carols have echoed off into the night as Julius slumbers beneath his bleak blanket, nestled in the bowels of the homeless shelter. A visitor will arrive to make his Christmas wish come true in a most unexpected way.

"Beware, have a care! For **Derek McFadden is back among the ghosts in *The Last Christmas Gift*, in which Travis is on the edge of despair while on a most unexpected boat ride. Look yonder, good gentlefolk, for *there*, just boarding... surely not Pops, his beloved grandfather departed these twenty years hence...?**

"Now, light ye all *A Winter Candle* as we partake of Bradley Harper's telling of Ben, newly retired from the military. What is an old soldier to do when he feels his family is lost to him? Why, folks, become a Santa Claus, of course! But who is it that detects the faintest flicker of hope in his heart? I tell you, someone up North is watching...

"But lo! Not all these gifts within are fiction. Oh, no, good folks! For within, there sit true-life encounters too. Hear Bradley Harper recount fact stranger than fiction! Hear ye what he's learned in *What Santa Has Taught Me*, an essay of experiences as a real-life Santa Claus.

"Good people, come close... let me whisper this to ye... 'Who among us didn't love Christmases when we were all but wee wildlings?' Ah, then relive the magic of your childhood in Maria O'Rourke's *Calling Us Home* as she lovingly recalls the magic of Irish Christmases of yore, where enchantment and excitement were magic unto themselves!

"Will Knight's *The Bear's Last Word on the Matter* fairly hales at the heartstrings in this final pull of Christmas crackers for one lad's special childhood friend at the "Bears Cares Home." With one last Christmas together, are their adventures truly concluded?

"And now, I ask you all, fair folk: *dare* you encounter the bitter-sweetness of *The Sugar Plum Redux*? Lilla Glass gifts us a fantastical fae, a tenebrous telling of *The Nutcracker* from a very different point of view.

"Ah, but all good things... Yet still one last journey, fair folk, where we must ask ourselves if Gus is not the hero in his own story, then who can it be? Andy, the 'real' and righteous writer? Or perhaps Daphne, the nonconformist neighbor? Before we reach journey's end, Erol Engin will show us how even the most selfish and insecure can provide a Christmas miracle in *A Tintoretto of the Soul*.

"Bless you, one and all, for your forbearance! Click ye a *buy now* button at those most wonderful of shops Amazon and B&N, and may your generous soul bequeath donations desired by that most worthy and hearty of hospitals, St

Jude! For, above all, 'tis surely the season for children. For who among us deserves magic more than they?"

Award-winning authors **Bradley Harper**, **Derek McFadden**, and **Erol Engin** lead this seasonal collection of magical storytelling!

100% of profits from sales going to
St. Jude Children's Research Hospital

This veritable Holiday treat, *The Bells of Christmas II*, is available for your delectation at:

Barnes & Noble

on

Nook

Amazon

in

hardback, paperback, and on Kindle

"For, above all...
'tis surely the season for children.
For who among us deserves magic more than they?"

– Darles Chickens

www.ingramcontent.com/pod-product-compliance
Lightning Source LLC
Chambersburg PA
CBHW060859250626
47159CB00008B/2810